THE SOULWEAVER

BOOK ONE THE SOULWEAVER SERIES

HEIDI CATHERINE

SEQUEL HOUSE

For Evan.
For Ever.

PART I

HANNAH

CHAPTER ONE

*H*annah's life began the day she died. It had happened before – both the dying and the beginning. She didn't know it, though. All she knew was now.

She knew the smell of spring in the fields around the forest. She knew the sound of whispering trees as she slipped beneath their canopy. She knew the feel of Matthew's hand clasping hers as if she were part of his soul. It was a hand that led her deeper into the forest. The deeper they went, the more she felt at peace. Here, the world could rage its wars and her ears would be deaf. It was her place to run when the world began to spin.

The world often spun for Hannah. She'd spent the sixteen years of her life feeling like she'd forgotten something of urgent importance. It was a nagging thought that pulled at her. If only she knew what it was she'd forgotten.

Something rustled in the leaves and Matthew drew in a sharp breath.

"It's just a wallaby," she laughed.

"I knew that," he said, leading her to a clearing where the ground was soft and prying eyes were far away.

Other residents of their small Australian town boasted of their seclusion from the rest of the world. It never felt secluded to Hannah. There always seemed to be someone poking about in her business and reporting back to her father. At these times she longed to live in a big city where no one knew her name. But she could never leave her forest. She belonged here.

It wasn't her first time in the clearing with Matthew. They'd spent hours here, talking, kissing and wishing for their day to come – a day when they could walk in public as they did when they were alone. A day when her father would accept his daughter's love for Matthew, instead of preaching the evils of lust.

She'd decided long ago that her father's preaching belonged in the small church he presided over. What could she learn about lust from a man who treated his wife as if she were a business acquaintance? She'd witnessed the longing in her mother's eyes, willing her husband to love her. *Desire* her. But her father didn't believe in that.

So, Hannah had taken her lust into the forest. She refused to live a life without feeling her heart race or stomach lurch when the boy she loved walked into the room. These were feelings not to be repressed. She felt that to her core.

When Matthew sank to his knees and pulled her to the ground, she didn't hesitate. She pressed her mouth to his and kissed him until she felt soft light filter from her lips down to her toes. Her fingers ran through his dark crop of hair then trailed over the strong line of his jaw. She knew every contour of his beloved face, had kissed every inch of it and stared into the deep blue of his eyes as if he were the only soul to walk the earth.

She loved him, and her love was as simple as it was pure.

Well, perhaps not so pure, she decided, as she allowed his hands to wander places they'd yet to explore. She knew he'd stop if she asked. She also knew she wouldn't ask. She'd dreamed of his hands upon her like this.

He broke their kiss as his breath hitched in his throat.

"I'll always love you." His gravelly voice created an intimacy beyond the beautiful words he spoke.

"And I, you."

He pushed a lock of blonde hair from her eyes. She leaned forward, wanting the taste of him once more. Her lips tingled at his touch, each cell in her body lighting with flames of desire.

She wanted Matthew in a way she couldn't imagine ever wanting another. When she was with him, she felt whole. The thoughts that usually nagged at her peeled away, falling to the ground in piles of dust. It didn't matter what it was she'd forgotten. When Matthew stood before her, he was the only thing that mattered. The world could be at war, but her heart was at peace when it was held in his gentle hands.

And that was exactly where she'd placed her heart – in his care and keeping. It felt safe there. He'd never hurt her. He'd sworn he'd love her until the day he died, and she believed him. It never occurred to her to believe anything else. Imagining him turning his back on her would be as impossible as imagining her doing the same. The trees in the forest would turn purple before that day would ever come.

She wished she could say it was love at first sight, only she couldn't remember the first time she'd seen him. In a town as small as theirs, he'd always been there. Had she first seen him as a toddler in his mother's arms? Perhaps they'd smiled at each other from their strollers. She was sure if she could go back in time and pinpoint the exact moment, her heart would've skipped a beat, even then.

He lay down and she slid on top of him, pressing her

torso to his. She could feel the beat of his heart through the thin cotton of his shirt. She smiled, knowing it was beating for her. They were connected in spirit. It was only natural for them to connect in body, too. His kisses trailed from her lips to the nape of her neck and she knew she'd give herself to him. The urge to join as one was growing beyond her ability to control it.

"I want you," she whispered.

He looked up at her, his soft lips parting to reply. Before the words could fall from his mouth, a loud noise crashed through the scrub just beyond the clearing. They scrambled to their feet and spun around, looking for the source of the disturbance. She hoped it wasn't her father. She couldn't bear to see this secret world shattered.

A stranger leaped into the clearing. Relief and fear flooded Hannah's body. She gasped for breath as she struggled to figure out which emotion to grab hold of. The stranger was only perhaps fourteen years of age, yet he wore the expression of a much older man. She wondered if he was lost.

His fair hair was wild and his clothes torn. Despite his disheveled appearance, he was extremely handsome, his perfect features unmarked by neglect. But it wasn't his appearance that startled Hannah. It was his aura. A warm energy pulsed from him and with each step he took, she felt it deeper in her heart.

As he approached, she saw he clutched a silver dagger by his side. Fear won the war and she felt her stomach drop.

"What do you want?" Matthew growled, his eyes darting around to see if this boy was alone.

He didn't reply, continuing to come closer. There was something in the way he walked that told Hannah he was there for a purpose. The hand that held the dagger was trembling, yet his eyes were filled with determination. He meant to use the dagger. Still, her mind grappled with the idea that he was a threat. She noted the fairness of his skin and hair, the blue of his eyes and for an instant wondered if perhaps they were related. They certainly looked alike.

His gaze was fixed on Matthew, who stood as rooted to the ground as the trees that surrounded them. Shock and confusion had etched their way across his face. It was clear this boy was a stranger to him.

He raised the dagger above his head.

"No!" Hannah screamed.

At the sound of her voice, the boy shifted his eyes to her. The pale blue of his irises flickered with warmth as he searched her face. She realized it was his eyes that made him seem older than his years. They shone with wisdom and she saw joy and sadness mingling with fear and courage. Something within her unraveled.

She knew this stranger. She felt both that she'd seen him a million times, yet she'd seen him never. *He* was what she'd forgotten. *He* was the thought that had nagged her since her earliest days. And he knew her, too. She could see it in his face as he dragged his eyes from her and fixed them once more on Matthew.

"Run!" Matthew yelled, thrusting her behind him and raising his fists.

She stumbled, finding herself unable to break the boy's gaze. Memories swirled in her mind as she struggled to pull the right one to the surface. They were too foggy. She couldn't get hold of the memory that would tell her who this stranger was.

"Hannah, run," Matthew cried. "Go. I'll be right behind you." He took her by the shoulders and turned her away, desperate to get her to safety.

She couldn't leave him. He was unarmed. What match would he be against that dagger?

"I'm not leaving you." She clung to the back of his shirt. The boy meant to kill him. She had no doubt about this. She was safe, but he was in grave danger.

She leaped in front of Matthew as she tried to shield him from the attack. A flicker of distress raced across the boy's face, but he held the dagger firmly in his grasp.

"Don't do this," she pleaded, looking deep into his eyes, trying to reignite the warmth she'd seen in him only moments before. How could someone so young be filled with so much pain that they would want to hurt someone like this? What had happened to this boy to bring him to this point?

Matthew pushed her behind him again. She stepped forward and tripped on a rock. She fell heavily this time, hearing the bone in her leg snap before she felt it.

As she looked up, she saw Matthew lunge at the boy, throwing him to the ground. Matthew was heavier and stronger, but the boy was faster, more skilled at fighting. He slid from under Matthew and within moments had him pinned to the ground using his knees as a vice. Matthew writhed and kicked, but the boy held him firmly to the forest floor.

Hannah struggled to her feet and cried out in pain. She had to save Matthew. She couldn't let this stranger take him from her, no matter how entranced she'd become by him.

She took her weight on her good leg and stepped forward with the broken one, only to find it give way. She collapsed on the ground. Adrenaline coursed through her body as pain shot up her leg. She pushed down the pain and dragged herself toward them.

"I'm sorry," the boy said to Matthew, raising the dagger above his head once more. The muscles in his forearm tensed as the dagger sliced through the air.

Hannah rose to her knees. As she threw herself toward

them, a ball of light rolled through the clearing, its brilliance turning the forest to white.

She crashed down on Matthew. She knew it was him, despite being blinded by the light. She knew his scent and the feel of him. What she didn't know was whether he was alive. And where was the boy?

Then she felt Matthew's arms wrap around her, pulling her tightly to his chest. She saw white flash upon white as another ball of light flew past, this one brighter than the first. Matthew was on her in an instant, sheltering her, protecting her from whatever came next.

"Mother," she heard the boy call. "No!"

Light became black. Then black became light.

Hannah was in a tunnel. Soft light filtered from its walls, chasing the darkness away. She peered ahead and saw a golden beam of light in the distance. She wanted to touch it and be near it, wrapped in its warmth. She took a step toward it, feeling weightless in body and mind. The pain from her leg had gone.

It was quiet. Each breath she took was a raging wind, shattering the tranquility. Then her breathing stopped. Now it was her heartbeat banging in a slow rhythm as it echoed down the tunnel. Then that stopped, too.

Silence. Peace. Euphoria.

The light called to her, whispering her name. She stepped closer. It was warm. It felt safe. She had no memory of how she'd come here. One moment she'd been pressed under the weight of Matthew's body, and the next…

Was she in heaven? Where was Matthew? Fear rose within her. Then the light shone brighter, drawing her in.

She forgot her fear. All she needed was to be close to the light. Nothing else mattered.

"Hannah," the light called. "Hannah."

She started to run. "I'm coming."

As she got closer, she saw the light was spinning in great circular movements like a breezeless tornado. Flashes of color sparked from the center. Her yearning to touch it grew and she reached out. Light pulsed to her fingers and they lit like torches, each finger a different color. The light traveled up her arms, spreading across her torso and down her legs in a wave of ecstasy.

It was pulling her forwards, drawing her in. She didn't struggle, she didn't call out. She floated to the light, certain she'd done this before.

Then she was within it. Encased in a warm cocoon, light pumping through her veins and love filling her lungs. There was no ground to stand on, yet her feet found their hold and she walked on.

"Hannah. Hannah."

She had to reach the voice. It was so beautiful.

An orange mist swirled into the light. Gradually, it took the shape of a figure. Soon an angel stood before her. Her gown glowed in golden hues and her blonde hair floated around the porcelain skin of her face, forming a halo. She reached out her arms and smiled.

"Hannah." The angel's voice flew into Hannah's mind as if it were a thought of her own. It was a voice that rang with hypnotic melody, despite no words being spoken.

She reached out and took the angel's hands. A spark of energy rippled through her body. She looked down and saw she was now clothed in her own golden gown of light. It warmed her, fed her, made her whole.

"I am Mother," the angel said. "I am the Soulweaver."

"Where am I?"

"You're in the Loom. You're safe here. Come with me. It's time for the knowing."

Hannah nodded. She'd follow this voice wherever it led.

The angel drew her in, wrapping her arms around her. Their gowns merged into a brilliant beam of light that shot directly upwards in a pathway to eternity. They rose, flying with the light, faster and faster.

She saw images of the life she'd lived and the people she'd loved. Matthew, her mother, her father, her brother. Then more images of faces she didn't recognize at first, but quickly knew to be from her past. She saw herself as a schoolteacher, a beggar, a priestess, a young girl in a desert. Each image of herself was different, yet equally familiar.

Her soul had lived for a thousand years, each of her lives filled with its own struggles, happiness and fortunes. She collected each memory as it flashed across the sky, reliving every moment, cherishing each soul that had touched her. There was one familiar soul, one burst of light that kept appearing. He was her son, her father, her brother, her lover. In each life he appeared as the other half to her whole. She yearned for him.

Now that all her lives had been returned to her, she could see herself as a complete soul. Her journey spanned so much more than her life as Hannah. She knew now she had more work to do, more lessons to learn. She hadn't reached her destination yet. Another life would need to be lived. The journey of her soul wasn't complete.

She flew higher and faster and the faces of loved ones blurred. The sky changed from gold to blue as she lost sensation of who she was or where. Secrets long held by the universe poured through her core.

Her energy merged with the light and she was no longer a single being. She was part of a huge tapestry of blissful energy that reached its arms from one side of the universe to the other. She was a small yet important part of a much bigger plan. The universe was nothing without her, just as she couldn't exist without it.

The light slowed and she separated from it, her energy returning to her own form. Soon, she stood still, her golden cloak wrapped around her once more.

"You've traveled well, child." Mother took her hand. It was a hand Hannah now knew to be an invention of her mind, existing only to keep the world familiar.

"Thank you, Mother."

"The knowing served you well, but as you saw, the journey of your soul must continue."

"Yes." Hannah looked at Mother, her eyes filled with love.

"You're ready now for your reflection."

"Yes, Mother."

A shimmering lake appeared before them. The water was black, the surface pricked with specks of bright light, giving the appearance of looking down on the night sky. Hannah recognized the floating lights as other souls completing their reflections. She knew the danger present here, remembered it from times gone by. Souls could be trapped, unable to tear themselves away from the temptations of the lake. She must be strong.

She turned to speak to Mother, only to find she was gone. The reflection must be done alone. This was her opportunity to look back on her lessons learned and say goodbye. A soul cannot move on to another life until it's prepared to let go of the last. She promised herself she'd find the strength to say goodbye. She wouldn't be one of those floating souls refusing to move on.

She knew what to do. She stepped into the lake.

The moment her feet touched the water, it swallowed her, dragging her under, transforming her body into a brilliant ball of light.

Images of her life as Hannah wrapped themselves around her. She saw herself as a young girl, lying on the grass watching the clouds float past. This was something she'd done often. She'd liked to imagine what else might be out there in the universe. She'd turn the clouds into soft hills and mountains and envisage a world of angels ruling the skies. Then she'd look beyond the clouds and imagine life on other planets. She never saw the little green men or flying saucers from the books she'd read. Instead she saw other planets filled with life, just like the planet she called home. She wondered if she'd ever get to see what was out there with her own eyes, instead of in the eye of her imagination. Would she fly with the angels, live more lives or visit life on other planets?

As she'd grown, her dreams became shaped by what she'd been told. Of course, angels didn't live in the clouds. Of course, there wasn't life out there beyond her small, blue planet. Of course, she wouldn't be born again. She'd go to heaven when it was her time and that was that.

Why had she allowed her dreams to grow narrower as her world had grown wider? She should never have let that happen.

Then the girl on the grass faded and she saw herself at school, at church, sitting on the branch of a tree. Her life had been simple, yet happy. She'd learned to value family over possessions, giving over taking, loving over hating. She'd been a good person. She'd known what was important in life and she'd tried hard to live by her family's rules, until her love for Matthew became her ruler. She would've done anything for him. Her love for him had taught her that standing up was sometimes as important as following along blindly.

The images of her past blurred and she was taken to the present. She saw her mother weeping in the forest, crouching with her head cradled in her hands. Hannah's little brother was standing by their mother's side, his hand on her shoulder, his face an image of distress and disbelief.

She saw her father standing before his small congregation. He was preaching at his pulpit, his eyes filled with confusion and rage.

She saw Matthew sitting alone, staring into the sky. He was alive. Whatever had torn her away from life had spared him. Although, he didn't look like someone who'd had his life spared. He was alive in body only. His beautiful spirit had been crushed.

Her parents would be all right in time. She knew that. They had each other and their faith to help them. They'd survive this. But Matthew was alone. He needed her. She couldn't leave him. It wasn't her time.

The reflection offered the chance to leave the Loom and return to Earth. Souls had been doing this for thousands of years. Her soul yearned for those she loved as much as anyone else's, maybe even more. Forgetting her promise to herself, she decided her next life could wait. This one wasn't finished yet.

She brought Matthew's face to her mind and concentrated all her energy into a single beam of light, stretching it out like an elastic band. Her soul flickered with the effort.

"Matthew," she called, visualizing herself traveling across the universe to sit by his side once more.

When her light could stretch no more, she let go. Energy poured into her soul and she felt herself race across the lake like a shooting star.

Cradled in a blanket of light, she began falling. She fell further and faster, spinning and spinning until all became black.

Then she was there. With Matthew. So real she thought she could touch him yet knew he couldn't see her. He was sitting in the garden of his parents' small house on the edge of the forest. He remained staring at the sky, his eyes unfocused, lost in thought. There was something different about him. She moved in closer. Silent tears were rolling down his cheeks.

"Matthew," she said, trailing hands that didn't exist across his face. "Matthew, my darling. I'm here."

"Hannah," he whispered.

She startled. Could he hear her? "Matthew?"

He closed his eyes. He could no more hear her than she could wipe away his tears. He was miserable, but he was alive, and she was glad. Lives shouldn't be extinguished so young. She wished she could ask him what happened in their last moments together. The knowing had hidden her death from her. That wasn't supposed to happen and it puzzled her.

Matthew's mother approached and sat next to him. She'd aged since Hannah had seen her last. Matthew's troubles were weighing on her heavily, sitting on her shoulders like blocks of iron.

"Come inside, sweetheart," she said to her son. "Jarred's listening to some music. I'm sure he'd love you to join him. He misses his brother."

He didn't reply.

"You can't spend your life sitting here as if she's going to come running to you from the forest. It's been over a month now. She's gone, Matthew."

A month? She'd been gone a month. That was the problem with the Loom. Time ceased to exist. An eternity on Earth could feel like the blink of an eye.

"Don't you think I know how long she's been gone?" His voice was harsh, unrecognizable from the Matthew she knew. "She's dead. She's dead because I couldn't protect her."

"God damn it, Matthew." His mother raked her hands

through her hair. "You were attacked and her heart stopped from fright. How could you protect her from that? We've been through this before. She was dead long before you carried her from the forest. You didn't cause this any more than you could've prevented it."

"Something else happened out there. Something I can't explain. There was the light. So much light."

"We don't know if that light was really there, you know that."

"Then how do you explain this?" He pointed to his eyes.

Hannah moved closer and realized what was different about him. It was his eyes.

He was blind.

"Oh, Matthew," she sobbed, trailing invisible kisses over his face. "Your beautiful eyes."

His mother reached out and placed a hand on his knee. "I can't explain it. Maybe the doctors are right and it was just the shock that made you think you saw a light. The mind can play strange tricks on us at times. You'll see again, just like the doctors said."

"I know what I saw out there. And anyway, what's the point in seeing when I can't see the one thing I want to?"

"Hannah," his mother whispered. "I know, darling."

"I'm here," Hannah cried out. "I'm here. I'll always be with you. I'll never leave your side."

CHAPTER TWO

*T*rue to her word, Hannah didn't leave Matthew's side. She was there holding his hand as he fumbled his way through his days. She lay beside him while he slept, sat with him in the garden and watched him as he ate his meals.

At times she was sure he felt her presence. Sometimes he even spoke to her, telling her he missed her and didn't know how to go on. She soothed him when nightmares haunted his dreams, wept when he cried and stroked his cheeks, whispering words he'd never hear.

She was sorry she hadn't been there with him in the first weeks after her death. From what she'd been able to piece together, those weeks had been torture for him.

Her father had visited him. Matthew's older brother, Jarred, had opened the door to find him standing there, shaking his fists and demanding to see the boy who'd killed his daughter. He didn't believe Matthew's account of the events. The police were suspicious, too. There wasn't a scrap of evidence to support Matthew's story of the stranger in the clearing.

Her father believed Matthew had lured her there. No daughter of his would willingly go into the forest with a boy. Her broken leg added fuel to his anger. She'd obviously tried to run away before he killed her. It didn't matter that all the evidence contradicted this. Her father believed the story he found easier to accept.

Unfortunately, the one person who could back up Matthew's story and clear his name was the stranger in the clearing – the boy who nobody had seen before that day or since. He'd vanished and Matthew had no idea who he was.

Matthew's parents had refused to let Hannah's father see their son again and the two families had avoided each other. This wasn't easy in a small town. Hannah had witnessed how people looked at Matthew and was glad he couldn't see it. It made her sad to think that this was how he had to live from now on, forever in doubt. If only people knew the truth. He hadn't killed her. He'd almost died trying to save her. There must be some way she could help him prove it.

She took comfort in the fact his friends and family believed him. They'd seen Matthew and Hannah together and knew he wasn't the monster her father was making him out to be. But would having the acceptance of a few outweigh having to bear the suspicion of the rest?

Whatever had taken the sight from Matthew's eyes in the forest also took the light from the eyes of his parents. Hannah watched their pain as they cared for their son. She saw the way they looked at each other, their sadness stretching between them, binding them in grief.

Jarred spent less and less time at home, preferring the company of his friends to the miserable family he'd found himself a part of.

"What's it like?" his mother asked Matthew once.

"What's what like?" he replied.

"To be blind." She leaned in toward him, really wanting to know.

"Close your eyes," he said.

She did as she was told and waited for him to speak, only to be met with silence

"Well?" she asked, her eyes still closed. "What's it like? Tell me."

"That's what it's like," he said. "Dark."

Her eyes sprang open. "Be serious, Matthew. I want to know. I want to understand what you're going through."

"Your eyes are open now, aren't they?" He turned his face toward her, grief pooling in his sightless eyes.

"Yes."

"That's why you'll never understand."

Without a word, his mother stood and left the room. She returned moments later wearing an eye mask, feeling her way in front of her with her hands. She sat next to him once more. He lifted his hands toward her face and felt the mask.

"What are you doing, Mum?"

"I'm going to wear this until I understand. If you won't tell me, then I'll find out for myself."

"That's stupid." He turned away from her.

"Why's it stupid? At least I'm trying."

"And you think I'm not." His voice filled with rage.

Hannah was surprised. She'd never seen him like this. He was normally so sweet and gentle. He shouldn't be treating his mother like this. She was only trying to connect with him.

"I've done nothing but try ever since this happened," he continued. "Every time you see me take a breath you're seeing me try. And you think wearing an eye mask is you trying. It's pathetic. Do you know why?"

His mother sat in silence, knowing he'd tell her whether she asked him to or not.

19

"It's pathetic because you know that at any moment you can remove the mask and you'll see. I don't have a mask to remove. My eyes are wide open and still, I see nothing. Forever, I'll see nothing. And the finality of that is what's hard to deal with. So much more than not being able to see in this actual moment. You don't understand and you never will."

She removed the mask and reached for his arm. He recoiled at her touch.

"Matthew, stop this. You're my son. I love you and your brother more than I'll ever love anything else. I carried you in my womb, I nursed you, I cared for you and watched you grow into the most magnificent young man I've ever met. I may not know what it's like to be blind, but I do know what it's like to lose a person who's precious to you. The day Hannah was taken from you was the day you were taken from me. The boy who returned from the forest wasn't the son I knew, yet still I continue to love you. You're my child, Matthew. You're *my child*. Watching you like this is killing me. I know you're trying. Please understand that I'm trying too. But you have to try harder. You have to lift yourself out of this."

Her words cut him deeply. Hannah wanted to protect him, but knew his mother was right. He was losing himself in his grief. He had to pull himself out before it was too late.

"I can't try harder." He choked out the words.

"You can. I can, too. Don't stop mourning Hannah but do stop mourning your sight. Learn to use your other senses. Make something of yourself. You can still have a wonderful life. Make Hannah proud. She wouldn't want to see you like this."

"Do you think she can see me?" His face filled with hope.

"Yes, I do. Maybe she's even with us now." She kissed him on the cheek. This time he didn't shy away.

"I think she can see me too," he said. "I can feel her some-times. I'm sure she's still with me."

"Oh, Matthew." Tears of light filled Hannah's eyes. She'd been right to return to him.

As days turned into weeks, then months, Hannah noticed a change in Matthew. His mother's words had affected him. He started to look at his situation from the perspective of others. He saw his parents' pain as well as his own. The anger that had invaded his soul ebbed away. He stopped feeling sorry for himself and his smile returned. Jarred returned too, opting to spend more time with his brother and less with his friends.

Matthew learned to trust his other senses and was able to make his way around the house without feeling in front of him. Slowly, he ventured out more often. Instead of making excuses to his friends as to why he couldn't join them in their activities, he said yes.

He began listening to classical music and his parents noticed him moving his fingers in the air as if he were playing it himself. So, his father bought him a piano, unaware that what he was actually buying his son was a new life.

Hannah had cringed when Matthew sat at the piano for the first time and a terrible mess of notes erupted from his fingertips, but as time passed the mess started to take order. Slowly at first, and then with great speed. It was like watching a butterfly emerge from a cocoon.

She sat next to him on the piano stool and urged him on, the music filling all the dark holes her death had left in his soul.

Encouraged by his passion, his father hired a music teacher. She didn't last long, however, being sent away after only a dozen lessons when Matthew overtook her. His kind of talent couldn't be taught. It came from within. Lessons were useless to him.

Jarred filmed him playing and posted it online, telling Matthew he was going to be an internet sensation – the boy who lost his sight and gained an extraordinary talent.

Matthew laughed at the idea. Hannah didn't. When he played the piano, it felt like he was speaking directly to her. She wasn't certain she wanted that shared with the world.

She watched the mixture of joy and trepidation in his parents' eyes, as Matthew's independence grew, no more so than the day he accompanied his friends to the beach. His father insisted Jarred accompany him.

"I'll watch over him," Hannah told his parents. Of course, they couldn't hear, and this reassurance did nothing to soothe their fears.

She stood by him in the waves, relishing the pleasure on his face as the cold water lapped at his legs. Jarred picked him up and threw him under the water and Hannah froze in fear as she waited for him to emerge. But when he did, he was whooping with joy and she knew he felt alive at last, like a whole person once more.

She also noticed the attention Tarryn paid him. The way she openly stared at him, knowing he couldn't see her. Hannah couldn't blame her. Matthew was incredibly handsome. Other girls had always tried to lure him away from her. It was to be expected. Now she was gone, there'd be another trying to take her place. Tarryn was an intelligent girl and surely Matthew would remember how beautiful she was. Even if he was oblivious to her attention at the moment, there'd be a day he'd take notice.

Hannah realized with a sharp pain that perhaps it was time for her to move on. The promise she'd made to never leave his side was a promise that now seemed more in her own interests than his. What would happen when the day came for him to fall in love again, get married, become a father? He wouldn't want her there to witness these events of his life. She knew that now. He no longer needed her. The time had come. Her promise would have to be broken. The Loom awaited her.

She spent one last night by his side, her head resting on his chest, listening to the beat of his heart, grateful he'd survived what she hadn't.

"Goodbye," she whispered. "I'll always love you."

"Hannah," he murmured, between deep breaths of sleep. His eyes flickered open. For the briefest moment, she was sure he saw her. His eyes closed and sleep claimed him once more.

At first light, she forced herself to leave, reminding herself she was doing this for him. He was still asleep. If she waited until he woke, she'd lose the strength to go.

She thought about going to her own house before she returned to the Loom. She longed to see her mother and brother, but the thought of seeing her father pained her too greatly. His lies were making it harder and harder for Matthew to live in this town. He was being unfair.

Instead of going home, she found herself making her way to the forest. She wanted to see the clearing once more before she left, to see the place she'd died. Perhaps then she'd remember what had caused her death.

Matthew had never gone back. His mother had asked him if he'd like to go, but he'd said it was too painful. She tried to encourage him by telling him the clearing had become some-what of a hangout place for the other students at their school. This disappointed Hannah. The clearing was a special place for her and Matthew. Its beauty was in its secrecy. She hoped the others hadn't destroyed it.

The forest was still and quiet. Early morning light broke

through the trees, making speckled patterns on the earth. She entered the clearing and was surprised to see splashes of color leaping at her. Bright ribbons and paper lanterns hung from every tree. Envelopes bearing her name had been tied to branches, and small figurines of angels peered at her from amongst the foliage. Her name had been carved into tree trunks and hundreds of small stones had been painted pink and laid out on the ground in the shape of a heart. Her school friends had built her the most beautiful shrine she could imagine, and it touched her profoundly. They hadn't destroyed the clearing; they'd made it even more impossibly beautiful. She wished Matthew could see it.

She took her time reading the notes her friends had left her. Their words were heartfelt and kind, and she felt sorry they hadn't told her how they felt when she was still alive. She'd had no idea how popular she was. She'd been so focused on Matthew she'd lost sight of how important these friendships were to her. She wished she could tell them how much they meant to her, too. If only her hands were made from flesh instead of light, she'd tie her own note to a tree, filled with words of love and gratitude.

Something caught her eye. There was one note she hadn't read, hanging high in a tree. It contained only five words.

HANNAH. COME TO ME. REINIER.

Reinier? She knew nobody of that name, yet it sounded oddly familiar. The memories of her past lives weren't as clear as her most recent life. Was he from a life gone by? A life before Hannah.

"Reinier," she said. A memory fought its way to the surface. He was the stranger in the clearing. The stranger who'd killed her, despite the fact she'd been sure he meant to protect her. He was the only one who could clear Matthew's name. She must go to him before she returned to the Loom. She shouldn't have waited this long. It wasn't right for the universe to keep the details of her death from her. Reinier was the key, able to unlock all the doors the universe had closed to her.

But could she face the boy who'd ended her life? The boy who'd taken her away from Matthew? She had to. Matthew's future depended on it. She didn't have a choice.

She brought him to her mind, concentrating on the torment that shadowed his eyes, for these eyes revealed the nature of his soul, and it was his soul she sought. She focused her energy in a single point and readied herself.

"Reinier, Reinier," she whispered.

She was in a dark room. The first thing she noticed was how small it was. It looked like some kind of boarding house. There were no personal possessions, just a single bed with a neatly-packed duffel bag beside it. The second thing she noticed was Reinier. He was asleep. The universe had delivered her with precision to the person she needed most. She wondered how long it would take her to get the answers she needed. How strange for him to ask her to see him when he had no way of knowing she was there. Perhaps he wanted to apologize for killing her. An unusual apology indeed.

She felt the same pull of energy she'd felt when he'd come near her in the clearing. This must be what happened when you met the person destined to take your life. Perhaps that's why she'd become certain he'd been the thing she'd forgotten all her life. All those nagging thoughts had been a premonition of her death. Why, then, did the energy that came from this boy feel so safe and warm?

She studied his face. It was stripped of the fear and anger that'd been present in the forest. He looked younger, more like the teenager he was. He reminded her of her brother and again she wondered if it were possible they were related. She certainly felt connected to him in some way.

It was strange to study him at such close proximity. She'd become accustomed to spending long nights staring at Matthew's face. This was a different face altogether. His hair had been cut short and it stuck up like a blond crown upon his head. A scar extended from the bottom of his left eye down to his chin. She didn't remember the scar on his face in the clearing. It changed his appearance, adding a dangerous edge to his angelic features. It was almost as if it had been put there to warn the world what he was capable of. For, as young and innocent as he appeared, Hannah knew he was not.

She reached out to touch his cheek, quickly withdrawing her hand when she realized what she was doing. It wasn't her place to put her hands on him, yet she felt strangely as though she'd touched his face before.

Sleep brought him an innocence she knew would be erased the moment his eyes opened. The boy lying sleeping in front of her was a killer. *Her* killer. This was the person who'd taken her life. He'd ripped her out of Matthew's arms long before she was ready to go. Why had he done this to her? She'd been sure she'd seen love in his eyes.

She had a sudden urge to slap him, to shake him, to beat him with her fists. But she knew these actions would have no effect. He would never feel her anger. He would never feel her pain.

His eyes opened, startling her. He blinked in the soft light, trying to find his focus.

"Hannah," he said, sitting up in bed, looking directly at her.

This wasn't possible. Living souls weren't supposed to be able to see those in transition. Perhaps he was dreaming.

She remained still.

"Hannah, thank goodness you came." He reached out toward her and the impossible became reality. He *could* see her.

She drew back, avoiding his touch. It felt strange to be spoken to after so long with Matthew. "How can you see me? This isn't possible."

"I see lots of things. You included. Oh, Hannah. I've missed you." He reached for her again. This time she let him, staring with fascination as his hand passed through her soul. Surely, he could hurt her no further, now that she was already dead.

"Have we met before? Other than when you killed me, of course." Her voice was cold. He *missed* her. What a ridiculous thing for her killer to say.

"You can't really believe I killed you. I'd never harm you. I was there to protect you."

"Protect me? Are you serious? You killed me. You must have." She could scarcely believe he was trying to deny it.

"You don't remember what happened. If you did, you'd know it wasn't me."

"Well it wasn't Matthew and you were the only other person there."

"True, but it wasn't me. I'd never do that to you." He was refusing to buy into her anger, seeming sure she'd believe him.

She wondered if that was how a guilty man behaved, or if it were possible he was innocent.

"How would I know what you would or wouldn't do?" she asked.

"Because you know me."

She couldn't deny that was exactly how she felt. "Have we met before?"

"Only a hundred times in a thousand years. I'm surprised

you don't remember." He smiled at her, affection plain on his face.

Now that his eyes were open, she found herself unable to look at anything else. How could a boy of a mere fourteen years or so have eyes teeming with such depth? He was full of contradictions. She'd never come across anyone like him.

"I feel like I know you, but I can't place where from." She felt herself being drawn in. There was something about his energy. Her intuition in the forest had told her he was there to protect her. Perhaps he was telling the truth. She clung to her guard as it threatened to drop.

"We were kept apart in your life as Hannah, but surely you saw me in the knowing? You must have."

That was it. Reinier was the burst of light that continued to appear as her past lives had flashed by. She'd seen him, always by her side. He was both her strength and her purpose. He was the other half to her soul she'd been yearning for all these years.

He smiled at her. "You remember me now, don't you?"

She nodded. He hadn't killed her. It wasn't possible. He'd protect her until the end of time, just as she would protect him. It was written in the stars. Something else must have happened out there. She knew it with the same certainty she knew her name had been Hannah. Reinier loved her and her soul loved him.

She reached out her hand, tentatively holding her palm toward him, her fingers longing to lace with his. It wasn't a romantic love she felt. It was completely different to how she felt with Matthew. This love was coming from the deepest part of her existence. It was almost the kind of love she'd describe as the love she had for herself. Like a critical part of her soul had been missing and now here it was before her, filling her with light and energy, making her feel whole.

He raised his hand to hers and the light of her soul

wrapped itself around him. She felt love and belonging flood through her core. How could she have forgotten him for so long, not noticing he was missing from her life? He would never hurt her.

So, if he didn't kill her, then who did?

"Please, tell me," she said, reluctantly pulling her hand away so she could think straight. "Who killed me? What happened out there?"

Before he could answer, the room filled with light, as if the sun was rising in seconds instead of the glorious minutes it took each day.

"What's happening?" She looked at him with fear in her eyes. There was something not right about this.

He turned to her and spoke quickly. "I've got so much to tell you, but we don't have time. I need you to remember one thing. One important thing. If you remember nothing else, always remember this. During the weaving, you must keep your mind blank. She can't erase what you don't supply. Don't let her take Hannah."

"What do you mean?" She knew the weaving was the final step in her soul's journey as Hannah. This was where everything she'd learned in the knowing would be erased, including her memories of the life she'd just lived. What she hadn't known was there was a way she could hold on.

She felt a strange sensation pass through her, a slight disconnection of reality. She was being pulled away against her will.

"Listen to me, Hannah. Think of nothing. Give her nothing. Otherwise she'll take everything." His voice was desperate, pleading with her to listen.

She was fading quickly now. A swirling sensation built within her. She fought it. She wasn't ready to go.

"I love you." He reached out, trying to grab hold of her. "I'll always love you."

Leaving Earth was painful. No soul ever chose this path until they were certain it was time to leave. She was anything but certain. She didn't want to go back to the Loom.

The light from within her, became her, stretching to the sky in a beam of agony. Her soul splintered into a million pieces. If she had a mouth, she'd scream. If she had a pulse, it would beat out of her chest. If she had fingers, they'd claw at the sky. She couldn't give in to the pain. She mustn't lose hold of herself. Something out there was trying to destroy her. If she was to survive, she needed to let go of Earth and fly with the currents of the light.

She relinquished her hold and sped upwards.

She flew higher and higher, the pain rushing through her, becoming her world. And when she thought she could continue no longer, she found herself breaking through the surface of the lake and floating in the blackness. The pain had been erased as quickly as it had been inflicted. Her journey was complete. Misery flooded her, threatening to drag her under. She'd broken her promise to Matthew and left him, and she'd failed to get her answers from Reinier. What would happen to Matthew now? She hadn't been ready to leave.

Her light flickered.

———

There are many signs of a soul in danger and Hannah recognized them all. When waking becomes more difficult than sleeping. When eyes prefer to be blind than to see. When living is harder than dying.

Her light continued to flicker in the lake. Time passed. The periods of blackness between each burst of light stretched longer and then longer still, until her light extinguished and her pain started to lift.

Her tired body filled with love. A comforting warmth pulsed through her, but a voice nagged at the edges. Someone was trying to break through. She ignored them. Strands of light wrapped themselves around her and she gave herself to it.

The voice nagged at her again. Stronger this time. She listened.

"No, Hannah. No. Don't let Mother take you. Fight this. Fight!"

The voice belonged to Reinier. She brought his face to her mind and as she did the strands of light fell away. She felt his strength fill her soul. Somehow, he was with her, healing her. Giving her the strength she needed to find her way through.

"You cannot take me," she cried in the darkness. "I'll fight you. This isn't the end."

Her words lit her soul like a candle. As her light returned, the entire lake surged with waves of energy. The other lights bobbing on the surface glowed brighter, pulling toward her like a magnet. She was back. She was strong, ready to face her next challenge. She'd return to Reinier and figure this out.

She focused her energy on an image in her mind of Reinier. The last time she'd done this, he was a stranger who'd filled her with confusion. This time he was a part of her soul, filling her with strength and love.

"Reinier," she whispered. Her whisper grew louder until she found herself shouting his name.

But her light didn't shoot across the lake and she didn't begin a journey to Earth.

"Reinier." Her shouts became sobs. The universe was working against her wishes. There was something going on here that was bigger than her. Reinier had said they were kept apart in her last lifetime and it seemed they were being kept apart still.

Her light pulled toward the edge of the lake. Mother was standing before her, shining with radiance, her arms outstretched. Hannah tried to pull back. She didn't want to be seduced by Mother's light. She no longer trusted her.

Pulling back proved useless. Her light continued to drift closer to Mother.

"Hannah. Come with Mother."

She tried to cry out. She tried to tell Mother to leave her alone. That she didn't want to go with her. She hadn't finished in the lake. But she could speak no words. All she could do was float silently toward her.

"Good girl, Hannah. Don't try to fight me. You can't fight a Soulweaver. Come now. It's time now for the weaving."

She was pulled from the lake and drifted to Mother's side, helplessly. She looked down at her body and saw her golden gown return, clothing her in warmth. Only this time, the warmth failed to penetrate the center of her soul.

Reinier's words came back to her. *Think of nothing. Give her nothing. Otherwise she'll take everything.*

She tried to empty her mind of each of her precious memories. Panic rose within her. The more she tried not to think of her loved ones, the more they swirled in her mind's eye. She couldn't let Mother take them from her. Matthew's memory was the one thing that kept her going. She couldn't possibly continue on this journey without him.

Mother smiled. "Don't worry. They can't hurt you when you know not who they are."

They approached an enormous glittering dome. Golden light sparked from its surface, sending out sharp rays in every direction. As they drew closer, Hannah realized the dome had no light source of its own. Instead, it was covered in millions of tiny mirrors, each one reflecting the brilliant light emitting from the gowns she and Mother wore.

Mother walked toward the dome and Hannah tried to pull away, not wanting to follow. This beautiful, shining dome may look enticing, but its purpose was to strip her of memories and steal Matthew from her mind.

Her protest was useless. She was being dragged along with powerful force. She'd be cleansed, whether she wanted it or not, just as she'd been taken from Earth against her will. As strong as she felt, she was no match for a Soulweaver.

Mother placed a hand on the dome and the mirrors parted, revealing a dark opening.

"No!" Hannah screamed in silence.

Mother stepped forward and the dome swallowed them up, taking them into its belly.

Darkness surrounded them. It was blacker than black. And silent. No sun to light their path. No air to transport waves of sound. Just endless miles of nothing.

This comforted Hannah. Darkness was preferable to Mother's blinding light. But Mother was still here. She could feel her presence.

Think of nothing. Give her nothing. Otherwise she'll take everything.

She tried not to think of Reinier, which made her think of him. She tried not to think of Matthew, which made her think of him. She tried to think of nothing and thought of everything. She didn't have long.

"It's time, Hannah. Say goodbye to your loved ones. Say goodbye to your life. Say goodbye to Hannah. Let the weaving begin."

In panic, she brought her father to her mind. He was the soul she was least at peace with. If Mother took him from her then perhaps she'd find a way to make that peace.

She pictured him on the pulpit, preaching to his congregation. She concentrated on every detail. The fall of his robes, the line of the stole around his neck, the way his eyebrows knitted together whenever he said the words *can't* or *don't.* She saw him clutching his well-worn bible and heard him quoting equally well-worn passages from within its pages. She studied the conviction in his eyes and the passion in his voice.

This was a man who believed the world was bigger than we can see and touch. He believed there was more to life than is lived on Earth. He was a man who was right about so much, yet wrong about just as much. She wanted him to know this. She wanted to tell him to look for the commonalities among the world's religions, instead of being so focused on their differences. Having faith of any kind was what was important. That was what prepared you for what was to come. It didn't matter what you called the Creator or how you chose to worship. What mattered was that you believed in something. *Anything.*

She consoled herself with the fact that one day he'd know all of this. Only when that day came, it'd be too late.

Her father's faith was strong. So strong it overshadowed his love for his family. Despite never having felt his love while on Earth, Hannah knew now that he loved her. His anger came from a place of love. His words were cruel, but his heart meant well. He wasn't a bad person.

She realized she'd been right. The weaving had helped her find peace with her father. Only now he'd be cleansed from her mind, she'd never be able to tell him that she loved him too.

"I'm sorry, Dad."

She felt her mind swirling, shutting down. The weaving was coming to an end. She floated further into the dome's abyss aware she was slipping away from herself. Her life as Hannah was drawing to a close. It was a life that barely had a chance to begin. It wasn't until she'd been taken from it that her eyes had opened and the fire in her belly had grown. The day she'd died was also the day she'd come to life.

An impossibly dark blackness engulfed her. It was quiet. Hannah was no more.

PART II

LIN

CHAPTER THREE

*L*in looked across the forest from her bedroom window, balancing her tiny frame on a stool. A possum scurried down the branch of a tree, making her laugh. She noticed the way the light fell on the highest branches, illuminating the leaves like torches. Other branches hung low with the weight of brightly colored flowers that had burst into life, and small birds hopped along the forest floor searching for food to feed their young.

There was an abundance of beauty in nature. Lin felt so much a part of the forest, she was sure she must have roots of her own that had threaded their way deep into the earth.

"You'll wear out your legs standing on that stool," her father always told her.

"I'm watching over my forest, Ah-ba," she'd say.

"Your forest is ugly." He'd smile, anticipating her response.

"You are ugly."

Her father would then lift her from the stool and tickle her until her sides ached from laughter.

Lin was born in Kowloon, Hong Kong, the only child of

hardworking parents who ran a convenience store on one of the city's many busy streets. They lived in an apartment building and from her bedroom window she had a view that unfolded for miles.

As a young girl, she thought of her city as a forest. The buildings were her trees. The colorful clothes on the washing lines that ringed the buildings were her flowers. The horns from the traffic were birds calling to each other, and she imagined the people below to be possums or wombats or wallabies. Her imagination supplied her with the view she longed to see, and she'd spend hours staring out, lost in a world of her own creation.

She tried to share this world with her father, but where she saw a forest, he saw the land for what it was – a city studded with concrete columns of life, stretching high into the sky.

As she grew older, her legs grew longer, and she no longer needed the stool. She'd press her nose to the window and stare at her city. She noticed how people's eyes remained focused on life at ground level, yet most of it was happening above their heads. Through the thin walls of her family's apartment she could hear talking, laughing, crying and shouting. All evidence of lives being lived, relationships being forged and people growing and changing.

She'd watch the people go about their day, and she'd wonder why she felt she didn't belong. The pages of her sketchpad were filled with drawings of a forest she'd never seen and faces of people she'd never met. When she slept, she dreamed of bright lights, dark skies and a woman with golden hair. She'd wake, confused and sad. Did everyone dream like this? Apparently not, she found out when she asked the girls at school.

Whenever she could escape the demands of school and working in her parents' store, she'd venture out on long walks to the woodlands on the outskirts of the city. Here, there was no need to imagine a forest. She felt at home sitting under the trees, with only her sketchpad for company.

She'd draw the trees or birds and notice how they differed from the forest of her dreams. She'd done some research on the internet at the library and been surprised to discover the forest she yearned for most closely resembled those found in Australia. It was strange to dream of a country she'd never been to. She'd never set foot outside Hong Kong.

The sheltered life she led didn't keep her thoughts from traveling across the globe. Her heart broke when she watched news reports and learned of wars that left people homeless and hungry as the innocence was stolen from their children's eyes. She wept as she learned of rainforests being devastated in order to graze cattle to supply the world with food that was clogging arteries and shortening lives. Precious species of animals were becoming extinct, crops were being sprayed with toxins and rivers pumped dry.

The world seemed to be filled with hurricanes and bush-fires, tsunamis and landslides, but here in the woodlands there was peace. Here, she was safe.

Some days she'd close her eyes and study the faces that plagued her thoughts. Then she'd sketch them. The faces belonged to westerners. They had kind eyes and fair skin. She wondered if they were from Australia, too.

Other days she wouldn't draw at all. She'd sit quietly and try to figure out what it all meant. Perhaps she'd seen an Australian movie when she was young and it had some kind of profound impact on her? Or perhaps not.

What she'd never been able to figure out was why, if she hadn't been to Australia, she felt as if her heart belonged there. Was it possible she'd lived a life there before? Many people in Hong Kong believed in reincarnation, but surely that couldn't be true?

Her parents often asked where she went when she disappeared, and she'd provide elaborate accounts of happy times spent with imaginary friends from school. The truth was she'd never had a friend from school or anywhere else. The other girls found her strange. They far preferred to keep company with clones of themselves than to listen to Lin's foreign ideas about the world and what their place in it might be. They kept their distance from her and although at times she was extremely lonely, she learned to value her own company.

The tourists who came to her family's store fascinated her. Her keen ears listened to their chatter as they passed by and she picked up English as though it was a language she'd been born to speak. She watched American sitcoms every chance she got as she perfected her skills. Her mother noticed her unusual interest, asking one day if her family wasn't good enough for her. How could Lin tell her that although she loved them, she couldn't shake the feeling she wasn't supposed to be here? There were times she wondered if she could be adopted. All it took was a glance in a mirror to push this thought from her mind. She shared an uncanny physical likeness to her mother. The same gentle curve of the brow, the same straight nose, the same high cheekbones. Why then did she relate more to the faces of strangers than those of her own family? At times she felt like two people sharing the one body.

There was one face in particular that haunted the depths of her mind. The older she got, the more the face pushed itself to the surface. She sketched it over and over trying to get the details right. Her pencil raced across the page shading his angular features. She pressed harder on the page as she traced the line of a scar that ran from his eye to his chin. His face seemed too young to be the owner of a scar like this. His skin was fair, his hair a dark shade of blond. But it was his eyes that captivated her. They reminded her of what it felt like to stare into the sky on a summer's day. They were full of depth and wonder, almost as though he knew all her secret hopes and dreams. She'd stare into his eyes and imagine what it would be like to look into them for real.

Faces like this weren't often seen in the streets of Hong Kong. The fairness of his features was in complete contrast to the people who surrounded her life, yet when she looked at him, she felt like she'd come home. She knew the boy who wore this face. She was connected to him somehow.

She kept her sketchpad hidden from her parents, tucking it in the bottom of the small chest she used to store her clothes. Her parents understood her need to draw even less than her need to conjure a forest from her window.

On the day of Lin's seventeenth birthday, she returned to her apartment to the sound of her parents shouting. Her mother was clutching her sketchbook to her chest, her face lined with tears. Her father was pacing the room, his fists clenched in frustration. They looked at her with sad, wide eyes.

It took her a few moments to realize they weren't arguing. Her parents' raised voices had been in harmony. They weren't upset with each other. They were upset with her. She stood in silence, waiting to be told what it was she'd done wrong.

"You lied to us," her father said.

"No, Ah-ba," she protested.

"You haven't been meeting your friends when you say you have."

"Have you been following me?" she asked, preparing to come clean about her trips to the woodlands. Surely, they couldn't be this upset about her need to draw, even if they didn't understand it?

"I don't need to follow you to know when you're lying." Her father looked disappointed. It was a look that broke her heart.

"I'm sorry, Ah-ba."

"You've been meeting the man from the market," her mother said, her eyes carefully avoiding her gaze. "You've disgraced our family's name." She stood and threw the sketchpad on the ground at Lin's feet. It was open at her latest drawing of the haunting face of the boy with the scar.

Lin bent to pick up the pad. "I don't know any man from the market. I haven't disgraced you."

"You lie," her father said. "The man you draw is the man from the market."

"It isn't true. I never go to the market. I go to the forest to draw. I don't know this man. Besides, the face I draw is of a boy, not a man." She knew the futility of her words as she spoke them. It didn't seem plausible she could be sketching a face she'd never seen. Had she come across this boy long ago and stored him in her subconscious? No. She'd remember a face like this. She'd remember the scar, if nothing else. She was sure she'd never met him.

"First you lie to us about where you've been going," her father said. "Now you lie to us about knowing this man. He followed your mother to our shop this morning and was asking for you. Do you still insist you don't know him?"

"You bring us shame." Her mother shook her head.

Her father stood, staring at her, waiting for her response. She knew there was nothing she could say to satisfy them. The truth would never be believed, and enough lies had already been told. She held her sketchpad tightly in one hand and looked from her mother to her father.

"I'm sorry."

With that, she ran to the door, down the stairs and onto the street below. She ran directly toward the market, her long, black hair streaming behind her. She wondered what she expected to find, or rather who she expected to find. The boy from her drawings was obviously known to her parents from the market, although they insisted he was now a man who'd been looking for her in their store. She had to find him.

The market was busy. She'd never spent much time there, finding any excuse not to accompany her parents on their regular trips for supplies. She hated crowds. This was just another quality of hers that those around her found strange. Craving personal space in a city like this was a pipedream.

She wound her way through the narrow lanes, studying the faces around her. If the boy from her drawings was here, he'd stand out. There weren't many westerners around. This market wasn't one of those frequented by tourists. He should be easy to find.

He wasn't.

After checking every market stall twice and scanning the faces of the crowds that milled around them, she realized she'd need to ask for help.

She fought the panic that had started surging through her veins, as she contemplated never finding him. She knew he must hold the answer to all her questions, otherwise she wouldn't know his face. How unbearable to come this close, yet still be so far away.

She approached a kindly-looking woman selling colorful reams of fabric and showed her one of her drawings.

"Have you seen this boy?" she asked in Cantonese.

The woman smiled and pointed a long, bony finger toward a small alleyway running behind the main thorough-fare. So, he *was* real. Her parents hadn't been mistaken.

She sighed, allowing the feeling of relief to restore her

calm. She thanked the lady and walked in the direction she'd been shown, carefully stepping on the uneven path, looking from left to right at the rear of the market stalls. It was dirty here, with the distinct smell of urine in the air. She stepped over a broken wooden box, almost slipped on a squashed orange and sat down on a bag of rice to catch her breath. She was close. She could feel it. She could feel *him*. He was very near.

She looked around. An old man with a hunched back and a pair of thick spectacles was staring at her from the rear of a small grocery store. He smiled and motioned with his walking stick for her to come closer. She stood and walked to him.

He either couldn't speak or chose not to as he motioned for her to step inside his store. She followed.

"Reinier," he said to her.

He pointed to a small camp bed that had been set up in the tiny back room of the shop. Pinned to the wall above the bed was a drawing. It was a drawing of a girl who looked unmistakably like Lin.

With a sharp breath of surprise, she looked down to the bed, to see a man sleeping. He was the boy from her own drawings, only older, just as her parents had said. As she'd been busy drawing him, he'd been busy growing into a man. A man who appeared to go by the name Reinier.

The energy she'd felt in the alleyway had grown stronger. It was bouncing off the walls of the small room where she stood. Her parents had always told her to be wary of strangers, but it didn't feel like she was in danger. The energy that surrounded this man felt good. She'd been right to come here.

"Reinier," the old man said, prodding him awake with his walking stick. "She's here."

He sat up, dazed, turning his eyes from the old man to

Lin. He jumped to his feet in haste, placing a large hand on each of her shoulders.

She flinched at the unexpected contact but didn't step away. He was taller than she'd imagined. She supposed that was what happened when you became a man.

As she looked into his eyes she felt a tingle run down her spine. This was the face of her dreams, the one she'd been unable to shake since the day she was born. She resisted a sudden urge to trace the familiar scar that marked his face.

The old man left them alone.

"You're here. You found me." His face radiated joy.

"Yes, I did." Her voice was a whisper. Her confidence and determination of only a few moments ago had evaporated the moment she'd laid eyes upon him. When she'd been searching for him so frantically in the market, she hadn't expected that finding him would knock the breath out of her lungs with such force.

"You speak English?" he asked.

She nodded, noticing the surprise on his face.

"You've always had a knack for languages."

"Who are you?" she asked, finding her voice. How would he know anything about her, let alone that?

"I'm Reinier. I've been searching for you," he said, cutting into her thoughts as he pointed to the sketch above his bed.

"Did you draw this?"

"Yes. It took me about a hundred attempts, but I eventually got your features right. Do you draw?" he asked, noticing the sketchbook in her hands.

Her shaking hands passed him her open sketchbook. He looked down and saw a younger version of his own face staring back at him.

"It worked. I knew you wouldn't let her take everything. I'm so proud of you." He threw the sketchpad onto the bed. This time when he put his hands on her it was to embrace her tightly. Her feet lifted from the ground as he swung her in a circle like a prize. She felt like a small child next to his tall, athletic frame.

He placed her down and she smoothed an imaginary wrinkle from her shirt, trying to disguise the blush that had risen to her cheeks. No man had ever laid his hands on her like this, apart from her father, and the man before her was most definitely not her father. Everything about him felt foreign, like he'd come to her from another world. Everything except his eyes. She looked directly into them, as she'd longed to for so many years. Her stomach tied itself into knots. Her drawing had come to life, only the eyes that stared back at her were even more soulful than she'd been able to capture on a page. She looked away, feeling embarrassed and not entirely sure why.

"What's your name?" he asked.

"Lin."

"Lin," he repeated. "Tell me, Lin. How exactly is it that no matter who you're born to, you're always the most beautiful girl in the world?"

The embarrassment she'd felt earlier crept further into the pit of her stomach. His over-familiarity was making her uncomfortable. She cursed herself for behaving like this. She had so many questions, yet here she was behaving like a young child.

"I don't understand," she said. "I don't know you."

"You do know me. How else do you explain your drawings? You just need to remember. Once the memories start, it'll all come back."

"What memories? I'm not..." Her voice trailed away as she contemplated escape. The only problem with that was she'd never get her answers. She'd come too far now to walk away.

"Don't go." He placed his hand on her forearm, sensing her desire to flee.

She pushed him away. "Okay. I'll stay, but I need you to do one thing."

"Yes?"

"Please keep your hands off me. I'm not used to men touching me like that." She couldn't tell him that every time he touched her she felt as if she might faint from the strange sensations it sent coursing through her body.

He smiled at her. "I'm sorry. Of course."

She sat down on the edge of the camp bed, folding her hands delicately on her knees. It was time to push down her nerves and ask some of the questions she'd been seeking answers to when she came in search of him.

"Start from the beginning," she said, finding her courage. "Who are you? And by that, I'm not asking your name. Why have I been drawing you? Why have you been drawing me? None of this is making any sense."

"Do you believe life continues after death?" he asked.

She nodded. "But what does that have to do with anything? I'm not dead and, by the look of things, neither are you."

"It'll make things easier, that's all. You already know my name's Reinier, but that's not always been so. My soul's been walking this earth for more than a thousand years, living different lives as different people." He paused, searching her eyes for a clue as to how she was taking this.

She sat quietly. He was speaking of a topic she'd often wondered about. If he'd lived before then it was more than possible she had, too. She waited for him to continue.

"Have you ever had the feeling you've lived before?"

"What do you mean?" His question made her nervous. He'd hit a nerve.

"I mean, do you ever feel like you've been here before?

49

Not as Lin, but as someone else with another life. Do you ever feel like this life isn't quite where you belong?"

"I feel like that all the time." She saw no point in lying. "How did you know that?"

"The last time I saw you, you were a girl named Hannah, living in Australia in a small town on the edge of the forest."

Her back straightened. He couldn't possibly know she dreamed of the Australian forest. He'd fallen silent, continuing to monitor her reaction to what he'd just told her.

"Go on," she said, feeling impatient.

He took a deep breath, clearly deciding she was coping with the direction of the conversation. "Your father was a preacher and you were in love with a boy called Matthew."

"Matthew," she repeated. She'd heard that name once on television and it had affected her. It was a name that felt important, only she had never known why. Occasionally, she'd find herself whispering the name, repeating it, noticing the way her tongue pressed against her front teeth when the name slid from her lips. How strange that this name would have such an effect on her, when the name Hannah had not.

"Yes, Matthew," he said. "He almost died trying to protect you. He loved you and you loved him. You know the name, don't you?"

She nodded, pointing to her sketchpad. "Is he in here?"

He picked it up and sat next to her on the bed as he flipped through the pages. He stopped at one of her earlier drawings and pointed to a sketch of a face she'd stared at for hours when she'd first drawn it. She'd become entranced as she'd traced her pencil along the strong line of his cheekbones. When she'd drawn the curve of his lips, she'd stopped still as she'd fought the urge to bend forward and bring her own lips to the page.

"Ridiculously good looking, isn't he?" he said.

She wondered for a moment who was better looking –

this boy called Matthew or the man who sat beside her. They were so different, yet both so striking that they equally filled her with feelings she didn't understand.

"Hannah was beautiful, too," he said. "Let me see if you're in here." He flipped through more pages, passing her the book when he found the picture he was looking for.

She studied the drawing for a moment. He was right. Hannah was beautiful. She looked like an angel. She felt electricity pass through her as she stared into the very eyes she herself had drawn. She knew what he was saying was true. This face *was* her face. It was the face she subconsciously expected to see every time she looked in a mirror. She'd never recognized her own dark eyes staring back at her. But how could this be true?

"Here's your mother." He pointed to another drawing of a woman with kind eyes and a warm smile. She ran her thumb gently across the page, caressing the sweet face that stared back at her.

"And my father? Where's he?" She wanted to know more. Despite how ridiculous it sounded, the more information she had, the more she felt at ease. Finally, these faces had names. They were people. *Real* people. She hadn't dreamed them up. She'd drawn them for a reason.

He flipped through the pages, turning each one slowly. "That's odd. Your father's not in here. Surely you've seen him in your dreams?"

"What did he look like?"

"He was some kind of minister. A preacher. I only saw him once. He was tall, stern looking."

"I've never seen anyone like that." How strange she'd seen so many faces, and never the face of the man who'd raised her.

"I wonder…" His voice trailed away. She couldn't tell if

he'd become lost in thought or changed his mind about what he was about to say.

"What do you wonder? Tell me."

"The weaving. I wonder if she took him from you in the weaving."

"What weaving? What are you talking about?"

"I'll explain that to you later. I don't want to bombard you with too much, too soon."

"No." She grabbed him on the arm, the contact taking him by surprise. "I've waited my whole life for these answers. This is the first conversation I've had with anyone that has actually made any sense. You can't stop giving me answers now."

Tears streamed down her face. The information he was giving her felt as important as the air in her lungs. For the very first time, she didn't feel different or crazy.

"Lin, it's okay. I'm going to tell you everything. As long as you've been waiting for these answers, I've been waiting to give them to you."

"Why have you waited so long? Do you know what torture life's been like for me? I thought I was mad." Her hand slipped from his arm and she clenched her fists in her lap.

"I had to wait until you were old enough to understand. How could I have told you this as a child?"

"Well, I'm not a child anymore. Please, you must tell me everything. Don't hold back. What's the weaving? Who took my father from me?"

He hesitated, an internal struggle visible on his face. "I just don't think it's right to tell you everything at once. I've already told you more than I'd planned to at first. If I tell you more, you might run away. And if that happens, we're all ruined."

"I'm not running anywhere. I'm here. I just have so many questions. You've hardly told me anything."

"Don't get upset, please. I've always hated to see you upset."

"Who are you? When have you hated seeing me upset?" She shifted to face him, looking deep into his eyes. They truly were windows to his soul. And it was a soul that grabbed hold of her heart and made her want to sob with joy.

"You feel it too, don't you?" He reached for her, his hand stopping only inches from her face.

She yearned for him to touch her. To feel his hands upon her face, his breath upon her cheek.

A jolt of energy passed through her as his skin connected with hers. With great effort she pulled away. "I asked you not to touch me."

"I'm sorry. I keep forgetting." His hand dropped to his knee. She looked at his long fingers and wide palms. These were hands that had a story to tell. He'd not been sitting idly by, waiting for her to come of age. His hands were the kind that knew hard work.

"Who are you?" she asked again.

"I'll tell you who I am but let me tell you about Matthew first."

"Okay." She would agree to anything just to keep him talking.

"Hannah loved Matthew. *You* loved Matthew. He was your intended. What you had with him was special. You were meant to have a child with him, and that child was destined to be very important to the world. It was a child that Mother was determined not to let you have."

"Hannah's mother?"

"No, not Hannah's mother. *Mother*. The Soulweaver."

"What's a Soulweaver?"

"It's exactly what you might think. She weaves our souls

into the lives we're meant to live. She's the one who decides what life we should live next for the benefit of humankind."

"I've dreamed of a woman with a glowing gown and halo of hair. She looks like an angel, yet somehow I always wake feeling uneasy."

"That's Mother. She wove the life you're living right now. You've met her many times."

"Just how many lives have I lived?" Her dark eyes searched his face for a hint of deception. Was he making this up? It seemed a little elaborate for a prank.

"You've lived dozens of lives."

"Then why don't I remember any of them? I only remember Hannah."

"You hung onto your memories of Hannah. You refused to let Mother take them from you," he said proudly.

"I'm not sure I did myself any favors there." Her words wiped the pride from his face.

"Why would you say that?"

"I feel like two people sharing a body. I can't separate where Hannah ends and where I begin."

"But that's exactly it. You can't separate them. You *are* Hannah. The one soul. You lived a life in her body and now you live as Lin. The only difference between you and Hannah is the body that contains your soul. Apart from that, you're exactly the same person."

"So why would Mother want to take my memories? What does it mean to her?"

"That's what she does. She gives each soul a clean slate with each new life. Can you imagine how complicated it'd get if everyone remembered their past lives?"

"Like me."

"Not like you. You only remember one other life and look how confused you've been. How'd you like to add another twenty or thirty to that? Trust me, it's not much fun."

"Is that what it's like for you?"

"Not as clearly as you remember being Hannah, but yes." He rose to his feet and paced the confines of the small room.

"So, you're telling me that with all the people you remember from all your lives, you've come looking for me. Why?"

"Because you're my soulmate. The other half to my whole." He looked at her with those eyes again and she felt herself being drawn in. Her soulmate? That sounded awfully romantic.

"I thought you said Matthew was my soulmate."

"I said he was your intended. That doesn't make him your soulmate. It's a common misconception that soulmates must be only of the romantic kind. It's possible to have a romantic relationship with a partner who isn't your soulmate, just as it's possible for your soulmate to be someone other than your partner."

Her cheeks flushed. "Right. I understand." It was like he'd read her thoughts. He didn't think of her in a romantic way. She was clear on that now. The feeling of embarrassment washed over her once more.

"You and I have traveled through each lifetime together, always finding each other no matter where in the world we've been placed. In some lifetimes I've been your husband – your intended – in others I've been your brother, your cousin, your son, your best friend. In each life, we meet and help each other on our paths. When our life is done we return to the stars and wait for each other before being born again. Except this time. Mother sent you back without me. She sent you far away, hoping I wouldn't find you. But as you see, even she's not powerful enough to keep us apart."

They sat in silence while she tried to absorb what he was telling her. His story was laughable. Then why wasn't she laughing? Each word he spoke made sense. Each piece of information filled a piece of the puzzle that'd been bothering her since her earliest years. She had to hear him out.

"If I don't look like Hannah, then how did you draw me? How did you find me? The world's a big place."

"Lin, I'd recognize you anywhere. It's not your face that's familiar to me, it's your soul. All I had to do was close my eyes and listen to my heart. Exactly like you did when you drew these pictures. I could see you and your surroundings. Soon your face became as familiar to me as your soul, I saw it so often."

"But I didn't draw your face as it is now. I drew you when you were younger. I pictured you as a boy."

"That's because you met me when you were Hannah, and I was a boy. Memories are far more powerful than conjuring a face you've never seen. All the pictures you draw are of faces as Hannah saw them, not as they are now."

"That doesn't explain how you found me once you'd seen my face."

"At first, I thought you were in China and I'd never find you, but then I closed my eyes and saw you with your father on a tram. You were pushed right back in your seat as if you were climbing the steepest mountain. You looked almost as if you were lying down."

She remembered that day. Her father had taken her on the tram that climbed Victoria Peak. Knowing how much she loved looking out on the city, he'd wanted to show it to her from its highest point. He'd been devastated when they'd arrived on the observation deck to find the city shrouded in clouds. She'd thought it was spectacular. She felt like she was on top of the world and had leaned out on the safety rails, letting the wind catch hold of her long hair and imagined she was an angel flying through the sky. How strange to think Reinier had also been with her that day.

"I knew immediately I'd been wrong," he continued. "I

saw a story on television once about that tram and recognized it instantly. I left for Hong Kong the next day. That was a month ago now. As soon as I arrived I knew you were near. I could feel you, like your energy was pulling me in your direction."

She wanted to tell him she felt the same, but she remained quiet. His words were more important to her at this stage.

"But this city has a lot of people in it," he said. "And you weren't so easy to find. Then I saw your mother in the market and I was sure I'd found you. You look so alike. I followed her to your family's shop this morning and asked if she had a daughter. I'm afraid I upset her. I was going to return later today to follow her home. I just knew she'd lead me to you."

"And instead I found you." She grinned, proud to have beaten him to it.

"How exactly did you manage that?"

"My mother was so upset at your visit that she went through my belongings to see if she could find evidence of some kind of secret affair. She found this." She pointed to the sketchpad. "Once she saw your face in there, she became convinced I've been shaming our family's name."

The door opened with a bang. Lin looked up, expecting to see the old man who'd led her here.

She was wrong.

CHAPTER FOUR

*L*in's father stood in the doorway, staring at his only daughter sitting with a strange man on a bed in the back of a grocery store.

It didn't look good and she knew it.

"Come here." His expression said more than his words. He was thinking the worst, and there was nothing she could say to reassure him.

"Sorry, Ah-ba." She crossed the room, standing silently to face him.

He raised his hand and brought it down across her face. She felt the blood rush to her cheek as the sting of the slap took hold. Pain burned through her. He'd never taken a hand to her before, except in love. Shock and shame sliced to her core.

"What have you done?" cried Reinier, rushing to her side, his eyes burning with hatred. He towered over her father, yet the older man held his ground, refusing to be intimidated.

"Please, Reinier. No," said Lin. "This is my fight. Not yours."

"Come," her father repeated, grabbing hold of her arm.

"I'll find you as soon as I can," she told Reinier, grateful for the privacy provided by her father's lack of English.

"Don't go with him. Come with me. Please, Lin."

"Not now. I have to make things right at home. My parents deserve better than this. I'll come back. Please, wait for me."

Her father was pulling on her arm now, dragging her from the store.

"I'll be here! Just make sure you return. You know I'll find you if you don't." He rushed to her and handed her the sketchpad. "You'll want this."

As her father swept her from the room, she met Reinier's eyes and held them. Light raced between them. There was a connection she'd never felt before. What he was saying was true. She'd known him since forever. He was part of her.

She walked alongside her father in silence. It was a silence that shouted at her so loudly she felt like covering her ears, as she tried to find a way to explain something that would be impossible for him to understand. She realized the truth wasn't the best choice in this situation. He'd never believe her, and it would drive a further wedge between them – a wedge too large to ever be dislodged.

She had no choice but to weave a clever web of lies. It was vital she regain her parents' trust, so she could return to the market and talk further with Reinier. Hopefully he'd wait for her. If what he was saying was true, and he really was her soulmate, then surely, he'd wait. But what if he didn't? He'd hardly told her anything. The thought of finding out as much as she had and no more, chilled her. She wouldn't be able to go on, knowing what she now knew and not having the opportunity to piece it all together. She'd never be able to do that on her own.

They approached the apartment building and climbed the stairs. Each step punched dread into the pit of her stomach.

Her mother would be waiting for her. She needed to think of a good story, and she needed to think of it fast.

Her father opened the apartment door and led her inside.

"Sit." He pointed to a wooden chair, placed opposite the settee her mother was sitting on. Lin did as she was told. Her father sat next to her mother. It reminded her of an inquisition.

Her father's rage exploded with sudden intensity, causing her to jump a few inches from her chair.

"You've shamed us. Shamed! You've lied to us many times. Then to make it worse, you ran away from us. We didn't raise you to disrespect us like this."

Her mother nodded in agreement, pausing occasionally to dab a handkerchief to her eyes, despite no tears seeming to be present.

Her father continued. "You've never been interested in your own family or culture. We've seen the way you look at westerners, like you think you belong with them and not with us. We've never been good enough for you. And now I find you alone with this foreign man whoring yourself on his bed. You're lucky I'm even speaking to you right now."

At this news, her mother wailed. Lin felt nauseous. Her father was so wrong, yet a lot of what he was saying was true. She did feel like she belonged in another world – Hannah's world. But she'd never thought her own family wasn't good enough. She loved her parents. She was proud of them and the life they'd managed to build for themselves and for her. She'd always felt their love. It pained her to have disappointed them like this.

"You're not saying anything," her father bellowed. "Are we not even worth your time to speak?"

She cleared her throat, still unsure what explanation she was about to give. *Help me, Reinier,* she thought. *Tell me what to say.* She sank to the floor and knelt in front of her parents with her head bowed. When she looked up, her cheeks were streaked with tears.

"I'm sorry. I didn't mean to lie to you. I love you. I'm young and I've acted badly. The man from the market is Reinier. He's a good man. He loves me and I love him. We're getting married. There'll be no shame on our family." Her mouth dropped in surprise. When she'd begun to speak she had no idea those were the words that would come out.

"Married! I don't think so. You're seventeen years old." Her father looked almost as shocked as when he'd found her on Reinier's bed.

"Which means I need your blessing, Ah-ba. I didn't intend to ask you like this. Reinier wanted to ask you himself."

"Tell him not to bother. Actually, there'll be no need for that, given you won't be seeing him to tell him anything."

"No. Please," she begged, noticing a new spark of hope in her mother's eyes. "Ah-ma?"

"It's not up to me." She looked at her husband and waited for him to speak.

"Please," Lin said. "Just think about it. We don't need to decide right away."

"I've already decided," her father said. "Now go to your room. You're the one who needs to think about things. Not us."

She rose to her feet and headed to her bedroom. Married? Where had that come from? She had to admit it was a genius idea. If Reinier were her fiancé, she'd be able to spend time with him without any shame being brought on her family. Then she could ask him each and every question that was burning her. The only problem with the plan was the actual marriage part. She never thought she'd get married. No boy had ever interested her before. Although, if there was one thing about Reinier, he was definitely interesting.

She lay down on her bed and remembered the sparks that

had flown through her body each time he'd laid his hands on her. He was older than her, but that didn't bother her. She'd always preferred the company of people who'd lived more years than she had. People her own age seemed so frivolous. And he was extremely handsome. The scar on his face made him seem dangerous. Mysterious. Yes, he was certainly more appealing than any man she'd ever met. And if she'd married him in past lives, then surely it made sense to marry him again?

Her mind turned to the activities married people did and heat rose to her cheeks. That wasn't something she could imagine herself doing. Would she have the courage to stand before him stripped bare of her clothes? What would it feel like to have his hands upon her? For him to touch her most private places. Her stomach clenched in a way that was starting to become familiar. He might not think of her in a romantic sense, yet she was certainly seeing him that way. She was already lying to her parents in an attempt to see him again. Was it possible to love someone you'd only known for ten minutes? Although if what Reinier was saying was true, she'd known him a lot longer than ten minutes.

A thousand years longer than ten minutes.

She rose to her feet and stood at her window. Night was falling and the sharp angles of neighboring buildings were starting to dull as they began their transformation into shadow and light. Where was Reinier? He was out there somewhere. Was he thinking of her?

He'd said Hannah lived in a small town on the edge of the forest. This explained why she felt such a connection to the forest. She looked out at the city, only this time instead of imagining the buildings as trees, they became the trees. She saw the forest with vivid clarity. Mountain Ash trees loomed overhead with large hollows in trunks that trailed with moss. Giant tree ferns lined the forest floor, with yellow robins hopping between their branches. She smelt the woody scent of the earth with hints of eucalyptus floating on the breeze. She heard animals calling to each other.

The forest she saw was Hannah's forest, and she missed it with an intensity that ached. She decided she'd go to Australia, somehow, some day. Maybe Reinier would take her there. If only he were here right now, she could ask him.

She picked up her sketchpad and looked at each drawing in turn. A few hours ago these sketches had filled her with confusion, but now they explained so much. These were the faces of people who'd helped shape her as the person she was today. She turned to the page with Hannah and looked into her own eyes once more.

"Hello, me." She wanted to know more about Hannah. More about the life she'd lived. Reinier had said it was possible to listen to her heart for answers. He said that's what she'd been doing, even if she hadn't known she was doing it.

She lay down and closed her eyes. She pictured Hannah in the forest. No, that wouldn't work. She couldn't *see* Hannah. She *was* Hannah. She took a deep breath and concentrated.

"I am Hannah," she whispered. She became aware of seeing the forest through a set of pale blue eyes. She felt her long, blonde hair shift in the gentle breeze. She felt her hand being held. Love and warmth were pouring into her whole body through the palm of her hand. She looked across and saw Matthew. He was smiling at her, leading her deeper into the forest. She smiled back at him. He was her life. He was her love. She ran with him into a clearing and they sank to their knees.

He was kissing her now. His soft lips pressed firmly against hers, his tongue seeking her own. Fire shot to her belly as she remembered how it felt to kiss the man she loved. It felt like her first kiss, experienced through lips that were her own, yet no longer existed. It was wonderful in ways she never expected. She felt powerful and vulnerable at the same time. Most of all she felt longing. A longing deep within her, to kiss Matthew until the world ran out of time. She'd never break away.

Then there was a noise and Reinier stood before them. He looked younger, like the boy from her drawings. His hair was wild, as were his eyes. He was holding a dagger. She felt herself as Hannah recognizing him. Only now, as Lin, she knew what it was she was recognizing. Not his face, but his soul.

This must be what Reinier had meant when he'd said they'd met before.

Matthew was trying to protect her. She cried out. He was the one who needed protection, not her. She felt a pain in her leg and saw Matthew and Reinier wrestling on the ground. The two men she loved. The image of them fighting tore at her heart. Reinier held a dagger over his head. She saw herself leaping between them. Then there was light. So much light. Then nothing.

She opened her eyes. Her room was dark now. The noise from the street below hummed into her consciousness. Her breathing was fast. Her heart was beating so hard it hurt. What had she seen? Reinier hadn't told her how Hannah had died. Had he killed her? Had he tried to kill Matthew? Perhaps that's why he thought she'd run when he told her who he was. She found it hard to believe he was capable of killing anybody. No. He said Mother had killed her. There'd been a light in the clearing that had something to do with her death. It wasn't Reinier.

Or was it?

Listening to her heart hadn't answered any questions. It'd only raised a thousand more.

The only thing she knew for certain was that Hannah had

loved Matthew. It was a deep and abiding love. A love that Lin felt in every cell. So, if she loved Matthew, how could she love Reinier too?

This morning she'd been in love with nobody. This morning, life was very simple, despite how complicated it had seemed at the time. Perhaps she'd have been better off not knowing anything she'd learned today.

Somehow, she knew that wasn't true.

———

It was five weeks until Lin saw Reinier again. They were five very long weeks and she was miserable. Her questions ate at her, robbing her of her ability to concentrate at school. She found herself unable even to draw a picture or read a book. Instead, she stood by her window or lay on her bed and recalled every possible detail about her life as Hannah. Memories flooded back, just as Reinier said they would. Sometimes she'd go into such a trance-like state, it came as a shock when she opened her eyes to realize she was a seventeen-year-old girl living in Hong Kong.

When she wasn't dreaming of Hannah, she was planning ways to see Reinier again. This wasn't proving easy. Her father had insisted on walking her to school in the morning and her mother was waiting at the gates at the end of the day. She felt like a criminal, not to be trusted. Her relationship with her parents had morphed from one of respect and love into one filled with resentment and suspicion.

Yet, still she believed she'd somehow see Reinier again. One day.

She wanted things to go back to the way they'd been before, but it was too late for that. She had to accept life was never going to be the same. Reinier had changed her forever. She ached to see him. To ask him questions, to feel the energy pass between them when she looked in his eyes, to spend time with the one person in the world who truly understood her.

She decided he couldn't possibly have killed Hannah. She would never believe that. His heart was too pure to have committed such a heinous act. Positive energy radiated from his soul. She'd once heard of someone who photographed auras. If this were possible, she thought such a photo of Reinier would rob the breath from her lungs, it'd be so beautiful.

She was sitting at the kitchen table doing her homework under the close supervision of her mother, when her father walked through the door. Waves of missing Reinier washed over her. It wasn't her father she wanted to see.

She didn't look up from her page. She rarely greeted her father anymore. It'd become too awkward. She knew he missed the days when as a young girl she'd drop whatever it was she'd been doing and run to him, throwing her arms around him and begging him to swing her around in endless circles. She missed it, too.

"Lin, we have a visitor," her father said.

She sighed, pushing down the sudden pang she'd just felt at Reinier's absence and glanced up. She wasn't in the mood to make small talk with one of her father's friends.

Her eyes widened to see the visitor was Reinier. He was standing next to her father, grinning. He winked at her and she felt the sparks from his eyes fly toward her, warming her from the inside. This was why she'd had a sudden, uncontrollable urge to see him. She'd felt his presence before her eyes had the chance to catch up.

She smiled her first genuine smile for five weeks. He was back. She'd forgotten just how attractive he was. Tall and strong, yet gentle and kind. And here he was standing next to her father, who didn't look at all like he was about to murder him. This was too good to be true.

"Sit down," her father said, motioning for Reinier to take a seat at the table.

"Thank you, that's very kind of you," he replied in perfect Cantonese.

"You speak our language?" Lin was shocked. It seemed there was nothing this man couldn't do.

"You're not the only one with a knack for languages. Besides, I'll do anything for the woman I love," he replied in English.

She blushed and looked across at her mother. She looked nervous, but not in the least surprised to see Reinier.

"Did you know about this?" she asked her mother.

"Listen to your father."

"Well, Ah-ba, what's happening here?"

"I thought you'd be happy," he said.

"I am happy. I'm just confused. Can you please tell me what's going on?"

"Reinier's been visiting me at the shop." His voice was matter-of-fact. It was the same voice he'd use to read her a shopping list or ask her to fetch him a glass of water.

"And you didn't tell me?" She sat forward in her chair, her eyes ablaze at how casually he was treating this.

"I don't tell you everything, just as you don't tell us everything." He raised an eyebrow at her, and she shrank back in her chair. So, that was it. His attitude was part of her punishment.

"At first I refused to see him," her father continued. "But he was very persistent. Eventually he persuaded me to listen to what he had to say."

She glanced at Reinier, who was still grinning.

"I got sick of waiting for you," he said.

"So," her father continued. "Reinier tells me he loves you.

He's convinced me his intentions are honorable. He'd like to marry you. From what you've said, I believe you'd like to marry him too?"

Her heart leaped. How did Reinier know that was what she'd told her parents? Her father must have said something. Was he really prepared to go along with her lie, or was it possible he wanted to marry her for real? No man had ever paid her much attention before. Why would a man like Reinier want to marry a girl like her?

Because they were soulmates. He'd told her so, himself.

"Yes, Ah-ba. I'd like to marry him." Her voice was a whisper as her nerves took hold. She wished she'd had more experience with men so she knew how to speak, how to act. She should have paid more attention to the boys at school.

"He's not a man of great means," her father said. "Nor is he the type of man I'd hoped for you to marry, but I believe he has a good heart."

"Yes, he does." Lin nodded. He did have a good heart. Although, she was surprised to hear her father speak like this. It was beginning to sound like he was going to offer his approval. The thought of him agreeing to let her marry a westerner was astounding. He'd always looked down on those from other cultures.

Reinier must have presented a very convincing argument. Perhaps the energy he radiated had an effect on other people as well as herself. Either that, or her father felt he had no choice. If she'd brought shame on his name, then marrying Reinier would be just about the only way for him to justify his daughter's actions.

"Life's been very unhappy over the last few weeks and that's not something I'm able to live with," he said. "I thought you'd snap out of your mood, but as time's been passing, you've been getting worse. Your smile has always been my joy and I can't bear to see it leave your face. I miss my d-daughter." The emotion he'd been hiding crept into his voice, causing his words to break.

"Thank you, Ah-ba." Her eyes welled with tears. She noticed her mother sitting very still. The only sign of her consent was her silence. However, silent consent was better than no consent at all. She could imagine it would have been difficult for her father to obtain her mother's agreement on this.

Her heart burst with love for her parents as she thought of them discussing her future, and ultimately deciding to give their daughter what she wanted, in order to keep her happy. That in itself was the definition of true love. She'd treated them terribly. They deserved so much more than she'd given them.

"Don't thank me yet," her father said. "I'm prepared to grant my consent, but not until you turn eighteen. You're still young. You must finish your schooling before you become a woman."

Lin knew this was a sore point for him. He'd never attended school. Her mother had some schooling behind her, but not enough to have earned her the kind of job she'd have liked. They wanted a better life for their daughter.

"Am I allowed to see Reinier before then?" This was her most pressing question. She could easily wait until she was eighteen to marry him. She could wait longer than that if needed. But waiting a year to have him answer her questions would be intolerable.

"You may see him once a week on Sundays. You'll meet in public, or here in our apartment when your mother or I are home. If you disobey these rules and bring further shame on our family, I won't grant you my permission for marriage."

She knew this would mean she'd have to wait until the legal age of twenty-one, which defeated the whole purpose of the marriage. By that age, she'd be able to get the answers she needed without the need to be married. But twenty-one seemed light-years away. She needed answers now. Besides, the idea of marrying the man sitting at her table wasn't one she found unpleasant, no matter how much she tried to quash her feelings.

"Yes, Ah-ba. I promise to respect your wishes. Thank you. I'm so sorry. To you too, Ah-ma."

"In this family we move forward, not backward," her mother replied, as she stood and walked to the kitchen sink. Her father stood also, pausing for a moment to place his hand on her head. She reached for his hand and pressed it to her cheek. He withdrew it, but not before she saw the sheen of tears in his eyes.

There she remained, at the table, with Reinier sitting across from her. Her parents were only a few paces away, yet the language barrier set them miles apart. She looked into Reinier's pale blue eyes. She had remembered every detail of his face, seen it in her dreams, stared at it in her sketchbook. It was hard to believe she was looking at him in person once more. She'd failed to return to him, so he'd found a way to come to her. She tried to figure out which of the hundred questions swirling in her mind she should begin with.

He spoke first. "I'm sorry, Lin. I know I was supposed to wait for you, but I got impatient. I've been searching for you for so long. It was torture to find you and then have you torn away. And I was worried about you. I thought your father might be harming you."

"That was the first time he's slapped me. He's not like that. He was upset." She felt it important to defend her father. She couldn't have anyone thinking he was a monster, when he'd just proven himself to be a man beyond reproach.

"I know that now. Although, I think you can see why I was worried. I'm sorry."

"Please don't be sorry. It's me who's sorry. I said I'd come to you, but then I couldn't. It was impossible to get away."

"Okay. I forgive you, then." He smiled his beautiful smile and her stomach lurched with affection for him.

"How did you know I'd told my parents we were to be married?"

He smiled. "After you left the market with your father I lay down on my bed and brought you to my mind. I sent you white light to protect you and keep you strong. I could feel your pain. I heard you call my name. You asked for my help, remember?"

She had asked for his help when she hadn't known what to say to her parents. The idea to say they were to be married had seemed to come from nowhere. Apparently, that wasn't so.

"How did you do that?" she asked.

"I've learned a thing or two over the last thousand years I've been here. I just concentrated on you and using every ounce of my soul, I projected my thoughts into your mind."

"Impressive."

"Don't worry. It's for emergency use only. I can't have you thinking I'm some kind of stalker." He pulled a face that made her laugh. It felt good to laugh. It eased the mountain of tension that had built up in her stomach.

"Well, thank you. I'm not sure what I would've said without your help."

"You would've thought of something."

"Yeah, something that would've ensured there'd be no way you'd be sitting here right now."

"Don't be so hard on yourself." His face filled with love and concern, causing her to shift uncomfortably in her chair. Was it possible she had the same effect on him that he had on her? He seemed so at ease.

"So," she said, desperate to turn the conversation around.

"You can learn to speak Cantonese in the blink of an eye, you can sketch faces like an artist, and you can project thoughts into people's minds. Is there anything you can't do?"

"I can't project thoughts into people's minds. Just yours."

"Then why didn't you tell me you were coming today? It would've saved me the shock."

"It doesn't work like that. It's not a telephone. It's more like sending ideas than actual words. Several times I did try to reassure you that you'd see me again. Did you feel that?"

She nodded. She had felt it. She'd known he'd find a way back to her.

"How exactly did you convince my father to let me marry you? I would've thought that was an impossible task. You make everything look so easy."

"It was anything but easy. Your father's a stubborn man, but it appears I'm even more so. I just kept trying until he listened. Convincing him was one of the hardest things I've done in any of my lifetimes."

Lin smiled. He'd fought for her. He really did love her. "Thank you. I'm so glad you succeeded. I was barely coping not being able to see you. Once we're married I'll be able to ask you questions until we're one hundred years old."

His eyes turned several shades darker and he looked away. She immediately wondered if his change of mood had anything to do with their nuptials.

"Do you really want to marry me or were you just trying to find a way we could talk?" She found herself desperately hoping he'd tell her that he loved her. Please, let it be true and not just a fantasy inside her head.

"We've been married so many times before, it doesn't seem to matter if we do it one more time."

This was far from the romantic response she expected. It seemed he did not, in fact, want to marry her for real. No man had ever made her feel the way he had. Unless she counted Matthew. But he could hardly count, given it was Hannah he'd loved, not her. She'd been naïve enough to think Reinier felt the same sparks pass between them. She sat in silence, scolding herself for being such an innocent.

"Lin, I didn't mean it like that," he said, noticing her change in demeanor. "I just meant that whether we're married or not, it changes nothing. The main thing is that we get to be together. I couldn't wait until you no longer lived under your parents' roof. I need to explain some things to you and the sooner I do it, the better. Being married just means we can get on with it right away."

"What's the hurry? You've waited this long." She was concerned. It didn't sound like he really wanted to marry her at all. She'd been foolish to think he'd felt the same way.

"Don't be upset. I love you. I've always loved you. It's just that there's a much greater purpose to our lives than getting married and living happily ever after."

"And what exactly is that?" She felt a little better. He did love her. But did he love her like a brother or like a lover? She knew how she felt.

"All in good time. There's a lot you need to understand first. Tell me, have Hannah's memories started to come back to you? They must have."

"Yes, although I still can't remember her father. *My* father. But the rest has been coming back. I remember my mother, Matthew, the forest. The memories are as clear as if they happened in this lifetime."

"That's wonderful. Not many souls have that ability, you know. You really are special."

"But there's still so much I'm confused about. You said Matthew almost died protecting me from Mother. In the memory I have of my death, you're the one who seems to have killed me. You were there with a dagger raised in the air, only I'm finding that hard to believe. What happened out there?"

He drew in a deep breath. "You were in the forest with Matthew. The conception of your child was imminent."

She blushed, remembering Matthew's hands upon her. It made her feel disloyal to Reinier. She remembered the love she felt for Matthew. The way she'd been prepared to give herself to him in body as well as her heart. If they hadn't been disturbed in the clearing that day, it was more than possible a child would've been conceived. A child that Reinier had said was destined to be very important to the world.

"What were you doing there?" she asked, embarrassed at what he must have witnessed. "If this child was meant to be so important, why did you try to prevent its conception?"

"The last thing I'd ever have tried to do was prevent it. I was trying to protect you, just like Matthew was. In the months before your death, I'd been having visions of you. We were yet to meet in Hannah's lifetime. Mother hadn't wanted us to meet, but I came to find you."

"But you were so young. How could you just up and find me?"

"Let's just say that the parents I was given in this lifetime didn't exactly care much about me. I ran away. I doubt they even looked for me."

She couldn't imagine anyone not caring for the man who sat before her. It made her incredibly sad. "I'm sorry to hear that."

"It's all right," he said, running his hands nervously through his hair. She noticed the strength in his forearms as he bent his arms back and looked away, feeling shy.

"What exactly were you hoping to achieve by finding me?" she asked, trying to steer the conversation back to more comfortable ground.

"I had to put a stop to Mother's plans for you."

"I thought Mother was good. You said she wove souls for the benefit of humankind."

"Mother's lost her way." His voice brimmed with sadness.

"What do you mean she's lost her way? What hope do any of us have if that's happened?"

"I don't know." He paused, his face etched with pain. "I do know she was aware of the importance of this child. That's why she decided to take your life. I couldn't let her do that. So, I got desperate and thought if I took Matthew's life, I could save yours. It was the only thing I could think of."

"You were trying to kill Matthew? How would that save me?" She sat back in her chair, horrified. Matthew had a pure soul, filled with light. She'd seen that through Hannah's eyes. The thought of someone taking his life was beyond cruel. No wonder she'd tried to protect him from Reinier.

"The child couldn't be conceived if Matthew was no longer there. There'd be no reason for Mother to kill you if he was already dead." He hung his head, clearly shamed by his actions.

"But you just said you wanted this child to be born."

"I know. However, if it were a choice between the child and you, I'd choose you every time. I'm sorry. Mother took you before I was able to act."

"How did she do it?"

"She reached out of the sky and lifted your soul directly from your body. I'd never seen that happen before. I was too late to save you. I'm not even sure I would've been able to go through with killing Matthew. Intentionally taking a life is the worst thing a soul can do. It's the only unforgiveable sin."

"What would've happened to you if you'd succeeded?"

"Simple. This life would be my last. My light would extinguish for good once it was done."

"You'd never have been reborn?"

"That's right."

"Why would you do that? Wouldn't it make more sense to let Mother kill Hannah and then we'd be together again in the next life? Like we are now."

"I knew she wouldn't let that happen. Mother had kept us apart when you were Hannah. She had other plans for us. I had to save you so we could figure this out together."

"But I *did* die, and you *did* manage to find me."

"And it took me years. It was a fluke that I found you at all."

"I don't think so. You were always meant to find me. I'm sure of it."

"Maybe. But I couldn't count on that."

"Why would Mother allow me to be born again if she was so determined to kill me?"

"That's not her decision. She had no choice. She couldn't keep you in the Loom forever."

"The Loom?"

"The place you go when you die. Most people call it heaven. Or hell."

"Which one is it?"

"Both."

She raised her eyebrows. This was an interesting concept. A place where reward and redemption could be rolled into one.

"So, who decided I had to come back?" she asked. "Who makes up all these rules?"

"The Author."

"What exactly did this author write to be so powerful?"

"Only the entire universe."

"You mean the Creator?"

"Some people call him that."

"You're saying Mother had no choice but for me to be

born again, so she chose Hong Kong in the hope we'd never meet?"

"Exactly. I don't think she expected me ever to find you here."

"There are plenty of places where I'd be more difficult to find than here."

"I suppose she thought this would be difficult enough. She underestimated us." He reached across the table and took hold of her hand, squeezing it gently. Touching his skin felt almost like touching a part of her own body. She placed her free hand on top of his and turned it over, studying the lines, callouses and sheer size of his hand. Again, he made her feel like a child in comparison.

Her father noticed the contact and approached the table. "Reinier, thank you for your visit," he said, making it clear he was now expected to leave.

"Not yet. It's too soon." Lin pleaded with her father with her eyes. But he refused to look at her.

Reinier stood. "It's okay," he said to Lin. "We'll meet again soon. You need to think about what we've talked about today."

He turned to her father, stooping slightly to lessen the height difference. "Thank you for allowing me to visit."

"You'll come next week?" Lin asked.

"Of course. And please, Lin, prepare yourself."

"Prepare myself?"

"Yes. What I have to ask you may come as a shock."

CHAPTER FIVE

*L*in stood and watched Reinier leave the apartment. Why had he said he'd ask her something that would come as a shock? The next week was going to be torture.

She hugged her parents, thanked them again for allowing him into her life and retreated to her bedroom to think about everything that had just transpired.

The vision she'd seen on that fateful day in the clearing had been true. Although, all hadn't been as it had seemed. Reinier had intended to kill Matthew to save her, only Mother had acted first and taken her life to prevent her baby being conceived.

But Matthew had lived. Perhaps he was still alive. The thought had never occurred to her. In all the time she'd spent thinking about Matthew, she'd concentrated on the past, not the present. If Matthew was alive, he'd be about Reinier's age. Had he married? She pushed down an irrational stab of jealously at that thought and wondered what he looked like as a grown man. Perhaps he had a beard. She smiled at the absurd thought. Of all the things she had to think about, Matthew's beard wasn't one of them. Yet still the image amused her. His strong, handsome face covered in hair seemed ridiculous. Oh, how she missed that face. Did he miss her? That thought wiped her smile away. She was sure he missed her.

She felt a pang in her stomach. The thought of traveling to Australia plagued her once more. It was more than the forest she missed. Once she and Reinier were married, she must return. Matthew wouldn't know her, of course, but she'd know him. It would feel like magic to stare into his soulful eyes once more.

She brushed away the confusion that clouded her mind. She mustn't think of Matthew in that way. She was to be Reinier's wife. Reinier. The man who made her heart skip beats, the man who'd rescued her from a life of confusion, and the feeling that there was something seriously wrong with her. He loved her. He'd said so. And she loved him. And in one week's time, she'd see him again. Perhaps her father would allow them to go for a walk. How proud she'd feel to stroll through the streets with such a handsome man by her side. That would open the eyes of the other girls at her school who thought of her as odd. She'd be the talk of the town for a whole new reason. The thought thrilled her.

Despite the foreboding words Reinier had left her with, she spent the week feeling happier than she had ever felt before. Finally, she knew who she was. She understood herself and celebrated her differences instead of bemoaning them.

When Sunday finally came, she rose early and put on a simple pink dress. She loved the soft feel of the cotton and knew it flattered her in a way that was both alluring yet conservative enough to please her parents. She sat on the small sofa in the living room and stared at the clock.

Her wait proved to be a long one. Morning became noon. Noon became afternoon. Reinier hadn't said a time. She'd assumed he'd be there in the morning. Surely, he hadn't expected her father to allow her out after dark?

Night fell and with it so did her hopes to see Reinier once more. He wasn't coming. Her mother sat beside her.

"What if he's had an accident?" Lin said.

"Maybe," her mother replied.

"Perhaps he's sick."

"Maybe."

"He couldn't have forgotten, could he?"

"No, no," her mother soothed. "He'll come next week."

She hoped her mother was right.

It was with a great sense of dread that she slipped out of her pink dress and pulled her nightdress over her head. She lay in bed and brought Reinier's face to her mind.

"Where are you?" she pleaded.

Instead of the usual rush of energy that passed through her body when she thought of him, she saw black. Dark clouds wafted into her mind. There was something wrong with him. He needed her.

The next morning, she asked her father to take her with him to the market. She had to see Reinier. She had to know what had happened to him. After much begging, her father agreed to check on him. He wouldn't allow her to miss a day of school to accompany him.

Each minute of her school day felt like an hour. Her teachers noticed how distracted she was and threatened her with being kept late. This was the worst punishment she could think of. She forced her mind back to her studies to satisfy her teachers, but her heart remained with Reinier. *Please, let him be okay.*

Eventually, the end of the school day came and she raced to the front gates to find her mother waiting for her.

"Where's Ah-ba?" she asked.

"He's at the shop."

"Did he find Reinier?"

"Yes."

"What happened?" She was desperate for information. It seemed her mother was holding back on purpose.

"Let's go to the shop and he can tell you himself."

Lin agreed. She knew her mother well enough to realize she'd get no further information from her. Whatever her father had discovered, it must be serious.

Her mother walked at the same slow and measured pace as always. Lin strode several steps ahead, willing her to hurry.

Eventually they arrived at the family store. Her father was serving a long line of customers.

"Please, Ah-ma."

Her mother nodded and took her father's place at the counter. Lin followed her father to the small storage room at the rear of the store.

"Did you find him?" she asked.

"Yes. He asked me to tell you he's sorry. He forgot." He shifted uncomfortably on his feet. There was more to this story.

"He forgot? I don't believe that."

"Lin, he didn't look well. I'm not sure he's thinking clearly."

"How exactly didn't he look well?" Fear built inside her. If anything were to happen to Reinier, her whole world would crumble. She couldn't lose him. She'd only just found him.

"He was pale. I think he may have a fever. He was coughing a lot."

"Where was he?"

"Working in the grocery store. The one where he sleeps."

"Will you take me there? Please, Ah-ba. I must see him."

"He's a grown man, Lin. People get sick. Let him rest. He'll come to see you when he's well."

"No, Ah-ba. Something's wrong. I can feel it." She felt panic rise like waves, stretching from her toes to the back of her throat. "Please. If you don't take me, I'll go alone."

Her father sighed and undid his apron, signaling his consent.

"Thank you." She kissed him lightly on his cheek and together they walked out of the store. Her mother nodded as they passed.

They walked in silence to the market, as was becoming their habit. She linked arms with him. "I love you, Ah-ba."

He smiled at her but didn't reply.

The market was busy, filled with color and noise. The many faces that filed past irritated her. None of them were the face she wanted to see. They approached the grocery store from the front entrance. It was a crowded store, filled mostly with fresh produce. The old man with the walking stick Lin had met the day she found Reinier, approached them, pointing with his stick to the back room.

"Reinier's sick," he said.

"Can we see him?" Lin asked.

He nodded.

Lin's father thanked the man and pushed open the flimsy back door. Reinier was lying on the camp bed, his brow covered in sweat, dry blood caked to his pillow. He seemed to be sleeping, yet was groaning softly, his hands clutching his stomach.

"Reinier," Lin cried, rushing to his side.

"Hannah," he said, opening his eyes, only to close them sharply again as he winced. She ignored his incorrect use of her name, hoping her father wouldn't notice. She felt enough like Hannah now that it didn't really matter what he called her.

"Ah-ba, he needs a doctor."

Lin's father nodded. "Come," he said to Reinier, helping him up from the bed. "We're going to the hospital."

Reinier draped his arms around both Lin and her father and they managed to help him through the grocery store, across the market and out to the main road. They sat him on the side of the road and Lin desperately waved at the traffic until she found a cab.

They loaded Reinier into the back seat and sat either side of him to keep him upright.

"Hannah," he said again. "Give her nothing or she'll take everything."

"Yes, Reinier," she soothed. He wasn't making any sense.

"Give her nothing, Hannah. Give her nothing." He broke into a coughing fit, yet was still trying to speak. "Han... Lin... nothing... nothing... "

"It's okay, Reinier. Nobody's giving anyone anything. We're taking you to the hospital."

He leaned his head back and closed his eyes. Blood dripped from his nose. The cab driver glanced nervously in his rear vision mirror and threw a box of tissues into the back. Lin held a tissue to Reinier's nose, trying to stem the bleeding.

"What's happening to him?" she asked her father.

"I don't know. Maybe it's typhoid."

One of their neighbors had typhoid. Lin remembered how sick he'd been and how worried his family was. But he'd survived. Reinier would survive too. He was a fighter. He hadn't come this far to be struck down by a disease like that. Unless...

Unless Mother had given it to him, to prevent him from asking her whatever it was he'd said he was going to ask. She might be trying to take Reinier's life, just as she'd taken Hannah's.

They got to the hospital and her father ran inside to get help. Whatever he said must have worked, as he returned only minutes later with both a nurse and a wheelchair.

They helped him into the chair and Lin ran alongside into the emergency room.

"Are you family?" the nurse asked.

"No." Lin's father shook his head.

"Please wait here." The nurse pointed to the crowded waiting room. "We'll let you know when there's news."

"But I'm family," Lin cried. "I'm his fiancée."

"We'll wait here," Lin's father said.

The nurse hesitated before nodding and wheeling Reinier through a set of double doors. Her father sat down, patting the seat next to him.

"Why can't I go with him?" she asked, refusing to take the seat next to her father.

"So you can get typhoid too?"

"It's a bit late to be worried about that." She held up her bloodstained hands.

"Go and wash." He pointed to the public bathroom.

She did as she was told. She soaped her hands and ran warm water over them, watching the basin turn red as Reinier's blood washed down the drain.

A hand grasped her lightly on her forearm. Her eyes snapped open to see a woman standing next to her.

"Are you all right?" the woman asked. "Do you need a doctor?"

"Yes. No. I mean, yes. I'm all right. No, I don't need a doctor."

The woman stepped away, looking confused.

"I'm fine. Thank you," Lin called after her.

She splashed some water on her face and returned to sit by her father's side. They waited four hours before a nurse came to them.

"Are you Hannah?" the nurse asked in Cantonese.

"Yes," Lin replied. Her father looked across at her, puzzled.

"It's just a name he has for me."

Her father nodded, although the puzzled look on his face remained.

"He's asking for you," the nurse said.

They rose to their feet.

"Only Hannah," the nurse said. "Your friend is very sick. He may only see one visitor at a time."

"Please, Ah-ba," Lin said. "I won't be long."

Her father nodded his consent.

She followed the nurse through a series of winding corridors to a ward containing several beds lined up against the far wall. She saw Reinier at once. He was lying in a bed, a crisp white sheet tucked under his arms. His eyes were closed. He was so still that for a moment she was filled with fear.

"He's resting," the nurse said, noticing her panic. "We've sedated him."

"What's wrong with him? Is it typhoid?"

"The doctor has ordered tests. We'll let you know when we have news." The nurse moved away.

Lin perched on the edge of Reinier's bed and held his hand. His eyes flickered at the contact. The energy she usually felt bouncing off him had dulled. It was as though the life force within him was struggling for air. The blood had been cleaned from his face and he looked almost peaceful.

She studied his sleeping face, feeling a sense that she'd done this before. Had Hannah watched him sleep? No, she couldn't have. She'd only met him once on the day she'd died, and then he'd been anything but asleep. He was unshaven now, with coarse bristles covering the lower part of his face. It suited him.

She decided to do something she'd been longing to do since the moment she'd first drawn his face. She let go of his hand and reached out, gently touching his scar. She ran her index finger down its length and felt rough skin meeting smooth. What had happened to him? Had someone hurt him?

He shifted uncomfortably in his bed and she withdrew her hand from his face.

"I'm here, Reinier. I'm here," she soothed.

"Hannah," he murmured.

"It's Lin, Reinier. Lin's here."

"Hmm, Hannah."

She smiled a sad smile. He seemed to want to call her Hannah. As far as he was concerned, Lin and Hannah were the same person. The name he used wasn't important. In some ways, it felt nice to be called Hannah. She decided not to correct him again.

She stroked his hand, turning it over and kissing him lightly on his palm.

"I love you," she whispered.

His breathing deepened and his eyes closed. He needed to rest, but she didn't want to leave so soon. She'd sit here forever if she were allowed.

She thought about the times he'd given her strength to face her challenges. Maybe it was time she did the same for him.

She placed one hand on his forehead and the other on his heart. She closed her eyes and used all her strength to summon the energy contained within her, concentrating on pouring it down her arms and through her hands into his body.

"Be strong," she whispered. "You can fight this. Come back to me, Reinier."

His eyes opened wide and she jumped back slightly in surprise. It had worked. Somehow his eyes looked clearer and the pink was returning to his skin. He tried to sit up.

"Lie down," she said, trying to push him back down on the bed. Even in his weakened state her strength was no match for his.

"Lin," he said, looking directly at her. "You must find Matthew."

"Matthew?"

"Find Matthew, Lin. You must find him."

"Okay, Reinier, when you're better, we'll find Matthew. I promise." She tried to lie him down again. Was he delirious or had her strength given him a moment of clarity? He'd called her Lin. Perhaps this was what he'd wanted to ask her. He wanted to take her to Matthew.

"Lin. Find Matthew. You must find him and have his baby. Lin, find him."

Lin lay on her bed with no memory of how she'd gotten home. Her father must have taken her. She could hear him speaking with her mother in the kitchen.

The shock of what Reinier had asked of her was robbing her mind of sense. He'd warned her that what he had to ask would have this effect on her. Even so, she hadn't expected it to be like this. Once again, she felt naïve. Of all the things she thought he might have asked her this hadn't once crossed her mind. He wanted her to have Matthew's baby, but how could that solve anything? She couldn't be married to Reinier and give birth to another man's child. Didn't he want her to have *his* child? Didn't he love her?

This had nothing to do with love. She knew that. Reinier

had told her Hannah had been destined to have Matthew's child and that child would be very important to the world. She also knew Reinier saw her and Hannah as the same person, the same soul. Reinier obviously believed that the same child could still be born if she were to conceive it with Matthew.

Where did that leave Reinier's feelings for her? He'd said it made no difference to him if he married her or not. Perhaps he didn't care for her at all. His only concern seemed to be ensuring this baby was brought into the world. Why, then, had he fooled her into believing he cared? What was all that talk about being soulmates, the other half to each other's souls? If he truly loved her, he wouldn't ask her to have another man's child. She wasn't ready to have anybody's child, least of all the child of a man she didn't know.

But she did know Matthew. She knew his every detail. She felt his lips press upon hers. She felt his hand holding her own. She knew him and she loved him, even if she'd never met him.

If she agreed to Reinier's plan and sought out Matthew, what made him think Matthew would want to have a child with her? He didn't know her. He didn't love her. He'd think she was mad if she turned up on his doorstep telling him she was Hannah and asking if he'd mind having a baby with her. He was probably already married with six kids of his own. Reinier was obviously delirious. Nothing he'd said made any sense since she'd found him so sick like that.

She knew that wasn't true. When he'd opened his eyes and called her Lin, he'd seemed to know exactly what he was saying.

The next day, she walked with her mother to their store.

"Would you like to go to the hospital?" her father asked.

"No," she said, picking up a box of crisps and neatly stacking them onto the shelf. "I'll just help here for a while."

"Okay," her father said, his brow furrowing.

The next day was the same. And the next. The following day, her father cornered her and demanded to know what was going on.

"I don't know," she replied. "I just realized that perhaps I don't know him as well as I thought I did."

"That's not good enough. You bring our family misery over this man until we agree to allow you to marry him. And now you say you don't know him. You're not allowed to change your mind about this, Lin. I don't even recognize you and the way you behave lately."

"I'm sorry, Ah-ba. I know. I'm sorry." Tears streamed down her cheeks. She threw her arms around her father and he held her. Here she felt safe. Her father wouldn't ask her to have a child she didn't want. Her father loved her. This was true love, not the strange love Reinier had offered her.

"Lin," her father said. "I went to the hospital today."

"What?" she stood back from him.

"We were right. He has typhoid. Whatever he said to you when you saw him, you mustn't listen. He wouldn't have known what he was saying. He didn't know who I was. I doubt he'd know who you are either."

She knew that wasn't true. "How long will he be in hospital?"

"A week or two. It depends on how things progress. He's in a lot of pain. I think you should go and see him."

"I'll see him when he's well."

That was all she'd say on the matter. She didn't like the idea of him in pain and felt guilty for not continuing to try to send him strength. It had drained her so much the last time, and she needed the strength herself to cope with what he'd asked of her.

Every few days her father would ask her to come with

him to the hospital and each time she'd reply that she was busy.

Days stretched into weeks and soon a month had passed. She was sitting at the kitchen table doing her homework when a knock came at their apartment door. She knew who it was before her mother had a chance to open it. She could feel the electricity from the other side of the thin paneling.

"Come in," her mother said.

Reinier stepped into the room. The energy that surrounded him had been restored. She had to stop herself from hurling herself into his arms.

His face was drawn, and he'd lost a lot of weight. He was now mere bones, held in place by pale skin. The strong layer of muscle that she'd secretly admired had vanished. He'd obviously been very unwell. Despite the anger and confusion she felt toward him, her heart wept. She shouldn't have been ignoring him. She'd been so selfish.

Her mother retreated to the kitchen and Lin offered Reinier a seat at the table.

"You look terrible," she said.

"Thank you," he said, his smile lighting up his face. She forgot she was mad at him. Forgot what he'd asked of her. She felt only this moment and the energy that passed between them. "You, on the other hand, look as beautiful as ever, Lin."

"Oh, you're calling me Lin today." She did her best to sound cross. He needed to understand that he'd upset her. There was a reason for her absence.

He looked confused. "What else would I call you?"

"Well, in the hospital it was Hannah. Either that or Han-Lin."

"Hanlin. I like that."

"You would." The anger slipped from her voice. He was impossible to have an argument with.

"You're mad at me. Why?"

"You don't remember what you said in the hospital, do you?"

"I don't remember you visiting me in the hospital, let alone what I said. I've been lying in that bed wondering where you were. Your father said you were busy. Of course, I knew that was a lie." His eyes were pleading with her. He clearly didn't remember what'd happened. "What did I say?"

"Nothing. Everything. Enough."

He looked worried now. "Listen. Whatever I said, don't pay any attention. I was delirious. I thought your father was my doctor the first time he came in."

"So, when you asked me to have Matthew's baby that was your fever talking?"

He turned a paler shade of pale. "Oh, Lin. I'm so sorry."

"Let me get one thing clear, Reinier. I'm not having anyone's child."

"But you must." He shook his head in despair. "We have to stop Mother. This baby is the chosen one."

"Chosen for what? How do you know this?"

"Because I've seen it. Just like I saw your face before I met you. Just like I saw Mother take your life in the clearing before it happened."

"She didn't take my life. She took Hannah's." It suddenly seemed important to retain her identity. She didn't want to be Hannah if it meant having Matthew's child.

"You *are* Hannah. You know that. It's your soul that makes you who you are, not your body. Don't you see? You having a child with Matthew is exactly the same as Hannah having the child. It makes no difference."

"How do you know this baby's so important? Calling it the chosen one sounds a little dramatic, don't you think?"

"No, I don't think. Look around you, Lin. Look at what humans are doing to this world. Everywhere you look we have wars, poverty and despair. We're killing each other, polluting our oceans, destroying our forests. It's gotten so bad even Mother has lost faith that we can be saved." His eyes burned with sincerity.

"How do you know that?"

"Why else would she be behaving like this? I think she believes the time has come for the human race to relinquish our rule over planet Earth. She'd prefer to weave souls for a peaceful race. One by one she's watching our souls extinguish and she's doing nothing to stop it because it suits her perfectly well. The last thing she wants to see is a chosen one undoing all the work she's done to destroy us."

"You really think one little baby can stop all of that? One child can save humankind from destroying itself? That's ridiculous." She shook her head, avoiding eye contact. Each time she looked into those eyes she was drawn into his spell.

"It's not ridiculous. I've never lied to you, Lin, and I'm not lying to you now. You know I speak the truth. You need to believe me. You and Matthew must have this child. He's our only hope."

"A boy?"

"Yes, a boy." He reached across the table and placed his hand on her arm. Sparks flew up her arm and raced to her heart.

"Don't touch me," she said. "I can't think when you touch me."

"I'm sorry." He retracted his hand.

"Does touching me have any effect on you at all?" He seemed to touch her so casually she was beginning to wonder if there was any meaning in his touch.

"Of course. Why do you think I'm always reaching out for you? It's what feeds my soul. I wish you'd come to see me so we could've sorted this out sooner. I missed you."

"If you really did miss me then you wouldn't want me to

have another man's baby." She dared to look into his eyes, only to find herself lost in them. She knew she'd do anything he asked of her, but that wasn't going to stop her pushing for another outcome.

"It's for the greater good," he said. "Besides, I see love differently to you."

"I don't understand."

"Souls love other souls. It's as simple as that. There's no romantic love or jealousy in the afterlife. You either love another soul or you don't. What other souls the soul you love chooses to love are of no consequence. Confused yet?"

"Very." He sounded like he was talking in riddles.

"It's hard to explain. Just trust me on this, Lin. I love you. My soul loves your soul. I would do anything for you. If you have a baby with Matthew, it won't change my love for you. Our souls are linked for eternity. Our love doesn't need to be romantic love for it to be real."

"What if it is romantic love for one of us?" Her cheeks burned. She had to ask. Her feelings were too strong to deny.

"You forget I'm still human, Lin. I'm a man standing before a beautiful woman. It isn't just one of us who feels this." He reached across the table for her. "Please let me touch you just for a moment."

Her resolve to be strong crumbled. She placed her hands in his wide palms and he gripped her tightly. She didn't pull away. She'd never be the one to pull away.

"Don't ask me to have Matthew's child. If I must have a child, then let it be yours. Reinier, please."

"It can't be my child. It needs to be Matthew's. We have to fight what we feel here, Lin."

She let go of his hands and saw him take in a breath of disappointment at the break in contact. He must feel it, too. "Take peace in knowing we'll be together again. We'll always be together. And besides, you love Matthew. You've just forgotten."

"I can't love two men at the same time."

"You can, Lin. But here in the world we live in, you can only have one of them. And it can't be me."

"Are you serious? You're asking me to marry you and then not only have another man's child, but to raise it with him? What about you? I'm not marrying you, then watching you walk away."

"I'm not really sure what I'm asking of you beyond having this child," he admitted. "Getting married is the best way to move this forward now. We can't wait any longer. Your parents will never let me take you to Australia to find Matthew if we're not married. Let's just find him and then we can work the rest out one step at a time."

"It feels more like a hundred steps at a time to me. Reinier, I'm not like you. You're stronger than me. I'm not sure I can do this."

"You can do this, Lin. You're stronger than you think. You're capable of so much more than you even know." He stood. "I'm going to leave you to think about this."

She looked up at him and they locked eyes once more. Memories from times gone by raced through her mind. She knew she trusted him. She knew she'd follow him to the end of time. She just didn't like where he was asking her to go.

He thanked her mother for allowing the visit and quietly closed the apartment door behind him. Lin buried her face in her hands.

"This man doesn't make you happy," her mother said.

"I know, Ah-ma. But I love him."

Her mother crossed the room to a set of drawers and returned with a hairbrush. She sat next to Lin and motioned for her to turn around. Lin turned her back to her mother and felt her slip the elastic from her hair and begin to brush out the long, black strands. As she brushed, she sang a lullaby about moonlight and fields and mountains. This was something her mother had done since she was a child. A woman of few words, she found it hard to express affection. This ritual had been her way of showing her love for her daughter.

Lin closed her eyes and accepted her mother's love.

CHAPTER SIX

*S*unday quickly became Lin's favorite day of the week. It was her day to see Reinier. A day to ask him questions and avoid answering the one question he asked of her. His question was always the same. She wasn't ready to give him an answer, holding on to the hope that if she avoided it for long enough, he'd give up asking. But he never did.

They didn't sit at the kitchen table to talk anymore. Instead, they'd venture out and walk the streets of Kowloon. Rarely did they eat together. Reinier was saving his money to take them to Australia once they were married. Sometimes they snuck past the attendant at the movies and sat together in the dark, Reinier watching the screen and Lin sneaking glances at the strong angles of his profile. She liked to sit on his left so she could look at his scar and remember what it felt like to trace her finger along it when she'd drawn him.

"How did you get your scar?" she asked him once.

"Trying to save a damsel in distress," he said.

"Did you save her?"

"No, but she's sitting with me now, so all wasn't lost."

"You mean, you got that scar the day Hannah died?"

"Oh, my little Hanlin," he said. "Who else do you see sitting here with me?"

Her eyes flickered with distress. It never occurred to her that on the day she'd lost her life, he'd been hurt so badly. It must have been quite some injury for the scar to be so vivid all these years later. Mother had been very serious about taking her life.

This story caused her to love his scar even more than before. It became a symbol of his love. Each time she looked at it, she saw him risking his life for her. It was unfair, really, for him to be constantly reminding her of that. How could she not fall in love with a man who'd fought so hard to save her?

As the months passed, her love for Reinier grew deeper still. Long gone were the days of him finding reasons to touch her. Instead, it became her looking for ways to touch him. His resolve was much stronger than hers.

She'd reach to hold his hand, only for him to squeeze hers and drop it by her side. She'd stand on tiptoes to brush her lips upon his, to find him turning his face to catch her kiss on his cheek. She'd loop her arm in his as they walked and he'd find an excuse to point at something, causing the contact to break. She found it hard to believe what he'd said about her not being the only one to feel the electricity between them. It seemed this man was made of concrete. But with one touch of his skin she knew this wasn't true. Warm energy bounced from his every pore, lighting fires within her body in places she didn't know could be lit. Yet still he insisted they fight their feelings for the good of the world. If it wasn't so frustrating, she was sure she'd find it amusing.

The day of their wedding approached. With no money for anything fancy, they chose a small ceremony at the marriage registry in Kowloon with only a handful of guests. Lin's parents would be there, together with her aunt and uncle and two sets of her parents' friends. She decided against inviting any of the girls from her school. Reinier's guest list was even shorter, consisting only of Feng, the old man from the grocery story.

Lin would wear the red gown her mother had worn on her own wedding day. It was a gown Lin had often tried on as a girl, parading around their small apartment as if she were Queen of China. She loved the feel of the silk against her skin and would run her small hands over the smooth lines of the dress as she admired the way the delicate gold leaf pattern wound its way from her shoulders to the folds of fabric bunched at her feet. She'd longed to be tall enough, with curves in the right places, to do the dress justice.

Now, here she stood at eighteen years of age, certainly tall enough. And the way color rose to Reinier's cheeks when he saw her at the registry office, she knew she had the curves as well. Her mother had pulled Lin's hair into a high bun and pinned it with a silver comb that had once belonged to her grandmother.

"You look beautiful," Reinier said, barely able to look at her. He wore a black suit made for him by a tailor at one of the market stalls. She noticed he wore it well. He'd long since recovered from his bout of typhoid and his physique had returned to the lean yet athletic form he'd had when she first met him. His blond hair had been combed neatly into place and his face was clean-shaven. Her heart leaped at the vision of this handsome man before her. A handsome man who was about to become her husband.

He reminded her of a prince from a storybook she'd loved as a child. It was as though the story had come to life. She'd never dreamed it possible. The men her parents had pointed out as potential suitors over the years most certainly didn't look like this. And they weren't strong and brave and wise like Reinier, either. If only this wedding were real. If only she could be sure he'd take her in his arms afterwards and make love to her like a real husband. She wasn't sure how she'd survive knowing she was married to the man of her dreams, yet unable to lay a finger on him.

She smiled at him, feeling suddenly shy. It seemed an odd way to greet the man who was about to become her husband. Shouldn't she kiss his cheek? No, definitely not. She knew the sparks would light her soul if that were to happen. She needed to keep a level head.

They walked with her parents to a waiting room where they sat in silence, staring at the checkerboard pattern on the wood-paneled walls. She heard Reinier draw in a deep breath and wondered whether he was nervous about marrying her or worried about what was to come afterwards.

She still hadn't given him an answer about Matthew. He just seemed to assume she'd say yes. He certainly wouldn't be about to marry her if he thought she'd say no. Hadn't he realized them being married would be an obstacle to Matthew agreeing to father her child? She hadn't wanted to point it out. But Reinier wasn't the sort to overlook a major detail like this one. So how was he planning to explain this?

Excuse me, Matthew, this is my wife, Lin. She's also your dead girlfriend, Hannah. Would you mind having a baby with her so we can save the world?

It was beyond ridiculous, which was why she hadn't let it plague her thoughts. She was confident Matthew would never agree to Reinier's plan. Then, finally, Reinier could let down his guard and be a proper husband. They'd find another way to put a stop to Mother. There was *always* another way.

She shifted her gaze to her parents. Her father was running his fingers along the lapel of his jacket. It was a nervous gesture she was familiar with. Her mother sat still, keeping her emotions to herself, as was her way. She looked beautiful in the lilac dress she saved for special occasions.

Lin's chest swelled with love for these two beautiful souls who'd raised her. They'd always loved her, always done the right thing by her. Had she always done the right thing by them? Deceiving them like this wasn't fair. They believed she and Reinier were in love.

She looked across at him. Color rose to his cheeks as he met her gaze. Perhaps it wasn't such a great lie. She was in love with him, and at times she was certain he felt the same. He definitely seemed to be affected by her today.

She was glad when the other guests began to arrive. Their presence seemed to relax her parents and shifted some of the focus away from her. She pretended not to notice the disapproving stare her parents' friends kept sending her way. This wasn't a traditional wedding, nor had she paid heed to many of the Chinese traditions. There'd been no setting up the bridal bed, no dowry paid, no fortune teller consulted about the wedding date. The only guest who seemed genuinely pleased for them was Feng. He smiled at them through the wrinkles on his face, his eyes alight with joy.

A tidy-looking woman with a clipboard appeared from the large door at the end of the room and called their names. The small group stood and followed her into a grand chamber. Rows of seats lined the room. Lin wished they had a smaller room. The empty seats were a further reminder to everyone how unconventional this marriage was. Where were the weeping relatives and giggling friends? They'd agreed to keep this wedding as simple as possible. Perhaps they'd taken it too far. She was grateful she'd never been the type of girl to daydream about her wedding day. If she were, she'd have been bitterly disappointed with this lack of fanfare.

None of that was important, she reminded herself. What was important was Reinier, the life she planned to build with him and the children she planned on having with him after Matthew rejected his ridiculous plan.

The celebrant entered the room from a separate door. He was a short, middle-aged man, dressed in an expensive suit. He welcomed them, glancing momentarily at the empty rows of seats. His glance automatically switched from the seats to Lin's trim waistline. She flushed, realizing he thought what everyone else must be thinking; that she was with child and being rushed into marriage.

For the first time since this marriage was arranged, she felt like running. She wanted to be far away from this event, far away from Reinier, even. She wanted to run so far she'd end up running back in time. Back to a time when she was a little girl with her life stretching before her like a promise. Back to a time when she didn't have the answers to her questions. The answers had satisfied her curiosity but had done little to satisfy her heart.

"Welcome," the celebrant said.

Reinier reached for her hand and held it, as if sensing her hesitation. He squeezed her gently and she felt tingles spread through her palm, up her arm and then move like waves through her body. All thoughts of running evaporated from her mind. She was safe when Reinier was by her side. He'd never let anything happen to her.

The ceremony began. She found herself only half listening to the words, instead concentrating on the warm flow of energy bouncing between her and Reinier. She spoke her vows in a whisper and fought back tears as Reinier spoke his. In that moment, she allowed herself to believe his words. Believe that he'd love her and care for her forever. She'd loved him since the beginning of time, and she'd love him until the end. Their souls had been bound together by far greater forces than a wedding certificate.

"You may kiss your bride," the celebrant announced, stepping back and grinning at Lin's parents, who remained in their seats, emotionless apart from a single tear that ran down her mother's face.

Lin stepped toward Reinier and lifted her face to his. He wouldn't be able to turn away this time. She'd finally know what his lips felt like on hers, even if it were to be for a few short, yet precious, moments. He bent down slowly, and their lips met. Sparks of electricity lit her every cell. She felt more alive at that moment than she'd ever felt before. His lips were firm yet soft, hesitant yet yearning. She closed her eyes preparing for the moment he'd pull away, only to find he didn't. His lips parted and his arms wrapped around her waist, pulling her body to his. Bliss bounced through her core and she gasped in surprise.

"I'm sorry," he said, breaking away, leaving her feeling dizzy.

"Don't be sorry," the celebrant said, laughing. "She's your wife. Although you could've waited for the honeymoon for a kiss like that."

Lin glanced at their small audience, embarrassed. For a moment she'd forgotten they were there. Each guest had a false smile plastered to their face in an unsuccessful attempt to mask their own shock. Except Feng, of course, who clapped his hands and laughed in glee.

Somehow, she managed to get herself through the remaining formalities, her knees buckling under the desire the kiss had punched into her gut. Now she knew for certain her feelings were not one way. Reinier loved her as a husband should love his wife. No man could kiss a woman like that without desiring her. She congratulated herself on winning the battle for his heart. It seemed the risk she'd taken in marrying him might pay off after all. He wouldn't be able to insist on taking her to Matthew now. She hoped he wasn't too disappointed with himself for letting his guard down like that.

The celebratory lunch at the restaurant next door to the registry office was as awkward as it was short. Her father had insisted on treating them all to a banquet.

The guests ate quickly and quietly, except for Feng who savored every mouthful of his food. Lin guessed it wasn't often he ate like this.

"Is this a wedding or a funeral?" Reinier had whispered in her ear. She giggled and forced another mouthful of food into her mouth, as keen for the lunch to be over as most of the guests were.

"Thank you, Ah-ba," Lin said as dessert was being served.

"It's only lunch," her father said.

"That's not what I'm thanking you for."

He looked at her with love in his eyes. "I'm sorry I couldn't give you a grander wedding."

"This wedding is perfect," she said.

"It will be more perfect when this lunch is over." A small smile found its way to his lips as he motioned for her to look at her uncle, whose eyes were drooping with fatigue.

She laughed. "The lunch is perfect, Ah-ba."

"The lunch is ugly, just like your forest," he said. It had been years since they'd joked like this about the forest she saw from her bedroom window, but clearly, he hadn't forgotten.

"You are ugly," she said, remembering her line.

He laughed.

"Ah-ba?"

"Yes."

"You do know that I don't think you're ugly, don't you?" she said, suddenly concerned he'd been taking her seriously all these years. "I think you're wonderful and handsome and the best father in the world."

"And I think you are drunk," he said, picking up her glass of water and smelling it.

Despite the casual way he brushed aside her compliment, she knew it had found its way to his heart. She could see it in the way his chest swelled.

"Reinier," he said, leaning forward in his chair. "Look after my daughter. She's my only child."

Lin knew this was his way of telling her he loved her, too.

She watched her father stand and make his way over to the waiter to pay the bill and organize a cab to take her and Reinier to a hotel in the heart of the city. She knew he could little afford to do this but refusing his offer would be an insult she wasn't prepared to throw at him.

Reinier had been busy organizing other things, including tickets for them to fly to Australia the following day. Clearly, he didn't want to waste any time. She could barely contain her excitement at the thought of visiting the forest she'd spent her life dreaming about. Meeting Matthew filled her with less excitement and more trepidation. Even so, it would be good to get this meeting out of the way. Until Matthew rejected Reinier's offer, they wouldn't be able to start the life Lin had planned for them.

Reinier checked them into their room. She felt a rush of excitement at being called Mr and Mrs Knight for the first time. She hoped she would always feel like that.

"Well, that was a fun lunch," Reinier said with a blank face as they stepped into the elevator.

She hesitated, then burst into laughter. He laughed, too. Just when their laughter took a turn for the hysterical, the lift arrived at their floor and the doors sprang open. An austere-looking man stood waiting for the lift with his equally severe-looking wife. This made them laugh further still.

"Good afternoon," Reinier said as he took Lin by the hand and led her from the elevator to their room. The couple did not reply.

"I don't think they were too impressed," Lin said as he opened the door.

"I think we made their day. We certainly gave them something to talk about." He stood back and motioned for her to pass. Their bags had been sent across earlier in the day and stood before them in the entryway.

They stepped into the room and came to a pause at the foot of the double bed before them. The soft, white bedspread had been decorated with rose petals, scattered in the shape of a heart. It was both the most romantic and heartbreaking sight Lin had ever seen. Would this be the night she became a woman, or would it be the night her heart broke in two?

"I'll sleep on the sofa," Reinier said, pointing to a settee in the corner of the room. She felt the first cracks appear in her heart.

"You don't have to," she said, powerless to prevent the pleading look in her eyes.

He turned to her, taking both her hands in his. "Lin, I'm so sorry. I should never have kissed you like that. I was weak. I should be stronger than that."

"It was our wedding. Of course you should've kissed me like that."

"Lin, that wasn't a real wedding. You know that."

"Tell that to the celebrant. Or my father." She yanked her hands away from him, feeling instant strength as the contact broke. It was almost impossible to stand up to him when her skin lay upon his.

"Please, Lin. You know I love you."

"Do I really know that? You say you love me. You kissed me at our wedding like you love me, but the rest of the time you treat me like I've just climbed out of a toxic swamp."

"I do not. Oh, Lin, if only you knew the truth."

"Well, we have all night," she said, sitting down on the bed. "You can start explaining now."

He hesitated and she crossed her arms in protest.

"I love you more than I've ever loved another soul," he said. "You are the reason I go on, no matter how difficult life gets. You've always been beautiful, but this time, your beauty is shining from every cell of your body. I've never seen anyone as exquisite as you. And believe me, I've seen a lot of people. When I'm near you I feel like I'm going to explode. The reason I move away when you touch me is because I just want to grab hold of you so tight I might break you in half."

"Then why don't you?" She stood and reached behind her, pulling down the zipper on her dress.

"Don't," he said, his pupils betraying his desire.

She slid the dress over her shoulders and it fell to the floor, leaving her standing before him, wearing only a set of very red and very sexy underwear. She'd begged her mother for some money the day before and purchased what she saw as her secret weapon. Let him push her away now. Let him tell her to have Matthew's baby. She was his wife. He loved her.

He stood before her. Frozen.

She'd imagined this moment hundreds of times. She thought she'd be nervous. She wasn't.

She closed the gap between them and trailed her hands up his chest to his shoulders. His mouth crashed down to hers and he kissed her. It was a kiss that made the one at their wedding seem staid.

He groaned and she knew she'd won.

CHAPTER SEVEN

*L*in woke. She knew she was alone before she opened her eyes. She could always tell when Reinier was near and when he wasn't. Perhaps he'd gone out for coffee or to organize breakfast. Their flight wasn't until the afternoon. They had plenty of time to relax in bed. She stretched out and smiled, remembering every moment of the night they'd spent together. He'd made her a woman in every possible way. It wasn't just the way he'd made love to her, it was the way he'd made her feel both beautiful and powerful at the same time. Her body ached for him just thinking about it. Where was he?

She opened her eyes to see a note on his pillow. He'd folded it in half and written her name in capital letters across the front. She smiled. As if the note could be for anyone else. She reached for it and propped herself up, leaning on the plush headboard. He must have thought she'd worry if she woke up and he wasn't there. He should know her better than that. If last night had proven anything, it was that he loved her.

As soon as she unfolded the letter, she knew it was bad news. The page was crammed with neatly formed letters. It was the length of the note that concerned her. It was far too long to tell her he'd gone out for coffee.

She quickly refolded the letter and clutched it to her chest. She didn't want to read it. Here, pressed against her heart, the letter could do her no harm. But once she'd read it her whole world could turn inside out. And right at that moment, there was nothing in her life that she wanted to change. Life was perfect. She'd found peace with her parents, she was married to the man she loved, and they were about to travel to the forest of her dreams.

She felt her hands begin to shake. How long could she ignore the letter?

She stood up, placed the letter back on Reinier's pillow and headed for the bathroom. What she needed was a long, hot bath. When she got out Reinier would be back and that note would be gone. If it were bad news he was giving her, she needed to give him time to change his mind. She'd pretend she'd never seen it and never need to know what was inside.

The tap turned on with a sudden gush and she stepped into the bath and lay down, enjoying the sensation of the water running across her naked body. She drew in a few deep breaths and noticed her hands were no longer shaking. As the water filled the tub, her mind filled with hope. Everything was going to be all right. Reinier loved her. He'd never leave her. She was being disloyal to even think that way. She'd tell him about this later and they'd have a good laugh about it.

She turned off the tap and floated in the water, enjoying the way it caressed her. She ran her hands across her breasts, remembering the way Reinier had cupped them in his hands. She moaned with the pleasure of the memory.

A knock at the door jolted her from her fantasy. That must be him. He'd forgotten to take his key. She hastily wrapped herself in a towel and padded across the room to the door, scolding herself for having panicked. Reinier hadn't left her. Everything was going to be okay.

Before her hand could grasp the door handle, it swung open.

She couldn't say who was more shocked. Was it her, standing there feeling very naked underneath a crisp, white towel, or the young man standing before her with a trolley laden with small bottles and over-priced grocery items?

"I'm sorry, ma'am. I was just checking the mini-bar," he said, looking at his feet.

She closed the door, not able to reply. Where was Reinier? He was supposed to be back by now. She was supposed to get out of the bath and find him there, grinning at her and calling her Hanlin.

She knew there was only one way to find out where he was. The note sat there on the pillow, looking at her, daring her to open it. She picked it up and sat on the edge of the bed, trying to calm herself. He couldn't have left her. There was nothing more important to him in the world than taking her to Australia to find Matthew. He'd been planning it for years. He wouldn't leave the morning it was about to happen.

If she had nothing to fear from the note, why couldn't she bring herself to read it? Because she *did* fear it. She feared it like she'd never feared anything else in her life.

She opened it.

My dear Hanlin,

I'm so sorry to do this on paper, but I have no strength to tell you this in person. When you are near me, I cannot think clearly. Last night was evidence of that. I should never have let that happen and I'm truly sorry. I hope you can find it in your beautiful heart to forgive me.

When you fell asleep, I lay here watching you breathe and thought about how much you are a part of me. I'll never love another soul in the way I love you.

This is our problem.

But our problem is nothing compared with the problems facing humankind. Only we can change the path Mother has set us on. I wasn't being dramatic when I told you of her intention to watch humankind destroy itself. The baby you and Matthew are destined to have is our only hope. He'll change what Mother has written in the stars. He's our future. And as much as I care for you, this is what's most important.

What I've asked of you is unfair. I know that. But I also know that you once loved Matthew and when you meet him again, you'll love him again. I realized last night that none of that will happen while I'm in your life. I was foolish to think we could travel to Australia together to make it happen.

Don't try to find me. You won't. I've left money and your plane ticket on the table. I beg you, please, fly to Australia today. Find Matthew. Convince him of your story. He'll believe you. I know he will. He'll love you and you'll love him. Mother won't stop you this time. I'll make sure of that. Do not fear.

Do this if you love me. Because if you love me, you must trust me. You must trust that I speak the truth. This baby must be born. It's the only way.

With all the love in my soul,
Reinier

Her hands were shaking. Tears streamed down her cheeks. A pit of anger swelled in her belly. He'd left her.

She leaped from the bed and dashed to the bathroom,

only just making it before she expelled the meager contents of her belly.

"Reinier," she cried. "Reinier." This was a nightmare. Surely this wasn't happening? He loved her. He wouldn't do this to her.

She returned to the bed and ran her hands across the cool space she'd thought he'd slept in. How long had he stayed and watched her sleep?

A sense of déjà vu washed over her. Once, she'd watched someone sleep and said goodbye. *Matthew.* She'd returned to him after her death. She was certain of it. She pushed the memories from her mind. She didn't want to think about Matthew now. He was the cause of all this. If he didn't exist then she'd be waking up next to Reinier instead of a note that had crushed her hopes for her future.

The memories of Matthew kept pushing to the surface. She remembered watching him struggle through his days without Hannah. She saw the pain in his mother's face. She saw him asleep in his bed and recalled how she'd laid her head on his chest and listened to his heart. It'd been so hard to say goodbye, but she'd had to. Was that how it felt for Reinier? Had he felt torn between what was the right thing to do and what he'd wanted to do in his heart? If only he'd talked to her about it, she'd have talked him out of leaving. They could've found another way to do what was right and still hold each other close. But that was exactly why he hadn't talked to her. He'd said so in his note.

She cursed herself out loud for her stupidity in seducing him. She should've just left things as they were. If she hadn't pushed Reinier into the very situation he was trying to avoid, then he'd still be here. It wasn't Matthew's fault.

It was hers.

Yet as hard as she tried, she couldn't regret her actions.

They were out of her control. She'd had to be close to Reinier. She couldn't have gone on with her life without knowing she'd held him so tight and been connected to him as one.

She fought back her tears. Her options felt limited. She couldn't possibly return home to her parents and tell them her husband of one day had left her. That would be shameful beyond imagination. Maybe if she did what Reinier said and went to Australia to find Matthew, he'd come back to her. She only had to have his baby. She didn't have to marry him. Anyway, she couldn't marry him. She was already married. Why couldn't she have Matthew's baby and raise it with Reinier? At the moment that seemed like the only possibility of ever having Reinier return to her life. Unless ... unless she was already pregnant.

Her hands flew to her belly and she rubbed the soft skin in circular motions.

"Please," she murmured. "Please let it be." Reinier would have to come back if she was pregnant with his child.

As her plan took shape, the sick feeling in her stomach lifted. She would get Reinier back one way or another. He'd searched for her and fought for her. Now it was her turn. He wouldn't leave her so easily. She'd prove her love for him.

She'd fly to Australia in the afternoon. She'd wait until she knew if a baby had begun to grow in her belly. If it had, Reinier would come to her. If it hadn't, then she'd find Matthew. She'd seduce him. Then Reinier would come to her. Please let the first option come true, she begged the universe.

"Are you listening, Mother?" she said. "Let me have Reinier's baby. Then you get what you want, and I get what I want."

Reinier's face flew into her mind with great force. Did he know what she was thinking? Could he hear her thoughts?

"Reinier," she screamed inside her head. "Come back. Don't do this."

PART III

MATTHEW

CHAPTER EIGHT

*M*atthew stared sightlessly out of the window. His attention was drawn by the distant sound of laughter, not the flash of color, as a group of schoolgirls passed by. Somewhere in the back of his mind, he remembered being young and carefree. That was long ago, in a time when his memories were made of pictures instead of smells, sounds and feelings.

He pushed the clouded memory of his youth away. It was another time. Another place. It felt like another world. His life was here now, in London.

"My life," he sighed.

The schoolgirls moved on and he found himself hoping the universe would protect their young lives and dreams. At their age, his life had shattered into a thousand pieces. In Hannah's case, the pieces had been stomped on and turned into dust. He tried to remember that always. No matter how sorry he felt for himself, he was the lucky one, although that didn't stop him from wishing he could trade places with her.

She was too beautiful to die so young. It was a rare beauty that penetrated from her clear blue eyes directly to her heart.

He'd accepted long ago that he'd miss her every day of his life. It seemed an added cruelty to have been robbed of his sight. How he'd love to look at a photo of her. It was getting harder to remember the details of her face. Instead, he was left with more of a feeling of her than an image.

He turned his attention to the piano in front of him and began to play. It was a slow, sad piece of music. One of the many he'd written himself. As his fingers swept over the keys, he lost himself in the music. He concentrated on each note, nodding his head when it rang in his ears as if confirming it told his story in the way he wanted it to.

How had he survived before he discovered music? How had he survived at all?

He continued to play, aware that large tears were rolling down his cheeks. The music had taken him back to another time when he could see Hannah's face. He was in the forest. She was by his side, her blonde hair flowing behind her as she walked, her soft lips teasing him with their innocence and promise. Beautiful Hannah.

It was no wonder that other women hadn't been able to compare. He'd had women, of course. They'd shared his bed, but none of them had ever occupied much space in his head. Not the way Hannah had. In the end, he'd given up on women. It always got too complicated when they became attached. That hadn't stopped them trying, but eventually they'd realize they could never compete with a treble clef for Matthew's attention and they'd give up.

It wasn't just the music that stood in the way of a relationship for Matthew. He was never sure if they were attracted to him or his money, of which he had plenty. How could they possibly be attracted to him? He felt ugly without his sight. He'd had to go so far as to hire a stylist to choose him a wardrobe, reminding him of a story he'd heard as a child about an emperor who'd had invisible clothes woven for him. Believing that only less intelligent people were unable to see the clothes and not wanting to admit he was one of them, the emperor had proudly marched down the street naked.

Matthew felt like the emperor. He didn't really know if his stylist had selected clothes in the latest fashion or if he was in fact parading around in purple checked pants. He had to trust, which was the hard part. Trust hadn't come easily to him since that day in the forest.

He was aware he was known as a recluse. The mad composer who filled his heart with music instead of a wife.

His music had taken him all over the world. Much to his parents' disappointment, he'd decided to settle in London. This new city had taken some getting used to. He'd spent the first months wishing he paid more attention to London while he still had his sight. He had vague images stored away of Buckingham Palace and Big Ben and longed to study their detail and see what everyone else could.

At times he felt homesick, but soon remembered his hometown came with either pitying or suspicious looks from people who remembered him from *before*. He didn't need to see to know that was how they looked at him. He could feel their eyes upon him, boring into him, making him feel like half a man. Although he'd never been charged with Hannah's murder, the investigation into her death was still an open case, which meant technically he was still a suspect, if not in the eyes of the police, in the eyes of certain people in the town.

In the early days, he tried to ignore them and live a normal life, but when Jarred had posted a video of him playing the piano online, his life had become anything but normal.

Just as Jarred had predicted, he became an overnight success, and his days were quickly filled with a blur of orchestras, concerts, movie scores and recording contracts. He had money and success beyond his dreams, yet his music remained haunted and his smiles remained forced.

"Pathetic," he mumbled as his fingers came to a sudden halt. He had everything the world could offer, apart from his sight. And Hannah. His first and only love. He'd give up the piano forever to spend one moment more with her.

He realized he missed her more now than he had when she'd first left him. In those early days, he still felt she was with him. He was doing fairly well back then. Life had felt positive; like he'd be able to survive. Then her presence had left him, a cloud being blown away in the wind. She'd disappeared and he'd felt the loss.

It was at that point he retreated. Why had she left him? That was if she'd even been there in the first place. It was a crazy idea to believe her spirit had stayed with him in those first few months. Perhaps it was because she'd been torn away so suddenly. Maybe her spirit had taken a while to realize it had been ejected from her young body.

Pain shot through his chest as he remembered carrying her, lifeless, from the clearing, stumbling in the darkness, only to find it was the middle of the day. He'd have never made it out of the forest if it weren't for the hand on his back guiding him. A hand he assumed belonged to the boy in the clearing who'd tried to kill him only moments earlier. He still couldn't understand why he'd been attacking him one moment and helping him the next.

He never found out who the boy was or whether he'd been responsible for Hannah's death. Maybe the doctors were right and his mind had invented the boy as a way to shield himself from what had really happened. It would be easy if he could believe that, but something in his gut told him it wasn't true. There *was* a boy in the clearing. He wasn't sure what he was doing there, but he hadn't harmed Hannah.

There was something in the way he'd looked at her. For a split second he'd thought he saw her return the look, almost as though she'd met him before. He had to resign himself to the fact he'd never know. Hannah was gone and the boy had vanished into thin air.

Believing the boy hadn't taken her life had only led him to one conclusion. It was the light. The light had taken her, just as it had taken his sight. So, what the hell was the light?

His fingers returned to the piano and thumped the keys in a furious rhythm. This was how he saw the light. Powerful. Relentless. Evil. That light had taken everything from him. When people spoke of the light at the end of the tunnel he wanted to scream. The light wasn't a comfort. It was a menace. Why could nobody else see that? Was he the only person in the world who knew its danger?

He drew in a deep breath, the oxygen fueling the fire in his belly and exploding in a volcanic rage on his hapless piano. He knew this passion was what he was famous for, yet very few people knew what torture lay underneath.

"I'll give you bloody light," he cried, his voice drowning in the melody of his grief.

A loud knock sounded at the door to his music room, jolting him back to the present.

"I've told you before, Maria," he bellowed. "I'm blind, not deaf."

"I'm sorry, Mr Sinclair," his housekeeper said, opening the door.

"What is it?" His voice softened as he heard the fear in her voice. He didn't want to upset her. She was the third housekeeper he'd had in as many months.

"You have a visitor. Shall I show her in?"

"Does this visitor have a name?" Frustration rose in his voice once more. It wasn't that hard to do a simple job properly.

"Her name's Lin. She says she knows you."

"I don't know anyone of that name. Give her Jarred's card and tell her to talk to him. Lord knows I pay him enough to deal with this kind of thing."

Jarred wasn't just his brother, he was also his manager. Matthew had thought it only fair, given he was the one who'd launched his career on the internet all those years ago.

"I've already given her Jarred's card, Mr Sinclair. It's just that she's very insistent she sees you. She's come all the way from Hong Kong."

"Oh, for goodness sake. That's a new one." He'd heard all kinds of stories over the years. Most of them were fabrications of the truth in an attempt for a crazed fan to meet him. Either that or they were a fresh-faced journalist looking for their big break. He didn't have time for either variety today.

"I think she's telling the truth, Mr Sinclair."

"Maria, I've told you I don't take appointments with strangers off the street. I don't have time for that. Tell her to call Jarred."

Maria paused. He could hear her standing very still, choosing her next words so as not to upset him.

"What, Maria?"

"I understand what you're saying, Mr Sinclair, but I really think you should see this girl. She's come such a long way."

"Well, she should've gotten in touch before she bothered." He turned back to his piano and waited for Maria to leave.

Once alone, his fingers returned to the piano. This time his music was restless. Edgy. Maria should know better than to disrupt him when he was working. An interruption like that could set him back for hours.

It wasn't long before he was immersed again and the agitation in his music was drowned out by notes tainted with heartbreak and loss. The tune of his life was not a joyful one.

Perhaps that was why his music was loved by so many. There was so much sadness in the world.

"I'm sorry, Mr Sinclair." It was Maria again.

His music came to a sudden halt. It seemed he was destined to achieve nothing today.

"What now?" he snapped. "Another girl from Hong Kong?"

"The same one. She won't leave until she sees you. She says it's urgent."

"That's what everyone says. And it never is."

"Please, Mr Sinclair. There's something unusual about this girl."

"I really don't have time for this." He did nothing to hide his frustration. He thought he'd been more than clear with Maria about what to do in this situation.

"I wouldn't insist if I didn't believe her, Mr Sinclair. I think you should see what she wants." Her voice quavered. It clearly wasn't easy for her to stand up to her new boss like this.

"All right, all right," he said, deciding to call the agency later and have Maria replaced. If she was going to succeed as his housekeeper, she needed to respect that he liked his privacy. He couldn't be interrupted just because she took a liking to a girl who appeared on his doorstep. He'd see this one visitor as a farewell gift to her.

"Send her in," he said. "Tell her she's got five minutes, so she'd better talk fast."

"Yes, Mr Sinclair. Thank you."

He heard the sound of her footsteps retreating and returning with another set. They were light footsteps. Unfamiliar.

The two women stood in the entrance to the room.

"I'll leave you to it," said Maria.

"No, Maria. You can stay. This won't take long."

He drew in his visitor's scent. Her perfume was light and floral. It was a cheap perfume, unlike the expensive fragrances of the women who moved in the same circles as him. It reminded him of something from his past. His mind began racing back to the place he'd dragged it from only minutes ago – the forest. This visitor wore the same perfume as Hannah. He hadn't smelled it for years. This meeting was sure to be a disaster. He wouldn't be able to hear a word she said.

"Hello, Matthew. I'm Lin. Thank you for seeing me." Her voice was timid yet determined. It was the voice of a woman trying desperately to mask her nerves. Her accent was only slight. She sounded more American than like a girl from Hong Kong.

"To what do I owe the pleasure of this interruption?" he asked, cutting immediately to the chase.

"I think this was a mistake. I'm sorry to waste your time." He heard her take a step toward the door. Her breathing was fast. Was she crying? For a reason he couldn't explain, he felt like reaching out to her.

"No, stop. Please sit down. I'm sorry. You caught me at a bad moment, that's all. My mind was elsewhere."

He heard her come closer, the floorboards creaking softly under her weight. To his surprise she sat next to him on the piano stool. She faced the opposite direction, her thigh pressing against his. He didn't move away, nor did he ask her to. She smelled like Hannah. She *felt* like Hannah. Would there be any harm in him pretending, if only for a moment, that she was Hannah?

"Thank you, Maria. You can leave now."

He knew letting Maria leave was a risky move, but the temptation to be alone with this girl for a moment was too much to resist.

"Yes, Mr Sinclair. I'll be right outside if you need me."

She closed the door behind her, leaving them in silence.

Lin's breathing was slow. He could feel her eyes on him, and he wondered why she was here.

Warm fingers threaded their way through his own and a surge of energy poured through his hand and into his body.

"Who are you?" His voice was a whisper on his breath.

"You know who I am."

He reached across with his other hand and brought his fingers to her face. Her skin was soft. Warm. Familiar yet completely foreign. He trailed his fingertips across her cheeks and brought them to her lips. She felt different to Hannah. So why did she remind him so much of her? He'd finally lost his mind.

"Matthew." She leaned closer and lightly pressed her lips against his. His mind swirled. The scent of her perfume was strong now, weaving its way through his nostrils and wrapping itself around the core of his soul. Her lips were soft and moist. He found himself responding to her kiss. He parted her lips with his own and deepened the kiss. He hadn't felt like this since the day in the clearing. He'd waited a long time to experience a kiss like this. He never thought he'd feel like this again.

His hands ran up her arms and to the back of her head, winding his fingers into her hair and sliding them through the long, slick strands. Something was wrong. Hannah's hair was thick and unruly. It didn't feel like this. *Of course, it didn't feel like this*, he scolded himself. It didn't feel like this because this wasn't Hannah.

He drew away, pushing himself back on the seat, breaking all contact.

"I'm sorry," he said. "I don't know what came over me. You remind me of someone, that's all."

"I remind you of Hannah, don't I?"

"What? How did…?" He stood. "I think you should leave."

"Matthew, please. I'm sorry. I shouldn't have done that." Her voice leached with desperation. "I hadn't planned to do that. I just wanted to talk. But when I saw you, I don't know what happened. I had to be close to you again."

"Again? I've never met you. I don't know you."

"You do know me. It's true, you've never met me as Lin, but you have met me."

"How do you know about Hannah? Are you a reporter? You know you're wasting your time. That story's been done to death." It had, too. The story of his girlfriend dying in his arms in the forest had been reported in many papers. According to the stories, he had turned blind with shock. A modern-day Romeo and Juliet. Lin was clearly a reporter trying to get a new angle for a story. How had she known about Hannah's perfume, though? He couldn't remember that detail ever being reported.

"I'm not a reporter, Matthew."

He cringed. There was an intimacy to the sound of his name on her lips.

"Sit down," she said, reaching for his hand once more. He crossed the room and sat on a settee. He couldn't think clearly with her in such close proximity.

"Your perfume," he said. "How did you know?"

"Let me tell you a story," she said, ignoring his question. "Once upon a time, there was a boy and a girl who lived on the edge of a forest."

"Enough," he said.

"They were in love. Madly in love," she continued. "They'd meet near a clump of violets. That was the place they always met. When the violets were in flower, the boy would pick one of them to tuck behind his love's ear."

Matthew sank back in the settee and allowed her to continue. He was certain nobody in the world knew this. He'd listen to what she had to say.

"On this particular day, the girl arrived first. She was wearing a pair of denim shorts and a purple tee shirt. When the boy arrived, he told her she looked like the violet bush. As they laughed, he took her hand in his and led her into the forest. It was quiet that day. A noise startled the boy and the girl told him it was only a wallaby. They laughed again. They were happy, you see. They were always happy when they were in the forest. It was their special place. Nobody could see them in there. The boy led the girl to a small clearing they'd discovered weeks before. There was soft grass there. The sort not usually found in a forest. The girl had said it was like an oasis in a desert. A mirage. She was afraid it would disappear as mysteriously as it seemed to have appeared. The boy had said not to worry. If it disappeared, he'd make her a new clearing. He'd cut down some trees, plant soft grass and water it every day until it was perfect."

Matthew's head sank into his hands. He remembered saying this. How could a girl from Hong Kong know this? It was as if Hannah was speaking from the dead. He let her continue.

"They knelt down on the grass and lay in each other's arms. He kissed her. She wanted him to make love to her for the first time. She wanted to be one with him and never let him go. Then there was a noise, and everything changed. A stranger leaped from the bushes. His hair was wild and his clothes were torn. He clutched a silver dagger in his hand. His face was tortured…" She paused as a huge sob escaped her lips.

Matthew stood and returned to the piano stool. "Please continue." He took her hand gently in his. "Please finish the story."

"There's not much more to the story, I'm afraid. The boy told his love to run. She wouldn't listen. He was scared for her, so he pushed her away and she tripped. Her leg broke. As she lay there on the ground, she saw the boy tackle the stranger. She couldn't let him get hurt so she pushed down her pain and dragged herself toward them. Then a giant light came from the sky."

She paused as he heard her voice break. This story didn't seem to be an easy one for her to tell.

"Go on," he coaxed. This was the part he wanted to hear most. Was it possible this strange girl could have the answers to all his questions? At this stage he was willing to believe anything.

"The light took the girl. It also took your sight." Her hands wrenched free from his grasp and she placed her fingers on his temples. He closed his eyes and she ran her fingertips across his eyelids.

"I'm so sorry," she sobbed. "Your beautiful eyes."

Before he had a chance to stop her, she leaped from the stool, ran out of the room and through the front door. Her footsteps were quickly swallowed by the noise of London passing by. Once again, Matthew cursed his eyes. Giving chase would be useless.

"Come back," he cried out.

CHAPTER NINE

*M*atthew didn't leave his house for many days after Lin's visit. She affected him so profoundly he wasn't certain what step to take next. He wondered if her visit had been real or if he'd imagined it.

"Maria," he called to his housekeeper. He'd decided not to let her go. He couldn't when her gut instinct about Lin had been so right.

"Yes, Mr Sinclair."

"Do you remember the girl from Hong Kong who visited me earlier this week?"

"Of course, I do."

Relief flooded him. He wasn't going crazy. She was real.

"Did she leave you any details? Surname, address, phone number, that kind of thing?"

"No, sorry."

"What did she look like?" he asked, needing to know more.

"She looked like a girl from Hong Kong," she answered in a tone that was so matter of fact he couldn't be offended.

"And what does a girl from Hong Kong look like?" he

asked, certain Maria must be looking at him like he was strange.

"Long, black hair, short, too skinny. You know the sort. Like she might snap in half in a strong wind."

"And how old do you think she was?"

"Young. Maybe sixteen. I'm not sure."

Fear punched him in the gut. Sixteen, and he'd kissed her like that.

"What were her eyes like?" he asked.

"Brown."

He sighed. She'd told him nothing he hadn't already been able to guess for himself.

"Haunted," she added.

"Haunted?"

"That's right. She looked haunted. Either she was petrified to see you, or she'd just seen a ghost. I can't be sure which one."

"Thank you, Maria."

Haunted was how he'd begun to think of her. Although he wasn't sure whether she was being haunted or doing the haunting herself. She'd certainly made him feel like he'd had a visit from a ghost. If only he knew where to find her. He needed to talk to her again.

He asked Jarred to keep a close watch on all the media for a story about the day he lost his sight. He needn't have bothered, really. He didn't believe Lin was a journalist. She'd barely asked him a question. All she'd seemed to want to do was tell him a story – a story she shouldn't have been able to tell. How had she known all those details? She'd spoken of things she couldn't possibly have known. He had to find her and speak to her again. But London was a big place. Perhaps she'd returned to Hong Kong. He hoped not. He'd never be able to find her there.

He called Jarred.

"Hello to my favorite hermit brother," Jarred said, picking up the call. "Ready to come out of hiding and make us both some money?"

"Any news on that media story?" Matthew asked.

"Listen here. You actually have to *do* something to make the news. You understand? They don't usually publish stories about composers who sit in their houses all day moping about. There are other celebrities out there who do things."

Matthew ignored his tone and pressed on. "Well, that's what I was calling about, in fact. Remember that idea you had about Trafalgar Square?"

"I sure do. Are you ready to play ball? Please don't tease me if you're not serious."

"I'm serious."

"When were you thinking? June's a nice time of year for a stunt like that."

"Actually, I was thinking a little sooner than that. What are you doing this afternoon?"

"My God, it's finally happened. You really have lost your marbles."

"You could be right about that."

"Well, let's just hope it doesn't run in the family." He let out a huge belly laugh. Matthew didn't join in.

Matthew took his place behind the grand piano that had been specially delivered to Trafalgar Square. Jarred had taken some convincing, eventually coming around when Matthew told him it would be this afternoon or never. It was too big an opportunity to pass up.

Jarred called in some huge favors to make it all happen. And happening it was. Thankfully, the police were yet to realize what exactly was going on. Busking was forbidden in the square. Not that this could be considered busking. He wasn't asking anyone for money. All they needed was an hour before they were moved away. With any luck, things would work out.

"How'll we get away with moving a giant piano into the square?" Matthew had asked.

"Easy," said Jarred. "We'll just wear fluorescent vests. Nobody questions anyone in safety gear."

He'd been right. A grand piano had made its way into the center of the square and was placed between two of the large bronze lions, without anyone so much as batting an eyelid. Concerts and protests were not uncommon in the square and passers-by assumed this was what was happening. It all looked very official.

Matthew hadn't performed in public for a long time, making this impromptu concert a very big deal. It was an idea of Jarred's from long ago, with him insisting it was a great way to gain publicity and boost his popularity with a younger audience. If the police tried to take him away, it would only add to the media frenzy. According to Jarred, there was no way to lose.

Thanks to a few phone calls Jarred had made on his way into the square, social media exploded with news of the performance and a small crowd had already begun to build. Not that Matthew particularly cared how many people came to listen to him play. As far as he was concerned, he was playing to one person and one person alone.

Lin. Let her come to him.

He felt Jarred's hand on his back.

"We're ready," he whispered. "Let the circus begin."

How apt, Matthew thought, aware of the huge lions looming by his side. He felt the cool air of their shadows. May they bring him luck.

He took a deep breath and began to play. Music poured

from his fingertips, telling stories of love and loss. Each person who listened heard their own story. Each note touched them in a different place. It wasn't unusual for his music to bring people to tears and today was no different. As the music built, so did the crowd. People stopped in their tracks. Even those who'd never heard of Matthew knew they were listening to something special and stayed to hear more. This was no ordinary busker. This was a prodigy at work.

Before long, the square was teeming with people. He could feel them in a way only a sightless person can. He knew he didn't have long. The police would move him soon.

He played a new piece of music he'd written after Lin's visit. The crowd pounced on the fresh energy and he felt them rise with the rhythm. The music spoke of hope and joy, of returning to the place deep within your heart that you called home. It was an uncharacteristically positive piece and he wasn't sure how the crowd would react to it. More specifically, he wasn't sure how Lin would react to it. Was she there in the sea of flesh and blood before him?

A hushed murmur spread through the crowd. Something was happening. The police must be closing in.

"Boo!" the crowd called.

He'd never been booed off stage. He stopped playing for a moment and pointed to himself questioningly.

"Matthew! Matthew! Matthew!" the crowd chanted. They were reassuring him, loving him, lifting him from his doubt. The jeering of the audience had been for the police. He was running out of time.

Jarred wouldn't be happy, but Matthew had other plans for this concert. And what he had planned had to be done now, before the police could stop him.

He rose to stand on his stool and tore off his jacket to reveal a white tee-shirt, emblazoned with a message he'd had

Maria write across the front in thick black marker, saying, *Come back!*

The crowd cheered even louder than before. Until that moment he hadn't realized just how many people were in the square. The noise was deafening. He felt strong hands grab him around the waist and pull him from the stool.

"You're coming with us," a deep voice said in his ear.

"Come back!" a man from the crowd called.

The rest of the crowd quickly caught on. "Come back. Come back. Come back," they chanted.

"That was brilliant. Brilliant. I swear it was just brilliant," Jarred gushed over the phone later that evening. "Where did you come up with the comeback idea?"

"Come back. Not comeback," Matthew corrected.

"Who cares what it was? It was brilliant. That's what it was. I couldn't have thought of anything better myself. What a stunt. They'll be talking about this for years."

"Who will?"

"They will. You know, everyone. You're the talk of the town. We were all over the news."

"I'm so pleased." His voice was flat. He wasn't pleased at all. So far it seemed the only person he'd wanted to come back had remained hidden in the shadows of London. Did she see his message and know it was for her?

"For God's sake, Matthew. For once in your life, try to sound happy. Just for a moment. Please."

"I am happy, Jarred. I'm just tired. It's been a long day. I've only just talked my way out of that police station. You didn't tell Mum about this, did you? You know how she worries."

"No, but she's bound to find out. You should call her and

tell her yourself. She's always complaining that you don't call often enough."

"Later. I'd really like to rest now."

"Well, for once I'm happy to let you. Well done today, little bro."

Matthew disconnected the call and took a sip of his brandy. He put on a CD he'd bought a few weeks ago. He'd already played it dozens of times and decided he'd like to meet the composer.

He relaxed into his chair and closed his eyes, trying to put some space between the hectic events of the day and the peaceful moment he now found himself in. The police had eventually let him off with a rather hefty fine. He wasn't really bothered by that. He wouldn't even have been bothered if they'd locked him up. He already felt like he'd spent most of his life locked up inside his head. How ironic that the only person in the world who seemed to hold the key, was the very person who'd vanished.

His doorbell sounded. He barely heard it over the music. Maria had long gone home for the day. He'd have to check who it was himself. Would it be another reporter, or could he dare to hope it was *her?*

"Hello," he called through the intercom. The video screen was useless. Whoever it was standing at his front gate would need to identify themselves.

"Hello, Matthew." He knew the voice immediately and pressed the button that would allow her to enter. Lin had come back. The concert had worked. It hadn't been for nothing. Joy filled him.

He heard her take the four paces that separated his front door from the gate and smelled her sweet perfume. It wasn't Hannah's perfume this time. It smelled of coconut and lemon. He guessed this was the perfume she usually wore.

"You came back," he said. "Thank goodness you saw the news. Come in." He stepped back and allowed her to pass.

"The news?" she said, heading for the music room where they met last time.

"This way," he said. "The living room's cozier at night."

She followed him. He could feel her eyes on his back.

"Sit down," he said, pointing to the large, leather sofa that dominated the room. "Would you like a drink?"

"No thanks." He could hear a tremble in her voice. He didn't need his sight to know she was wearing the same haunted expression as last time.

He sat next to her and turned the music down.

"If you didn't see me on the news, where did you see me? Were you there today?"

"I'm sorry, Matthew. I don't know what you're talking about. What's happened?"

"You mean…" He started to laugh. A soft, gentle laugh to begin with and then as the reality of what she'd said set in, it became louder. "You mean, I did all of that for nothing?"

"Did all of what? I really don't know what you mean."

"Oh, it doesn't matter, I suppose. I just staged one of the world's biggest media stunts today to get your attention and here you are, completely oblivious to all of it."

"I hope it wasn't too elaborate." She sounded worried.

"No, no. Look it up on the internet later. Just a small event. You'll see."

"Okay. Well, sorry about that."

"Anyway, you're here now. It doesn't matter." And it didn't. All that mattered was she'd come back to him. Now he could get some answers. But it was more than that. He'd been yearning for her. Her last visit had filled a wound deep in his heart. When she left, the wound had felt raw and exposed, causing him more pain than it had before.

"Why were you trying to get my attention?" she asked.

"Because you disappeared. How else was I meant to find you?"

"Does that mean you believe what I had to say?" She sounded eager, reminding him of a young girl.

"How old are you?" he asked, remembering Maria's estimate of sixteen.

"Eighteen," she replied. "I turned eighteen a few months ago."

"Good." He breathed a sigh of relief.

"You didn't answer my question. Do you believe me? Have you thought about what I said?"

"I've thought of little else since you ran out of here. I don't know what to believe. You feel like Hannah. I mean, not your physical form, but the aura you have about you. And you know things only Hannah would know. I can't work it out. Either you really are Hannah, or you're playing a cruel joke on a blind man."

"I'd never do that to you." She sounded sincere. If only he could be sure.

"I have so many questions to ask you."

"I know what it's like to have questions. Ask me anything you like."

"First, I need to get something straight. Before you ran out last time, you were saying that the giant light that took Hannah returned you in her place. It all sounds a little ridiculous."

"Please don't mock me. I'm Hannah, but I'm not. My name's Lin and I was born and raised in Hong Kong. I don't share Hannah's life, but I do share her soul. When Hannah died, she was born again in my body. Normally I wouldn't remember my past life except Hannah blocked her memories from being taken away. As a result, I remember my life as Hannah almost as clearly as I remember my life as Lin."

"I don't know about all of this." He'd once heard a discussion on late-night radio about a young boy who'd believed he was a fighter pilot in World War II. He knew his name, rank and how he'd died. It was convincing, but in the end, Matthew had decided it all sounded too bizarre to be true.

"I understand your confusion," she said. "It took me a long time to figure out, too. I spent my whole life as Lin confused. I had memories of the forest, of my mother, of you. I didn't understand what these memories were until…"

"Until what?"

"Until I had them explained to me."

"And who exactly managed to do that?"

"Reinier." She was unable to disguise the pain in her voice when she said his name. "The boy with the silver dagger. He came to find me. He asked me to come to you."

Matthew took a deep breath and stood. He began pacing the room. Lin's story was made from madness. He couldn't possibly believe it. Except it was the only thing that made any sense. When the doctors told him the boy in the clearing was a figment of his imagination he wanted to scream at them. He hadn't imagined him. He had been there. Nobody had believed him, no matter how much he'd insisted.

Until now.

"I know it's hard to believe," she said, crossing the room and taking him by the hand. "Please, sit with me. Ask me some questions. I'll tell you everything I know."

He allowed her to lead him back to the sofa. Maybe she was right. He should ask her some questions. He wasn't obliged to believe her answers.

"What happened to Hannah after she died?" he asked.

"She went to the light. What happened after that isn't important."

"You just said you were going to answer my questions. And the first one you avoid."

"Well, what exactly is it you want to know?"

"What did Hannah do after she died?"

"You mean, did she visit you?"

He nodded. "Yes."

"She did. She stayed by your side for many months. She didn't ever want to leave you."

"But she did leave, didn't she?"

"Yes. She saw your life moving forwards. There was a day you went to the beach with your friends. You had a good time."

"How could that be important?" He shook his head wondering how she could know this. It was seeming more and more likely that what she was telling him was true. It was the only explanation.

"Hannah realized you didn't need her anymore. She was being selfish staying. Would you really have wanted her there watching you fall in love, marry, have children? You needed her to leave."

"Well, as you can clearly see, none of that has happened." His voice was etched with hurt as the pain of Hannah's leaving rose to the surface. "There are no wives or children hiding in my closets here. So no, I didn't need her to leave. The reason I was doing well was because Hannah was there. I could feel her. She was the one making me strong. When she left, everything fell to pieces. I didn't know how to go on."

He heard Lin gasp. What he'd said had hurt her, but it needed to be said. If she really was Hannah, then she needed to know the truth. Her leaving had almost destroyed him.

"I'm sorry," she said. "I didn't know. I wanted to stay. I left for your benefit, not mine. Leaving you was the hardest thing I've ever done."

She clutched at the front of his shirt and pressed her wet cheek to his chest.

"Why did you run away last time you visited me?" he

asked, trying not to melt into her embrace. He had to keep a level head about this.

"It was too much. It took me by surprise. I thought I'd feel differently about seeing you as Lin. But I didn't. I felt exactly like Hannah again. I just wanted to climb into your lap, wrap my arms around you and never let you go. Then I saw your suffering. Your eyes were always so beautiful. They still are. Only now they can't see and it's all my fault."

"It's not your fault. You didn't need to run."

"I had to get some space from you. I didn't plan to run. If only you knew the trouble I had finding you. Anyway, maybe it was a good thing I left. It's given you a chance to think. I'm not sure you were ready to believe my story last time."

"I'm not sure I'm ready to believe it now."

"Then why aren't you pushing me away?" She brought her face to his and pressed her cheek against him. Warm waves of joy pulsed through his body. Her skin felt electric, like it was a part of his own body returned to him at last.

"Matthew, I know what it's like to have questions." She pulled back, breaking the contact. He instinctively leaned forward, only to find clear air instead of the warmth of her cheek. "I thought I'd go mad when I first had the chance to ask questions. My answers were given to me slowly. Painfully slowly. And now I see that was for the best. If I'd been told everything in one day, I'd never have believed it. It's a lot to take in."

"Are you telling me you're going to run away again?"

"Not yet, but soon."

"What are you afraid of?"

"I'm not afraid."

"You can't fool a blind man. Your voice is quavering, your body is shaking. I can feel your fear. Please don't be afraid of me."

"It's not you I'm afraid of."

"Then what is it?"

"Everything." She wept. "I don't want to cry." She sucked back her tears in large gulps.

"You can cry," he said, pulling her back to his chest and stroking her smooth hair.

"You don't understand. If I start crying, then I'm afraid I'll never stop."

"Then don't stop." He held her closer still, and almost felt her let her guard down. Her small body was wracked with fear and pain. He felt her spirit breaking apart in his arms. What had this poor girl gone through? If what she was saying was true, her life must be torture. It was hard enough dealing with the pain one lifetime could bring. He couldn't imagine having to feel someone else's pain as if it were your own. Especially when the pain was as great as Hannah's.

After several minutes her sobs faded.

"I'm glad you can't see me," she said. "I must look a mess."

"I don't need my eyes to see you, Lin. You look beautiful to me."

He heard the hesitation in her breathing and knew she was about to kiss him. Every fact he'd learned today told him to run, yet his instincts told him to stay, to hold her in his arms and keep her there, safe, forever.

He leaned forward and this time he made contact with her. Not the soft warmth of her cheek, but the moist comfort of her lips. This kiss was different to last time. In the music room he'd been kissing Hannah. Now, he was kissing Lin. A beautiful lost girl from Hong Kong, who'd walked into his house and turned his world upside down, in a way he never imagined possible.

"I'll come back tomorrow," she said, breaking away, the fear returning to her voice.

"Don't go. Please. Let me look after you."

"I have to go."

"Then tell me where you're going. Where are you staying?"

She hesitated. "It's a hostel on the South Bank."

"Does it have a name?" He couldn't let her leave without a way to find her again.

"It's called Saint Poppy's." Her voice was relaxed now. In trusting him, she'd found her calm.

"I've never heard of a Saint Poppy."

She laughed. "I'm not sure there ever was one. There's not much that's holy about that place, let me tell you. Unless you count the carpet, of course."

"Then stay here. I have plenty of room as you can see."

"Thank you, but no. That wouldn't work."

"Okay. The offer's there if you change your mind."

She stood. "I'll see myself out."

"Well, I can't exactly see you out, can I?"

"Sorry?"

"It's okay. It was a blind joke."

"Oh, right. Funny."

"Bye, Lin." He reached out his hand and felt her place her hand in his. Sparks shot up his arm. Would she always have this effect on him?

"Bye, Matthew."

And she was gone, taking her light and energy with her. He instantly felt empty inside and realized that was the way he'd been feeling for the past eighteen years. How would he be able to get used to that feeling again, now he knew it didn't have to be like that? There was a way to lift the darkness from his soul.

And that way was Lin.

CHAPTER TEN

*M*atthew fell asleep with Lin on his mind and awoke the next morning as if time had failed to pass. The thought of her was still with him.

He knew he couldn't wait to see if she'd visit him again. He'd go to Saint Poppy's and find her. If he went early hopefully she'd still be there. It didn't sound like the sort of place anyone would want to hang around. Whatever did she do all day? See the sights of London? He smiled as he imagined her climbing to the top of St Paul's Cathedral or roaming the grounds of the Tower of London.

Hannah had always wanted to travel. She'd had grand plans for them to see the world once they finished school. Why did the light have to ruin those plans? There was so much Lin had failed to tell him. So many questions that burned at him. The light was the question that plagued him most. He had to know what it was that'd changed everything so profoundly that day.

He arranged for a car to take him to the South Bank. He wanted to get there quickly and finding his own way was a challenge he didn't particularly feel like. His usual driver, Thomas, arrived almost immediately.

"Waiting for my call, were you?" Matthew asked as he slid into the back seat.

"I'm always waiting for calls from my favorite clients."

Matthew liked Thomas. He was always pleasant, always discreet. He had a way of knowing when to talk and when to let him sit with his own thoughts. He also knew every shortcut in London.

"Where to today?" he asked.

"The South Bank. There's a hostel there called Saint Poppy's. Do you know it?"

"Not a place my clients usually frequent, but yes, I know it." There was no judgment in his voice. There was a hint of curiosity, but he didn't ask any questions.

Matthew took a pair of dark glasses from his pocket and slid them on. He didn't like wearing glasses, but found it made others more comfortable – particularly strangers. And who knew how many people he'd need to speak to today to find Lin? He had his cane with him too. Another item he hated, but it was a necessary evil. Without it he'd be lying flat on his face in no time. Or worse, he could trip and catch himself with his hand, and break his wrist. There'd be no playing the piano then. He had to protect his hands.

It didn't take long to arrive at the South Bank.

"Want me to wait for you?" Thomas asked.

"It's okay, thanks. I might be a while. I'll call you if I need you." Matthew had already decided if Lin wasn't there, he'd wait. All day and night if necessary.

He made his way up the front stairs and felt at the door handle trying to figure out if he was meant to push, pull or slide it. It pushed open and he stepped inside, listening for the sounds of a computer humming or phone ringing.

"The front desk's over there," a male with an Australian accent said.

He felt a hand at his elbow.

"Thanks," he said, allowing himself to be led.

"Margaret, you've got a customer." The man walked away.

"Hello. Can I help you?"

By her voice, Matthew decided Margaret was in her fifties, slightly overweight, with blonde hair, and too much make up. Assigning faces to strangers was a habit he'd developed over the years. It helped him remember who was who. And it amused him. Particularly when he got it right, which was often.

"I'm looking for a friend of mine who's staying here. Her name's Lin."

"Does she have a surname?"

"Oh, I don't actually know it." How stupid of him to think he could find her with only her first name. "She's from Hong Kong. She's eighteen, very pretty."

"Right. Well, I can't help you without a surname, I'm afraid." He could hear a change in tone. Clearly, Margaret wasn't impressed by him coming in and asking after a young woman.

"She's a friend of my sister," he said, wondering why he needed to lie. He felt some need to protect Lin's reputation. "I'm sure she's staying here. Do you mind if I wait?"

"There's a sofa behind you. Suit yourself. You might be waiting a while, though. I'm not even sure she's staying here."

He heard the clicking of fingers on a keyboard, an indication Margaret had finished the conversation. He turned and felt his way to the sofa.

"You're looking for Lin?" It was the Australian again, who was proving to be more and more useful by the minute.

"Do you know her?"

"Sure. I know everyone around here. I can take you to her if you like. I know where she hangs out most days."

This sounded too good to be true.

"That'd be great," he said, deciding to take his chances. "Thank you."

"Are you all right to walk? It's a few blocks."

"My eyes might not work, but my legs are just fine." He tried to keep the venom out of his voice, but suspected he wasn't successful.

"Sorry, mate. I didn't mean to offend you."

"No, no. You're being very helpful. I'm sorry."

"Bummer about your eyes. You're that piano dude, aren't you?"

Matthew smiled. He'd been called many things over the years but couldn't recall ever being called a piano dude. "Yeah, I'm the piano dude. Matthew."

"I'm Sean. I saw you on the news last night. Awesome stunt you pulled. You're all over the papers today. I'm from Australia, too. Up north, though."

"Nice to meet you, Sean. Thanks for your help with this." He put out his hand only to experience an extremely awkward handshake with what he was sure was Sean's left hand.

"What you can't see," said Sean, "is that I'm missing my right arm. Left one works a beauty though. Except maybe when it comes to handshakes."

"Between the two of us, we have a full working set of body parts. We'll be fine, I think."

"You didn't ask me how I lost my arm. Most people are dying to know."

Matthew frowned. He'd never ask someone such a personal question. "You didn't ask about my sight, so I thought I'd let it go."

"Only reason I didn't ask was because I already know. I read about it in the paper years ago."

"Well, you have one up on me then. Shall we go and find Lin?" He heard Sean breathe out through his nose and knew his briskness had offended him. "You can tell me about your arm on the way."

"It's a great story," Sean said, his enthusiasm returning. He opened the door for him, and they walked down the stairs.

"Which way?" Matthew asked.

"We'll take a left."

"How far did you say?"

"I said a few blocks, but it may be a bit more than that."

"Okay. Umm, Sean. Do you mind if I keep my hand on your elbow so I can put this cane away?"

"Spoils your image, hey?"

"Something like that."

"Of course, mate. Although you'll need to stand on my other side. No elbow on this side."

They switched sides and continued on. Matthew felt instantly better without his cane. It was nice to hear an Australian accent, even one filled with the kind of slang that made him cringe.

"So, anyway, I'm out surfing one day," said Sean, and Matthew realized he was going to have to hear the story of the missing arm. "And my mate, Cookie, starts screaming like a little girl. I look over and there's this bloody fin in the water. Never been so scared in all my life. So, we start swimming for shore, kicking and thrashing around like frogs in a blender. Useless we were. Pathetic."

"Understandable," said Matthew to show he was listening.

"So, the next thing I see is this giant mouth, with these enormous teeth. So many teeth. And it's open wide about to bite Cookie in half. That's how Cookie got his name, you see. Anyway, me being the genius I am, I reach out to push

Cookie out of the way. I don't know what I was thinking. I mean, an eight-foot white pointer is about to attack and there's me trying to push him aside like I'm a superhero. Then all I can remember is the bastard's jaws snapping closed, and I look down and there's blood spewing everywhere. No pain whatsoever. Doctors reckon I was in shock."

Matthew grimaced. "Doctors claim a lot of things happen to you in shock. They're not always right."

"Yeah well, this time I think maybe they were. Cookie kicked the shark in the nose, grabbed me and dragged me out of the water. He's the superhero."

"Cookie would probably be dead if it weren't for you."

"That's what he reckons."

"Tell me about Lin," said Matthew, hoping now that the story was out of the way he might be able to find out a little more about her. Conversation had never been his strong point.

"What do you mean? I thought you said she's your sister's friend."

"She is. I just wondered how long you've known her?"

"I met her about a week ago. Well, I found an excuse to meet her, to be honest. I suppose your sister's told you how cute she is? I just had to talk to her. Not that she seemed very interested in me. She was polite, but you always know when a girl really wants to talk to you or not. How does your sister know her, anyway?"

"She worked in Hong Kong for a while. Anyway, if Lin didn't talk to you, how do you know where she spends her time?" He was keen to steer the conversation back to Lin and far away from his fictitious sister. Sean was a nice guy. It felt wrong to lie to him like this. Undoing the lie seemed too difficult, at this stage.

"I've seen her down at Hyde Park, sleeping on one of those deck chairs. She was pretty jetlagged when she first arrived from Australia, and Lord knows, nobody gets any sleep at night at Saint Pop's."

"Australia? I thought she came from Hong Kong."

"Are you sure she's your sister's friend? You don't seem to know much about her."

"My sister's always sketchy on details like that. So, what was she doing in Australia?"

"I'm not sure exactly. She said she was holidaying, but when I asked her where she'd been, she didn't seem to know anything about Australia. She said she spent most of her time in a small town there, somewhere near the forest in Victoria, doing some research."

Matthew started to feel ill as the information he'd just been given sunk in. So, Lin had been researching in a small Australian town near the edge of the forest. That sounded very much like she'd been in his hometown, researching him. Was that how she knew so much about him? Were his instincts all wrong? Perhaps she was a reporter after all.

"You all right, mate? You look like you've seen a ghost. Well, if you could see, that is."

"I'm fine, thanks. I just have a lot on my mind at the moment."

The truth was he'd had nothing but Lin on his mind since she first walked into his life and made his head spin. How could she have fooled him like that? She was so convincing. Was she after money or a story? He'd been sure she was genuine. It seemed all it took to trick him was some cheap perfume and a few stories about the past. She'd made a real fool of him.

"So, tell me," Sean said, "What's it like being famous?"

"Not a whole lot of fun, actually."

"I think it'd be so cool."

"For a start, there are a lot of people out there who try to take advantage of you." Matthew's voice was hard.

"Yeah, but you must pull the chicks. Know any you can introduce me to?"

"Plenty, and you can have them all." *Including Lin.*

"You serious?"

"Sure. Actually, there's an event at the Tate I was supposed to go to tonight, only I'm not much in the mood. You want to go in my place? There'll be plenty of women."

"Really? Yes please. I can't play the piano though."

"It's not that kind of event." Matthew pulled his phone from his pocket and called Jarred, asking him to add Sean's name to the list on the door. Jarred was less than impressed to hear he wouldn't be attending himself. Thankfully, he was still in a good mood from the events of the day before and agreed to arrange it.

"Be there at seven," Matthew said to Sean. "And wear something nice."

"Thanks so much. I don't know what to say."

"That must be a first."

"You're funny. A bit of a rude bastard, but I like you."

"Well, it's the least I can do. You've already helped me out more than you know."

He had, too. Without Sean, he'd never have known about Lin's trip to Australia. He'd still be under her spell, believing her to be Hannah. Giving Sean a night out surrounded by beautiful women was the least he could do. Besides, he hated feeling in debt to people. This evened the score.

Sean came to a sudden stop. "She's over there," he said. "She's asleep."

"Brilliant. Thanks so much."

"No. Thank you. Really, I mean it."

"Would you mind taking me over to her quietly and then leaving me to wake her?"

"Your wish is my command. Give me a hug, man." Sean wrapped his one arm around Matthew in a firm grasp. He wasn't wrong when he'd said it was a good arm. Matthew tolerated the hug, relieved when Sean broke away. He wasn't great with physical contact these days, except when it came to Lin. But that was all in the past now he knew the truth.

Sean led him several steps and patted him on the back to indicate his departure. Matthew nodded his appreciation and stepped forward, his leg making contact with the hard timber of the chair frame.

"Hello," he said. "Lin."

He felt the chair rock as she woke.

"Matthew. How did you find me?"

"Research." His voice was icy. Every guard he had was firmly up. She wasn't going to break through this time.

"Here, sit in this chair. I'll bring another one over."

He sat and waited until he heard her sit beside him. He felt it more than he heard it. Her mere presence affected him, like a pebble causing a ripple to spread across a lake. *Don't let her in.*

"What's wrong?" she asked. "You look terrible."

"Why, Lin? Is Lin even your name? Why did you do it?"

"I don't understand. Why did I do what?"

"You know what I'm talking about. Why did you come to my doorstep and feed me this ridiculous story? Why did you make a fool of me? Why did you give me such hope?" He realized that was it. That was the source of his hurt. He didn't really care if she'd hurt his pride. It was the hope she'd given him, and the hurt he felt when it had been so swiftly taken away.

"What's happened since I left you?"

"What's happened is I've realized how badly you fooled me."

"I was telling you the truth. I swear it, Matthew. I don't understand why all of a sudden you're doubting me, when only last night we made so much progress."

"Progress? So, that's what this is for you. Progress toward what, exactly?"

"Sorry, that was a poor choice of word. Please remember English isn't my first language."

"You haven't exactly seemed to struggle with the language until now."

"Please don't pick on one word I used. I just meant that last night I felt so close to you, and today you're so angry. Something must've happened to make you like this. How did you find me? Who have you been talking to?"

"An Australian guy called Sean took me here."

"Really? Did he tell you about his arm?"

"Of course. He couldn't wait to tell me that terrible story about the shark."

"It'd be a terrible story if it were true. He confessed to my roommate that he lost his arm in a car accident. He tells that shark story to impress people."

If Matthew weren't so angry, he'd have laughed. To think he'd been feeling bad about saying Lin was his sister's friend, and all the time Sean was lying through his teeth. He couldn't believe he hadn't picked up on it. Normally he could hear a lie in the way someone spoke. He'd been so distracted by the prospect of finding Lin, he'd been only half-listening to Sean's story.

"Another liar," he said, bitterly.

"Are you calling me a liar?" She sounded hurt.

"Did you go to Australia?"

"Yes, but what does that matter?"

"Is that how you found out all those things about me and Hannah?" He needed some answers.

"No. I went to Australia because, stupidly, that's where I expected to find you. It wasn't until I got there that I realized it was so naïve of me to expect you to be sitting exactly where I left you. I visited your parents to find out where you were, but they were suspicious and wouldn't tell me anything."

"Of course, they were suspicious. Perhaps they're smarter than I am."

"I asked around town and people were only too happy to talk about their most famous resident. They told me you'd made it big and lived in London now. They're a bit upset about that, you know. Still happy to brag about you, though."

"Well, they didn't seem too thrilled about me when I did live there, let me tell you. People are such hypocrites. No wonder I don't trust anyone."

"Matthew, please. I don't understand how me going to Australia changes anything. I mean, I had to find you somehow. I didn't realize you were a famous musician. All I could see were memories from Hannah's past. I couldn't see you in the present."

"So, you weren't researching me?"

"Well, I suppose I *was* researching you. For a start, I was trying to find out where you were. And while I was there, of course I tried to find out more about you, and what happened to you after I left. Besides, I had other reasons for wanting to go there."

"Such as?" He felt his guard dropping and tried desperately to put it back up in place. What she was saying so far was making sense.

"I had to see the town I'd lived in as Hannah. The place I'd dreamed about all my life. I wanted to go to the forest. To the clearing. To see my family…"

"You saw your family? What was that like?" His curiosity was getting the better of him now.

"It broke my heart. My brother wasn't there. He's grown up now with a family of his own, although I saw my parents. I didn't tell them who I was, of course. I just went to the church and said I was on holiday and wanted somewhere to worship. My mother was so beautiful. She looked me straight in the eye when we met and then hugged me tight. She apologized and said she wasn't usually so familiar with people. I wanted to tell her – I almost bit my tongue off not telling her – but I know she'd never have believed me, and it would just have upset her."

"Did you see your father?"

"Of course. He was there standing at the altar. I didn't talk to him, though. It's strange, but he's the one person I can't remember. I felt no connection to him whatsoever. Reinier told me once he thought my memory of him was cleansed. And after seeing him preaching, I think I know why. He didn't strike me as the sort of person Hannah would've kept close to her heart."

"Reinier? He's the boy from the clearing, isn't he?" *Damn it.* She was slipping under all his defenses. Soon he'd probably be kissing her, and there was nothing he could do to stop himself.

"Yes."

"Where's he now? And who the hell is he, anyway?"

"He's an enlightened soul. He knows things. Sees things. He saw danger for me in the clearing that day."

"Why would he care if you were in danger?"

"Because we're soulmates. We've been connected in all our past lives. He came to the clearing to protect me."

"By attacking us with a dagger? Great way to protect someone." He was jealous and he knew it. Soulmates? The idea made him want to vomit.

"It wasn't like that." Her voice was defensive. He'd pushed too far.

"It was exactly like that. What else do you think he was doing with that knife? He wasn't trying to make a salad."

"He didn't kill Hannah. The light did. It was you he was

trying to kill." He heard the regret in her voice. This wasn't something she'd been planning to tell him.

"Oh, well that's all right then. He sounds like a perfectly lovely guy. I can see why he's such a good friend of yours."

"He didn't want to hurt you. He'd never hurt anyone intentionally."

"I'm pretty sure being stabbed to death would hurt."

"He thought if he killed you then Mother wouldn't kill me."

"Mother? This is absurd, you realize."

"Mother is the Soulweaver. She's the one who decides which soul is born to which person. You and I were intended to conceive a child that day in the forest. She didn't want the child to be born, so instead she took my life. Reinier thought if he took your life first, then there'd be no reason for Mother to take mine."

"Well, that clears it up then." Matthew's voice dripped with sarcasm. "This Mother doesn't sound like she's very effective at her job. Taking an innocent girl's life to prevent yet another innocent life being born. I hope this Mother doesn't have performance reviews, because I don't think she'd pass with flying colors."

"Do you see now why I didn't want to tell you this yet? You're mocking me. You don't believe a word I'm saying." Her voice was shaking. He'd really upset her now.

"What was the light, then?" He might as well ask, he decided. It was the one question he'd really wanted to know all these years.

"That was Mother. She came down and lifted my soul directly from my body. That's why my autopsy was inconclusive. There was no actual cause of death. My heart stopped because my body no longer contained a soul."

"And my eyes? Did Mother decide to take those with her as a souvenir?"

"Your eyes are still in your head, as you very well know. No, you were blinded by Mother's light. It's very bright. It's not intended for any human to see. Maybe you'll see again one day. Maybe your eyes just need time to recover."

"Now you sound like my doctor, and I don't believe him either."

"Matthew, just think about it. What I'm saying makes sense. Why else would Reinier throw down his dagger after I died? He didn't want to kill you, and once I was dead, he had no need. That's why he helped you from the forest. It was his hand on your shoulder that guided you."

"How do you know that? Nobody knows that. Not even my parents."

"I know it because Reinier told me. He was there, Matthew. I'm not making any of this up."

"I'd like to meet him. Where is he? Did he come with you?" Maybe if he met the boy from the clearing he could start to believe this story. Not that he'd be able to recognize him without his sight.

"I don't know where he is. He disappeared." Her voice quavered. He could tell she was only just holding on to her composure.

"That's very convenient. You have no idea where he is?"

"No. Believe me, I'd like to know."

"You love him, don't you?"

She hesitated. "So much it hurts."

"Then why the hell have you been kissing me?"

"You don't get it, Matthew. The part of me that's Lin loves Reinier, but the part of me that's Hannah still loves you. I can't separate the two parts. I love you both."

CHAPTER ELEVEN

*M*atthew and Lin arrived at his apartment later that morning. After she'd told him she loved him, his feelings for her had begun to shift. If this was an act, she deserved an award for her performance. He still couldn't figure out any possible way she could've found out the information she knew, unless her story was true.

He'd convinced her to stay with him. He needed to make sure she didn't run away again. She agreed, saying she was worried that if she left him alone he'd jump to the wrong conclusion again about some innocent piece of information. That scene in the park had rattled her.

Besides, he liked the idea of her sleeping under his roof, her energy bouncing off his walls. No matter how hard he fought his feelings, she'd burrowed her way into his heart. Actually, burrowed was not the word. Exploded was more apt. She'd taken him completely by surprise and awoken feelings in him that he'd repressed for far too long.

Maria made up one of the spare bedrooms for her. If she thought it odd that the girl who'd knocked on the door was now a guest in Matthew's home, she didn't say so.

Matthew had left her to settle in, saying he had some business to take care of. He asked Thomas to take him to an address Jarred had given him for a private investigator. Matthew had never used this investigator's services before but had heard Jarred speak highly of him when he had his wife trailed the year before last. The investigator had indeed uncovered exactly why Jarred's wife had been returning from her weekly yoga class with flushed cheeks and a healthy glow, having never actually attended a single class.

The investigator's name was Fraser Fraser. An odd name, thought Matthew, although he supposed it was a rather odd profession, so perhaps it suited.

As he was ushered into his office, he immediately realized there was more about Fraser Fraser that was unusual than just his name. He could tell by his handshake the man was exceptionally tall. How did he manage to sneak around spying on people with such a large frame? Surely, he'd stand out in any crowd.

Matthew took a seat across from Fraser's desk and thanked him for seeing him on such short notice.

"Not a problem at all," Fraser said. "I'm a big fan of your work."

"Thank you. Jarred speaks highly of you."

"I love a happy customer. So how can I help you today? Your wife hasn't taken up yoga, has she?" His tone was smarmy. Matthew wasn't sure he'd made the right decision to trust him, but the thought of trying to find someone else gave him a headache. Fraser Fraser would have to do.

"No, I don't have a wife, thankfully. I was just wondering if you could find some information for me on a couple of people."

"Of course. That's my job. Who exactly are you interested in finding out about?"

"Well, you see, I had a visit recently from a woman who

claims we met in the past. Only I can't remember that meeting. I just wondered what you can tell me about her. I've been thinking that maybe she's a reporter."

"Right. Of course. No problem. We'll go through her specifics in a moment. How many others are on your list?"

"Just one. Only I don't know much about him, I'm afraid."

"What do you know?"

"His name is Reinier."

———

Matthew spent the next hour providing Fraser with every detail he knew about Lin and Reinier. It was precious little. He decided if Fraser could come up with even one piece of information then he was a genius. Thankfully, he seemed confident.

He returned to his apartment without feeling any guilt. Lin had researched him. All he was doing was a little research of his own.

He found her asleep on the settee in his music room. He heard her heavy breathing the moment he set foot in the room, so he sat in an armchair across from her and listened to the soft noises she made. She was sleeping deeply, and he imagined her dreams flickering behind her eyelids. Was she dreaming of him, or was she dreaming of Reinier? If what she said about loving them both was true, then perhaps she was more like him than he'd had initially realized. After all, he loved two women at the same time. Only one was dead, and the other was asleep before him right now.

Did he love Lin? He wasn't even sure he knew what love was. Was it feeling like you'd rather die than see harm come to a person? Was it as though they'd taken up residence in a corner of your heart, and no matter how you tried they remained lodged there? Was it when a person occupied all the crevices of your mind, leaving you unable to hold another thought without them seeping through? If that was love, then Lin certainly qualified.

Her breathing lightened. She'd wake soon and they could talk once more. Now that she'd told him what she believed the light to be, he wondered what question was burning most at him now.

The baby.

Why had Mother been intent on preventing the birth of the baby he was supposed to have conceived with Hannah? It wasn't hard to believe a baby would've been conceived. He'd wanted Hannah with every cell in his body. She was different that day, too. Instead of gently moving his hands away, she'd let him explore her soft curves. If they'd been left alone, they'd never have been able to stop. The thought of her aroused him even now.

Yes, it was very likely a baby would have been conceived in the clearing that day. He could only imagine what Hannah's father would've said about that. They'd have had to run away. Life would have been tough, but they'd have been together. That seemed a luxury, compared to the lonely life he'd led without her. He'd return every extravagance of his decadent lifestyle to have Hannah back.

Lin stirred. Did he have Hannah back, after all? Her spirit certainly felt the same, even if her lips did not.

"You're back," she said. "How long have you been here?"

"Not long. You sure sleep a lot."

"So would you, if you'd traveled all this way only to land in a hostel where sleep is a novelty."

"Fair enough. You have a lot of catching up to do."

"It's nice here. Your home is beautiful. You have great taste."

"I can't take the credit, I'm afraid. My interior designer

did it all. Not sure why I bothered paying her that fortune. I can't see any of it."

"Well I can, and I love it."

"It was worth every penny then. So, Lin, tell me about the baby."

"The baby? How did you... Oh, you mean the baby you were meant to have with Hannah."

"What other baby would I have meant?"

"No. No. No other baby. I just woke up. I'm confused."

"Okay. So, now we know which baby I'm talking about, how about you fill me in? Why would Mother want to stop Hannah and me from conceiving a child? Was it a devil child?"

"No! The complete opposite, actually. You see, Mother's turned against us. By us, I mean humankind. She decided if we can no longer look after ourselves, each other and our planet, then she also has no interest in looking after us. She's decided to sit back and watch us destroy ourselves."

"How does a baby change any of that?"

"Because it isn't just any baby we're talking about. This is a special baby. He's destined to alter the course of the world."

Matthew's jaw dropped at this outlandish statement. "Hang on a minute. I think I wrote the score for that movie last time I was in Hollywood."

"This isn't a joke, Matthew. It's true. I don't know how it's possible, but I know it's what's meant to happen. This baby is our only hope."

"Is? Don't you mean *was*?"

"Is."

Silence hung in the air. What did she mean? He could hardly have a baby with Hannah now. Unless... She didn't mean...?

"Are you serious? Are you saying what I think you're saying? You want to have a baby with me?"

"I had a feeling that would be your reaction."

"I'm glad, because if you expected any other kind of reaction, you'd be delusional. In fact, maybe you're already delusional. Don't you think it's a little farfetched to believe a baby could save the world?"

"Well, I'm sure he won't do much when he's still a baby."

"You think one person can solve all the problems our planet is facing? That's a tough job."

"One person *can* change the world. We're all so much more powerful than we realize."

"Just how exactly is one person going to do this? What big, amazing thing is he destined to do that will save us all? You did say *he*, didn't you?"

"Yes, a boy. I don't know how he's going to do it. I just know that he is. And maybe it's not one big, amazing thing he's going to do that will make the difference. Maybe it's lots of big, amazing things. Or maybe it will just be one tiny, innocent act that will have an effect that ripples across humankind."

"Like the butterfly effect. One small flap of the wings and bingo, there's a hurricane."

"It sounded a lot more beautiful the first time I had it explained to me, but yes, that's exactly what I mean. You know, you have a way with words – a way of making things sound terrible. You express yourself so beautifully on a piano, yet you turn words to mud."

"Because music doesn't lie. Even terrible music speaks the truth."

"And I'm speaking the truth to you now." She stood and crossed the room, sliding herself onto his knee. He tensed at her touch.

"Are you trying to start the conception immediately?" he asked.

"Of course not." She pulled back.

"Well, what's all of this, then?"

"Oh, for goodness sake, Matthew. I thought we were more grown up than that." She got up and returned to the settee

"You're barely more than a child, Lin."

"That's not true. I don't think I've ever been a child. I was born with all of Hannah's experiences. Being a child always seemed so pointless to me. I'd look at the other kids and wonder what they were doing playing their silly games. I was more interested in my sketches or talking to the customers in our store about their travels or their life."

"You draw?"

"Yes. I've drawn lots of pictures. Lot of pictures of you, too. Long before I even knew who you were. The first time I drew you, I was nine years old."

"I wish I could see your drawings."

"I wish I could show them to you. I have them here with me. Maybe one day, your sight—"

"My sight won't come back," he said, cutting her off. "Anyway, we were talking about you and the unhappy childhood you had."

"You're wrong about that. I had a confusing childhood, but I was happy. I had parents who loved me. We had an income to support us and a roof over our heads. Just because I didn't skip or play with dolls, doesn't mean I didn't have a good time. I was just different to the other kids. That's why they didn't like me, I suppose."

"I'm sure they liked you."

"No, really, they didn't. They said I thought I was better than them. That wasn't it. I was just aware that I was different. I couldn't explain it to them. I couldn't even explain it to myself."

"What sort of store did your parents own?"

"A convenience store, like a small supermarket. They still

own it. They work hard. It's a good business." Her voice softened at the mention of her parents.

"You miss them, don't you?"

"Of course, I do."

"Do they know where you are?"

"They think I'm in Australia."

"Why haven't you told them you're in London?"

"Be serious! You think you're having a tough time believing what I'm trying to tell you? You try getting my parents to understand. No. It's better they don't know at the moment. It'd upset them too much."

This time Matthew crossed the room and sat next to her. He reached for her, his hand gently stroking the back of her head. His fingers entwined with her hair and he raked them downwards, enjoying the way they slipped through the sleek strands without catching. She smelt of lime, a fragrance he recognized from the shower gel in the spare bathroom.

"You showered," he said.

"Nothing gets past you."

He noticed a shiver in her voice. Was his touch affecting her as much as it was affecting him? The stories she'd been telling him were beyond ludicrous. So why did he keep finding himself reeled in? Believing her. Wanting her.

"Lin, about this baby. I…"

"You're not ready right now."

"I don't think I'll ever be ready. There's so much I depend on other people for as it is. I couldn't look after a baby."

"That's rubbish. Plenty of blind people have babies. Plus, I wouldn't expect you to look after it."

"It's not going to happen, Lin. I'm sorry. There has to be another way to save the world."

"Stop doing that."

"Doing what?"

"Saying *save the world* like that. You're making fun of me."

"Sorry. I don't mean to. I'm just finding it a little hard to believe, that's all."

"I get it. You need time. Believe me, I get it. When I first heard about the baby, I freaked out. You're actually handling it a thousand times better than I did. I couldn't imagine having a baby. Now I understand there's a bigger picture. Whether or not I'm ready to be a mother is of absolutely no importance, compared to the challenge being faced by humankind."

"Do you think it's really that bad? I mean, the way we're treating the Earth?"

"Of course, it's that's bad. When was the last time you heard the news and nothing bad had happened? Countries are fighting countries. People are killing people. We steal, we rape, we lie. And all the while, we destroy the very planet that's giving us life. The trees give us air, so we cut down our forests. The oceans give us food, so we poison our fish. The atmosphere protects us, so we fill it with smog. Our planet is dying and all we're worried about is which celebrity is getting divorced and who won the football. We've all gone mad."

"You agree with Mother?"

"Of course not. No. I can see why she's started thinking that way, and something definitely needs to be done, but I'd never give up on the human race. I think she's forgotten what it's like to be human."

"She was human?"

"I think so. A long time ago." Uncertainty crept into her voice. It seemed she was not so sure about everything, after all.

"And you really think the Earth's become so bad that something drastic needs to be done?"

"It's obvious. Every year it's worse than the last. How long can that go on? We might be all right for this lifetime, but what about the next?"

"Maybe if people knew they were coming back again, they'd take better care."

"Lately, I don't know. People have become so selfish that all we care about is what's happening in our own little part of the world in the next five minutes."

"You know, Hannah used to speak like this sometimes. She was always worried about the world. She could barely watch the news on television. I think that's why she liked the forest so much."

"It was. You forget who you're speaking to."

"I haven't forgotten. My brain just hasn't reconciled you and Hannah as the one person yet." He wasn't sure that would ever happen.

"You have trouble putting us together. Reinier used to have trouble pulling us apart. He called me Hanlin sometimes."

"Cute." He was being sarcastic. He still wasn't sure about Reinier. Lin had said he'd disappeared. Did that mean he could return and snatch her away as quickly as she'd appeared? He hoped not. Perhaps the information Fraser dug up would shed some light on this.

She laughed, missing the sarcasm in his voice.

"So, Hanlin," he said. This time the sarcasm couldn't be missed. The words were dripping in it. "If you really are the one person, doesn't that mean you cheated on me when you fell in love with Reinier?" He was being cheeky now, although he had to admit he was genuinely curious about her answer.

"Technically yes, I suppose. But you need to remember the feelings I developed for him happened in a time of great confusion for me. He rescued me from that. It also happened at a time before I'd met you as Lin."

"You think it might have been different if we'd met?"

He heard her draw in a deep breath before she answered. "Perhaps," she said.

He knew he had to decide if *perhaps* was going to be good enough for him.

Fraser Fraser had told Matthew he'd need one week before he'd be able to present him with a report on his findings. Matthew didn't mind waiting – as long as the report contained the answers he needed.

He kept Lin at arm's length as much as he could. They spent hours talking and somehow, he refrained from kissing her. He was determined that wouldn't happen until he'd read Fraser's report. There was plenty of innocent touching, though. The tracing of his finger down the smooth skin of her cheek or the placing of his palm on her shoulder as he pulled her close. The feel of her hand in his soon became as familiar as breathing. He knew the feel of her. He knew the scent of her.

As the week grew old he came to realize the touching was not so innocent after all. She was slowly seducing him, whether intentionally or not. He was a fish on her line, being pulled closer and closer until it would be too late. His fate felt sealed.

If Fraser's report showed her to be dishonest he wasn't sure how he'd react. He suspected it wouldn't be good. He'd be devastated. The more he talked with her, the more he came to believe she was being honest with him. He tried to get her to contradict herself or slip up on a fact she should know, but it never happened. Nobody could possibly know that much about Hannah, and his relationship with her, unless they actually were Hannah. Or a mind reader.

Finally, the day had come for him to make his way to

Fraser's office. He'd told Lin he needed to attend to some personal business, and she hadn't questioned him. This made him feel sick to his stomach, until he reminded himself it wasn't a lie. He did have to attend to personal business – the personal business of finding out for sure if she was telling him the truth.

He took a seat in Fraser's office as instructed and sat quietly listening to him shuffle some papers about.

"I'm sorry, Matthew. I'm not used to having to present these reports verbally. Normally, I'd hand it to you, and we'd run through it together."

"No problem. Sorry to trouble you. I didn't go blind to be a nuisance."

"Oh, no, no, no. Sorry. It's no trouble. Now, where do I start? Okay, yes, I found Lin's records. She was indeed born in Kowloon, Hong Kong, a little over eighteen years ago. Her parents are Shen Sung and Mei Chan. They run a grocery store. Lin's their only child. Is this all adding up?"

"Perfectly. Go on."

"Lin attended Shun Chin International College, graduating with excellent grades, although her final report card noted her concentration levels weren't up to scratch and she was somewhat of a loner."

Matthew nodded. So far there were no surprises. He held on to the relief that threatened to flood his body. He must hear the full report first.

"Now, here's what I call the pearler."

"The pearler?"

"The hidden piece of information you're going to love. Or not. You know, the reason you hired me."

A sick feeling took hold in his stomach. He breathed deeply and prepared himself for the so-called pearler.

"Well," Fraser continued. "Lin was married the day after her eighteenth birthday. Did you know that?"

Matthew shook his head as he concentrated on maintaining his composure. The thought of Lin being married made him sick. "Please go on. Who did she marry?"

"Well this is where it gets interesting. She married Reinier Knight in a registry office in Kowloon."

"Lin's married to Reinier?" He couldn't believe it. How could she have kept that information from him? That was huge. What else was she keeping from him? There was a lot more to Lin than she'd revealed.

"Yeah but hang on. That's not the pearler."

"That's not it?" What could possibly be more shocking than what he'd already heard?

"Right. Well, it turns out that Reinier died the day after the marriage took place."

Matthew's head spun. Reinier was dead. And he died the day after he married Lin. There had to be a mistake. Lin had said she didn't know where he was, which meant she was either hiding more information from him, or she really didn't know.

"You with me here?" Fraser asked.

"Yeah, just taking it all in. That's some pearler. Are you absolutely positive he's dead?"

"I have his death certificate right in front of me."

"How? What happened?"

"It was suicide. Threw himself off a bridge. Terrible business."

"The day after the wedding?"

"Yeah. Awful. Lin must be really messed up after that. Especially given the baby."

"Hang on. What baby?" This was getting worse by the minute. First, she's married, then she's a widow, and then she has a baby. Did he even know her at all?

"Well it turns out she went on her honeymoon alone. To Australia. She spent about two months there. During that time, she had an early miscarriage. Looks like the wedding was consummated, if you know what I mean."

"How the hell do you know this?" Anger sent bile shooting to the back of Matthew's throat and he stood. How dare Fraser speak about Lin like that. Like she was some character in a soap opera and not the woman he loved. Then he remembered he was upset with her and sat back down. He couldn't possibly love her. He didn't even know who she was.

"Hey, don't get upset with me. I'm just doing what you paid me to do."

"Sorry, you're right. I just didn't expect that level of detail."

"People rarely do. Although if you remember correctly, I did ask you if you were sure you wanted to know whatever I found out." He could hear nerves in Fraser's voice. He hadn't meant to intimidate him.

"Yeah, yeah. Of course. Is that it? No more pearlers? What did you find out about Reinier?"

"Okay, he was a little harder to track down, until I found his surname on the marriage certificate. Reinier Knight. Born in Melbourne, Australia, to parents Richard and Montana Knight. He was one of seven children. At the age of three, he was put into the care of a foster family. This was the first of many. He was a runner, and I don't mean the athletic type. Constantly running away. The authorities lost track of him after his thirteenth birthday. He was listed as a missing person, only I don't think they tried awfully hard to find him. Somehow, he managed to fend for himself all those years, until he turned up in Hong Kong about a year before his marriage to Lin."

These words made Matthew wince. He hated to think of Lin married to anyone. He wasn't sure how to process it. This was going to take some getting used to.

"A mysterious character indeed," Fraser continued. "I'm

afraid I couldn't dig up a lot more in the week you gave me. Happy to continue on if you'd like me to."

"No thanks. You've given me everything I need and more."

"I can give you this report if it's any use to you."

"Sure, I'll take it. I've paid enough for it." He heard Fraser shift uncomfortably in his chair. "Worth every penny, of course," he added. "Thanks for your time, Fraser. Jarred was right. You're very good at your job."

"No problem. I enjoyed it. Sure beats trailing rich women around town. I've spent so much time sitting outside nail salons I think I could just about do the manicure myself."

Matthew shook Fraser's hand, silently wondering yet again exactly how tall he was. He seemed so much taller than any ordinary man. He'd have to ask Jarred. Not that he'd judge someone for a peculiarity. He wasn't exactly famous for being ordinary.

He left the building and made his way to a nearby café he'd been to once before. He didn't want to return to his apartment immediately. He needed some time to absorb what Fraser had told him. There was no way he could face Lin until he'd sorted out his thoughts.

He ordered a coffee and asked to be taken to a seat near the back where he could be left in peace. The waitress was only too happy to oblige. He wasn't sure if she knew who he was. He hoped not. He wasn't in the mood to make small talk or sign autographs. He was never in the mood for signing autographs and almost always declined, mainly because he could never be sure what it was he was actually signing. Thankfully the waitress didn't say anything, apart from commenting on the beautiful weather outside. She left him with his coffee and his thoughts.

He didn't know where to begin. There was so much to take in. He remembered how angry he'd felt at the park when he confronted Lin about going to Australia. And she had a perfectly logical explanation for all of that. Perhaps she'd be able to explain this, too. Although explaining away a marriage, a suicide and a miscarriage was going to be a little more challenging. It all left him feeling rather numb.

He'd felt anything but numb when Fraser had spoken about Lin consummating her marriage. He'd felt rage. He'd wanted to protect her. Was that what love did to you? Had it rendered him even more blind than he'd already been? Had it blinded his ability to make good decisions?

He groaned, as the pressure of making the right choice weighed on him. He should give her the chance to explain.

"Is the coffee all right?" the waitress asked, taking his groan as a complaint.

"The coffee's great, thanks," he lied.

He'd drunk half of it and not tasted a single drop. It reminded him of how his life had been before he met Lin. Like he'd been cloaked in anesthetic. She'd awoken him from his deep sleep, and he'd felt alive for the first time since that day in the forest. He had to talk to her. He was in way too deep to walk away now, without at least hearing her out.

He took another sip of his coffee, and this time he noticed the sharp bite of the caffeine as it slipped down his throat. Life was happening all around him. It was time he started to take more notice. Lin had had a life before she found him. He couldn't hold that against her.

The time had come for a very honest conversation.

CHAPTER TWELVE

*M*atthew didn't return to his apartment until nightfall. Once he'd unscrambled his thoughts, he needed to sit with them. He was certain of two things. Lin wasn't a reporter and she believed her story to be true. But did he? Did he really believe she was Hannah in a past life? Was it really possible they were destined to give birth to the chosen one? He could handle the Hannah part. The baby part was proving to be a lot more difficult.

There were so many things she'd hidden from him. Her marriage to Reinier, his death and her miscarriage. She had to have known Reinier had died. That was why she sounded so sad every time she said his name. Why hadn't she told him? If he was completely honest with himself, in some ways, it was a relief. At least he didn't have to worry about him turning up on their doorstep and whisking Lin away.

She'd also spent a lot more time in Australia than she'd led him to believe. Fraser had said she was there for two months. That seemed an extraordinarily long time to find out he was in London. Even with all the reminiscing about her past that she claimed to have done. He suspected it had something to do with the miscarriage. She must have taken it very badly. Either that or she'd been very ill. Again, he wondered why she couldn't have been honest with him about this. Plenty of women have been married, widowed or lost babies. He hadn't been searching for the Virgin Mary. It wouldn't have changed the way he felt about her. Hiding it from him was what had upset him.

His conclusions left him confused about how he should feel toward her. It appeared she'd been honest with him. She'd just omitted an awful lot of vital information. Was that the same as lying? If so, maybe she could accuse him of the same thing. He hadn't told her about hiring Fraser. Although, somehow, this lie didn't seem quite as significant as what she'd hidden from him.

He needed to come clean with her. He'd give her the report Fraser had provided him with and gauge her reaction.

As he opened his front door, the first thing he noticed was the delicious aroma that hung in the air. Maria had been cooking his meals since she'd arrived and although they were wonderful, this smelled different. The combination of spices made his stomach groan. Lin must have been cooking. He felt selfish for his late return.

No, he reminded himself. What he'd been doing that day was important. It needed to be done. Lin had appeared in his life like a leaf on an autumn breeze. He'd had to find out if she was genuine.

"You're home." Lin found him in the entryway and gave him a light peck on the cheek. "I was starting to worry about you."

"Sorry. I got held up. Something smells great." He smiled. Would this be what it'd be like if he made a life with her? It was most definitely not unpleasant. Maybe he could put off showing her the report until after they'd eaten. One last meal together before the roof blew off.

"I hope you don't mind," she said. "Maria's cooking has been terrific this week, but I've been missing my food from home. I went to the market and couldn't help myself."

"How did Maria take that?"

"I don't think she was too impressed. I hope I didn't offend her."

"She'll cope. You didn't wait for me to eat, did you?"

"Well, actually I did. It's okay. I've set us up at your dining table. I know you don't normally eat there, but it's such a beautiful room. I thought we could enjoy it."

"That's fine," he said, changing direction and heading for the dining room. He didn't like the acoustics in that room, which was why he rarely used it. There weren't many soft surfaces to absorb the sound and he found voices bounced off the walls. He didn't want to upset Lin, though. It was likely he'd be doing enough of that later.

They took their seats at one end of the enormous table.

"What are we eating?" he asked, not liking to stick his fork into anything until he knew exactly what it was.

"It's a vegetarian curry. Fingers crossed you like it."

"It smells great." He scooped some into his mouth, which tingled in response. "It's got a kick to it."

"Oh, sorry. Don't you like spicy food?"

"No, it's great. I love it. Are we drinking anything with it?" He felt in front of him for a glass, wanting to cleanse his palate of the spice. The meal was delicious, but definitely hotter than what he was accustomed to.

"Of course. Let me pour the wine."

"You're not vegetarian, though," he said, while she poured.

"Actually, I am."

"But Maria's been cooking meat for you all week." He took a sip of the wine and relaxed for a moment before continuing with his meal.

"No, she hasn't. We talked about it when I arrived here.

She looked at me like I had two heads, but she's been coming up with great variations to the meals all week."

He frowned. It was times like this that he wished for his sight. What other things did he miss that were right in front of his face? He knew it wasn't right to think like that. There were plenty of other things he noticed purely because he was reliant on his other senses.

"Are you sure it's not too spicy?" she asked, noticing his expression.

"No, it's wonderful. Delicious. I'm just a little tired, I suppose. Tell me, how long have you been a vegetarian? You know Hannah never ate meat, don't you?"

"I thought as much. Meat has never tasted right to me, even as a little girl. I kept seeing the animal's big, brown eyes staring at me from my plate."

"Do you look down on me for eating meat, then?" The thought of her looking at him in any way other than with the adoration she'd been expressing since he'd met her, disturbed him.

"Of course not. It's just not for me."

"Do animals have souls? Is that the reason?"

"I believe they do."

"So, we might all come back as chickens in our next life?" He laughed nervously, wondering how much longer he could put off the conversation they needed to have. It didn't seem fair, after all the trouble she'd gone to with dinner.

"I don't have all the answers, you know. But I don't think it's like that. I believe life is a lot simpler for animals."

"How so?" He was genuinely interested. She had some very definite ideas on topics he'd never given a moment's thought.

"I've always thought animals are reborn quite quickly, and always as the same species. They kind of bypass the Loom, or heaven, or whatever you want to call it."

"You mean the poor dung beetle never gets a shot at being a lion or a tiger? Now, that's sad."

"It's not sad. It is what it is. I'm sure a dung beetle is perfectly happy being a dung beetle."

"Where are all these new souls coming from, then? I mean, look at the population of the world and how it's grown over the years. Who are all these people?" He was rambling now, and he knew it. It was something he did when he was avoiding talking about something. Either that or he retreated into silence. He didn't think silence would get him very far tonight.

"There are old souls and new souls. I'm not sure where the new souls come from. Maybe one day we'll all find out."

"What about me? Am I an old soul? Have I been here before?" He took another mouthful of his curry and waited for her to reply. The idea of having lived before was fascinating. He hoped he'd been someone interesting.

"I think you've been here a few times before, yes."

"But not as many times as you."

"No."

"How do you know I'm not a brand new soul? Maybe I've come from Mars or Jupiter."

"It's in your eyes," she said, ignoring his last comment. "I can see other lives still sparkling behind the surface."

"Who was I? King of England... Jack the Ripper... an exotic dancer maybe?"

She laughed. "Gosh, I hope not. I don't know who you were. I don't think we've met before, though."

"How do you know that?"

"When I died as Hannah, I saw my past lives flash past. I never saw you."

"How would you recognize me? I wouldn't look like me, would I?" He was trying to convince her. To put the possibility in her mind. She'd already told him Reinier was her soulmate who'd been by her side throughout her lives. He wished it were him.

"I'd have recognized your soul," she said.

They lapsed into silence. As he finished the last few mouthfuls of his meal, he thought about the answers she'd just given him. She'd come out with them far too quickly to have invented them on the spot.

"Lin," he said reaching for the leather satchel he'd walked in with. "I have a confession to make."

"Confessions aren't normally good." He heard her place her cutlery down, giving him her full attention.

"I hired a private investigator to tell me more about you."

She gasped. "I suppose he told you I'm telling you the truth about myself. Or did he tell you I'm a reporter? Or a prostitute?"

"Lin, stop it. Please. I just had to be sure. He did find out you've been truthful with me, although he did tell me about some things you left out of your story. Do you have any confessions of your own to make?"

"You're talking about Reinier, aren't you?" Her voice was cold. He'd hit a nerve.

"Yes. I'm talking about your husband, Reinier."

"So what? It's not like we ever had time for him to be a real husband."

"Was it an immaculate conception?" he asked, failing to keep the bitterness from his voice. Was she really trying to deny it?

"What are you talking about?"

"The baby you miscarried in Australia."

She gasped. "You must've paid that investigator a fortune. How on earth did he find out about that? My family doesn't even know about it. Nobody knows."

"Why didn't you tell me, Lin?" His voice was soft now. He

didn't want the screaming match this was setting itself up to be. He wanted her to open up to him. To trust him.

"I wanted to tell you, but... it was just too painful." He didn't need to see her to know there'd be tears rolling down her soft cheeks. "We were only married for one day before he..."

Matthew waited. Would she tell him? There was no point in her keeping it secret now.

"Here," he said, placing Fraser's report on the table in front of her. "Read it for yourself. I'll be in the living room when you're ready to be honest with me."

He heard her pick it up.

"Thank you for dinner," he said and left the room.

He'd only just taken a seat in the lounge when he heard her scream. The sound of it echoed across the dining room and raced around the house like a tornado, turning his blood to ice. It was the sound of grief. It was the sound of a woman in pain.

"Reinier," she sobbed. "No, Reinier, no."

He found her balled up on the floor. Her sobs frightened him. He sat beside her and reached out, wanting to soothe her pain.

"Don't touch me," she spat at him. "Leave me alone."

He retracted his hand but found himself unable to leave her side. So instead, he drew up his knees and rested his back against the wall. He'd wait until she calmed down, or until she killed him, whichever came first. She hadn't known about Reinier's death after all. What did she think had happened to the man, when he'd disappeared the day after their wedding?

He felt terrible about having handed her the report before they had a chance to talk it through. What an awful way for him to have broken the news to her. It was no wonder she was upset with him.

"I'm sorry, Lin. I thought you knew."

She ignored his apology and continued to sob.

After several minutes, he shuffled over and tried reaching for her again. She flinched at his touch, but this time she didn't tell him to stop. Very slowly, very carefully he placed the palm of his hand on her back. He could feel her agony. It poured into him, blackening his soul.

She shifted, unfurling slightly, and rested her head on his knee. He stroked her hair, combing it with his fingers.

"My mother used to comb my hair when I was upset," she said. Her voice croaked as she spoke, but the sound of it flooded relief through his core.

"I'm really sorry, Lin."

"Why would he do it? Why?"

"Who knows why anyone takes their life. He must've been in more pain than you realized."

She sat up. "He had a lot to deal with, but he was stronger than that. And besides, he knows the consequences of taking a human life, even if it was his own."

"Consequences?"

"It's an unforgiveable sin. Reinier has taken a life. His soul will be extinguished. He'll never be reborn." Huge sobs wracked her body and Matthew pulled her to him, wrapping his arms around her.

"He must've had his reasons, Lin."

She didn't reply, disappearing once more under her blanket of grief.

He stayed with her as the night slipped away, eventually carrying her to her room and tucking her into bed. She was awake yet lost in a world of silence. He took a pillow and blanket from his room and curled up on the chaise longue beside her bed, hoping his presence would comfort her.

He didn't sleep. He lay there, listening to her fight her emotions as her brain struggled to accept Reinier's death.

She'd loved him deeply, that much was clear. He wondered exactly what her relationship with him had been like. The baby was evidence that their marriage had been more than one of convenience. He thought of Reinier's hands upon her and felt ill. He knew he had no right to be jealous, but the feeling was getting harder to fight. The more he found out about her relationship with Reinier, the more inferior he felt. He'd been with his fair share of women since Hannah's death, but none of them had come close to what she'd had with Reinier.

How could she say she loved him, when her heart belonged to another man? He doubted she'd react like this if he died.

Just why did Reinier choose to die? Lin had said the consequences would be dire, so from what Matthew knew of him, he wouldn't have done this without a good reason. Was it too much for him to have to witness his wife having another man's child? Why would Reinier impregnate Lin with his own child, if what he was supposed to want more than anything was for her to have a child with Matthew?

There were no simple answers to any of these questions. The more he tried to solve them, the more questions he added to his list. By morning he was sure if he wrote them down, the list would be a mile long.

"It's morning," Lin whispered.

"I know." Matthew sat up and yawned.

"How do you know if you can't see the sun?"

"The same way you know you're hungry, even though you can't see your stomach."

"That's a stupid analogy, you know." There was a hint of a smile in her voice, although he could tell she was still gripped by grief. She may not have slept, but the night's rest had served her well.

"Welcome back."

"I'm not back yet, but thank you. Thank you for staying with me."

"I wasn't sure you wanted me to."

"I did."

"I'm glad. Are you okay?"

"Of course not. Although I'm still breathing, so that's a good sign."

"You're very confusing, you know."

"I don't mean to be." He heard her moving in the bed and guessed she'd sat up.

"Maybe it's me who's confused." He rubbed his temples, trying to find the right words. "Lin, I realized last night that I'm in love with you. Seeing you fall apart like that broke my heart. Your grief reminded me of how I felt when Hannah died. The pain of that loss never left me. Until you arrived. You pulled away from me last night and I thought I was going to lose you all over again. I'm not sure I could cope with that."

"You haven't lost me." She moved from her bed and sat next to him on the chaise longue. "I wasn't in control of my emotions last night. Perhaps I'm still not. I'm sorry if I hurt you. I'm just so shocked and angry, and so desperately heart-broken. Reinier was such a pure soul. So good, so strong. He saved me from a life of confusion. Without him, I'd still be running around in circles trying to figure out why nothing in life made any sense. I loved him."

"Hopefully, one day, you'll feel the same about me."

She took his hand in hers. "But I do, Matthew. I do. This is what I was trying to explain to you in the park that day. I know we're not meant to love two people at once, but that's how I feel. You and Reinier are both so important to me in such different ways. It's impossible for me to choose between you. Don't think because you witnessed my tears for Reinier last night that I love you any less."

He felt relief at hearing this. She had such a way of allaying his fears. "Why do you think he did it? What happened the last time you saw him?"

"It was the day after our wedding, as you know. I woke up to a note on his pillow. He'd gone."

"Would you read me the note?" He didn't ask if she still had it. He knew she would, despite the few possessions she'd arrived with in London. A girl like Lin wouldn't throw out such a note.

He heard her open the drawer beside her bed and unfold a piece of paper. She began to read. She kept her voice level, although her breathing gave away her pain. She was struggling to keep herself together. Matthew listened to Reinier's last words to her. It was difficult to hear him tell her he loved her. This time he pushed down his jealousy. It wasn't fair to be jealous of a dead man.

How strange it was to hear Reinier speak of Matthew himself, and the baby he was supposed to have with Lin. Reinier had not only accepted that his wife needed to have another man's baby, but he was actively encouraging her to. He must truly have believed in this baby and the path it was destined to take.

He flinched when Lin read the words about her not being able to fall in love with him while Reinier was in her life. These words were true. Reinier had known her well. Lin was certainly capable of loving them both, but even he doubted she could find the room in her heart if they were standing before her at the same time. If Lin's soul could somehow clone itself and he had both Hannah and Lin standing before him, he'd be a mess. Hearts were easier to divide when they were only required to offer themselves to one person at a time.

Reinier had exited Lin's life so she could fall in love with him and have a child. No wonder he'd said not to try to find him. He wanted her to be strong and not spend her life grieving over him.

Then Lin read the words, "Mother *won't stop you this time. I'll make sure of that,*" and Reinier's decision became clear. He was concerned Mother would take Lin's life, just as she'd taken Hannah's. His fear made a lot of sense. He was determined to stop Mother this time. He'd failed Hannah when he'd tried to protect her on planet Earth. It seemed now he was going to try to stop her from the sky above.

Had this also become clear to Lin? All night she'd been asking why. And the answer had been with her the whole time.

Lin let out a wail. "He went to fight Mother."

She knew.

CHAPTER THIRTEEN

*M*atthew had figured out early in his life there was one lesson he'd need to learn in order to survive. That lesson was patience. He'd needed patience to carry on after Hannah's death. He'd needed patience to learn to live without sight. And now, more than ever, he needed patience to watch the woman he loved grieve for another man.

She'd loved Reinier, but she also loved him. It was in the way she gently touched his cheek as she said goodnight. It was in the way she stumbled to find the simplest words whenever he came near. Most of all, it was in the way she tried her best to put his needs before her own. He noticed the effort she put in her voice to sound cheery, even when clouds of doom hung from her shoulders. She might have gotten away with this with a sighted person, but not with him. He could pick out the truth in her words and mood with ease. Not that he let her know.

He also noticed the way she molded her daily activities around him. She gave him time alone with his music, just as she was there waiting for him at the dinner table. She never complained when he went to a meeting or a performance yet was pleased when he asked her to accompany him.

The only thing he wished he didn't notice was the way she cried when she was alone in bed at night. He'd stand on the other side of her closed door with his hands pressed to the timber and cry with her. Great silent tears would roll down his cheeks, as he resisted the urge to race to her side and hold her to his chest. She needed space and she needed time. He mustn't rush her.

He knew only too well what it felt like when someone tried to rush you through your grief. His parents had been so understanding at first when Hannah died, yet after several years their patience grew thin. Surely, he was over her by now, they'd ask. They hadn't seemed to understand that he'd *never* be over her. You don't get over losing someone you love with all your heart.

Now the girl he'd spent so many years grieving for had reappeared in his life. How ironic that just as she'd healed his wounds, her own wounds had opened.

Several times he heard her talking on the phone to her parents in Hong Kong. He didn't need to speak Cantonese to know they were angry with her and that their harsh words cut her deeply. He longed to know what the argument was about, but never asked. He guessed it had something to do with him. And Reinier. It was always about Reinier. Their three souls seemed to be linked in a way that was impossible to separate.

"Have you told them he died?" he eventually asked, as she ended a long phone call and sighed in frustration. He'd waited long enough for her to raise the subject. It didn't look like that would ever happen and he was tired of staying silent.

"How did you know we were talking about him?" she

asked, sounding more curious than annoyed. "Don't tell me you speak Cantonese."

"Of course not."

"Reinier did. I couldn't believe how quickly he learned it."

He tried to hide his frustration. There was Reinier again. All roads led back to him.

"Well, I'm sorry I'm not as clever as Reinier," he said, failing to keep the jealousy from his voice.

"Don't be like that. I've just had my father giving me a hard time, and now you." She sounded disappointed. He should've tried harder to keep his emotions to himself. "So how did you know we were talking about him? I don't remember using his name just then."

"What else would you be talking about? The last time they saw you, they were sending you off on your honeymoon."

"I never told you that. Did your investigator find that out for you? What else did he tell you?" Now it was her turn to feel annoyed.

"I've already apologized for that. If you'd like me to do it again, I will. Sorry. Are you happy now?" He hated going over old ground. He thought they'd cleared that up.

"You're asking me if I'm happy? I think you know the answer to that."

Her words punched him in the gut. There was nothing he wanted more in the world than to make her happy.

"I'm sorry, Lin. Let's not argue." He reached for her, finding her hands tightly clasped in her lap. "I just figured it out, that's all. You've said before that your parents have never left Hong Kong and you left the day after your wedding."

"Oh, of course." She squeezed his hand briefly and let it go.

"Have you told them he died?" She hadn't answered his question, so he decided to push a little harder. Now that he'd let the words out, he wanted an answer.

"I've told them, but they don't believe me."

"What do you mean, they don't believe you?" That seemed impossible. What parent wouldn't believe their daughter when she told them her husband had died?

"Exactly that. They don't believe me."

"Then what do you believe?"

"They think he ran out on me and I'm too embarrassed to admit it."

"That's not embarrassing." There was something he wasn't getting. This didn't make sense.

"Things are different in my culture. You don't just get married one minute and divorced the next."

"That's my point. You didn't get divorced. He died. Why wouldn't they believe that?" His parents had believed his innocence when Hannah had died in the forest. They'd never questioned him. It seemed strange to think a parent could be so suspicious of their child when it came to such a serious matter.

"I told you, it's different. If Reinier *had* left me, I probably would've made up some kind of story. I'm not sure I could've told them the truth. That's why they don't believe me now. People make up all kinds of stories to hide their shame."

"Couldn't they check the death records or something?"

"I suppose so. If they were really that motivated, which they aren't. They already think they're right."

"Do they know about me?" He knew they did. He'd heard her say his name once, but he wanted to hear it from her.

She hesitated. "Yes and no."

"What does that mean?"

"They know I'm staying with you."

"Who do they think I am?"

"I told them I work as your secretary and I'm given my room as part of my salary."

"Oh." He wasn't sure what to say about that. He was a

little offended. If he meant as much to her as she did to him, she wouldn't lie about it. He'd told his parents he'd met someone special, resulting in his mother asking him a thousand questions. A thousand questions he wasn't sure how to answer. Maybe Lin was the clever one, to avoid the topic and therefore the inquisition.

"As far as my parents are concerned, Reinier left me some time during our honeymoon and I ran off to London to hide my face."

"Will you ever tell them the truth about me?"

"What? That I met you in a past life? Definitely not."

"Not that. I meant will you ever tell them that I'm more than just a boss to you?" He wanted to ask if she'd ever tell them that she loved him, but that sounded a bit presumptuous. She hadn't talked of love lately. It felt like their relationship had taken a step backward since she'd learned of Reinier's death. He longed for her to kiss him like she had the day she'd first appeared in his music room, wearing Hannah's perfume as well as her soul. He'd begun to live for the small signs of affection she offered him as he waited for her to be ready to offer more.

"In time I'll tell my parents about you. Not that I expect they'll ever understand," she said.

"Do you miss them?"

"Of course, I do. My father mostly. He was the one I was close to."

"The opposite to Hannah."

"Yes, it seems Mother went to great lengths to ensure everything about my life was the opposite of Hannah's. Maximum confusion."

"Hopefully not everything's the opposite to Hannah." He ground his teeth. Hannah had loved him. Was she saying the same wasn't true for her?

"No, Matthew. I didn't mean *everything*. I love you. I do.

I've just had so much going on in my life and my mind that I need to slow everything else down. My feelings for you haven't changed. They never will."

He drew in a deep breath. "I'm glad to hear that."

"Although, I must tell you that you're a very different person to the Matthew I knew as Hannah."

"Of course I'm different," he said. "When you were Hannah, I was sixteen and had never had a trouble or a worry in my life. A lot's happened since then. Besides, you're not exactly the same as you were back then, either."

"Good point. You still love me though, don't you?"

He realized he wasn't the only one who needed reassurance. "I'll always love you. Never doubt that."

"It's just that you've been so distant lately, I thought maybe you'd changed your mind about me."

"What do you mean?" He couldn't believe what he was hearing. "I've been trying to give you space. Slow things down, as you said."

"I've heard you outside my bedroom door at night. Why haven't you come to me to comfort me like you did the night I found out Reinier died?"

He could hear her fighting tears. She was doing her best to remain strong, but clearly the well-meaning distance he'd put between them had hurt her.

"I knew you needed time to grieve," he said. "Trust me, if I'd gone into your room at night, I'm not sure I'd have been able to give you the space you need. You're forgetting that I'm a man. A man who's head over heels in love with you. You know I'm not great at these conversations, Lin."

"You're actually quite good at these conversations, when you try." She stood up indicating she was finished talking. He'd pushed her far enough. "I'm going to make some tea. Would you like some?"

"Sure. That'd be lovely." The truth was he hated her tea.

He just liked the idea of her making it for him. It made him feel loved, reminding him of how his mother had fussed over him when he'd lived at home. He was getting better at masking his grimace as he swallowed it down.

He went to his piano and sat down to tinker with a new piece he'd been working on. He didn't want to get too involved, knowing Lin would be interrupting shortly. It felt good to keep his hands busy. It slowed down his mind from processing his conversation with her. He didn't want his thoughts to wander down the path of thinking about her parents giving their blessing to her marriage to Reinier yet believing he himself was just her boss and landlord.

His hands fell from the piano keys and into his lap. Would he ever feel worthy when being compared to Reinier – a man who'd taken his life to protect her from the heavens? What had *he* done for her? He had her investigated and crushed her with devastating news in the most heartless fashion. He knew he needed to stop comparing himself to Reinier. This wasn't a competition he'd ever win.

It was far preferable to think about when she told him she loved him. He couldn't believe she'd been upset he hadn't come to her at night. He wished she hadn't ended the conversation right when they were starting to get somewhere. He didn't even want the cup of tea, although he couldn't hear any sound of her in the kitchen. Perhaps she'd changed her mind and gone upstairs, expecting him to follow her. Had their conversation rattled her, and was now one of those times she needed him to comfort her? He had no idea how he was supposed to know when to go to her and when to leave her alone. Women were such complicated creatures.

Perhaps he should've left things alone. This was exactly why he hadn't pressed her earlier. But how would their relationship ever move beyond what it was now, if he didn't push a little? It was torture having her living here in his home, without being able to take her in his arms, or to his bed. No, he was glad they'd talked. At least now he felt reassured of her feelings.

He got up and headed for the kitchen, only to find she wasn't there.

"Lin," he called, finding only silence in return.

He wandered through the house, moving slowly, as was his habit since losing his sight. He went upstairs to check for her, anxiety rising within him. He'd have heard her if she'd gone out. She must be in the house somewhere.

"Lin, are you okay?" he called.

He stopped for a moment and listened to the sounds of the house and heard the faint noise of water running in the guest bathroom. Lin's bathroom. He headed in that direction, only to pause at the bathroom door, torn between wanting to make sure she was all right and wanting to give her privacy.

He knocked quietly.

"Lin?"

The shower turned off and a few moments later the door opened. They stood in silence. She was obviously studying his face and he longed to be able to study hers. What did she look like? He was sure she was beautiful.

"Hold me," she said.

He stepped forward and reached for her, his hands landing with precision on her bare shoulders, still wet from the shower. His hands jolted away in surprise. Was she naked?

"Hold me," she said again.

He returned his hands to her shoulders and slid them down the curve of her back as he pulled her close. She was most definitely naked.

"What are you doing?" he asked, as she wrapped her arms around his neck and drew his face down to hers.

"I'm kissing you."

Her lips found his and he felt his body light with desire. For one moment, he wondered if he should stop. Was she in the right frame of mind to make a decision like this? It only took until the next moment for him to lose his train of thought. All he could think of was Lin. Her smooth skin under the roughness of his hands. Her moist lips pressed to his own.

She had him. He was hers.

———

Matthew decided patience was most definitely a virtue. He thought of all the years he'd waited for Lin to appear in his life, and all the time after that he'd waited to join as one with her. Being so close to her had fueled his love even further, to such an extent he wondered if it was possible to die from love. He loved her so much he thought at times his heart might explode.

After taking so long to get going, their relationship quickly grew into one of complete adoration. He could no longer imagine his life without her. All the sadness of his life had now been replaced with joy. She filled the dark holes in his soul with light.

He even wondered if perhaps his sight would be returned to him. If this much happiness had healed his soul, then perhaps it could heal his body too.

Although, he had to admit that, apart from the odd moment when he was overwhelmed with the desire to look into Lin's eyes and hold her face in his hands, he was grateful for all that his blindness had given him. It was his blindness that had opened his eyes and enabled him to recognize Hannah within Lin. If he'd had his sight, it was more than likely he'd have dismissed Lin as a lunatic and not given her a second thought.

His blindness had also given him the gift of music. He'd never be able to see the notes so clearly in his mind if he had other objects in his field of vision to distract him. For that he was grateful. It was almost as if his blindness was meant to be.

Lin seemed to share his newfound joy. He no longer heard her crying at night, for now that she slept in his bed he could wake her from her nightmares and hold her tight, soothing her fears and restoring her calm. He noticed a new tinkle to her voice, which he was sure was mirrored within her eyes.

There were many times he felt as if he were sixteen years old again, roaming through the forest with Hannah. Young. Innocent. In love.

As the days slipped by, he realized he needed to do more for Lin to keep her happy than simply to provide a roof over her head and arms to hold her close. She needed some independence, and a chance to explore some of her own areas of interest. It wasn't fair of him to expect her to wait around while he played his music. She needed a passion of her own.

She'd told him she loved to sketch, so he bought her tickets to the opening of a new exhibition at the National Gallery, and insisted she attend. While she was gone he called an art supply store and offered the manager an obscene amount of money to fill a van with easels, blank canvasses, paints, brushes and any other supplies she thought an artist might need.

He then organized for his dining room to be cleared. He'd never liked this room and, after the awful scene that occurred in there the night Lin had learned of Reinier's death, it had become a place he despised. It was time to put some new energy into this room that Lin had once said she thought was beautiful. It would make the perfect studio for her.

There was another table in the family room that adjoined the kitchen, where he preferred to eat. So what if he was no longer able to offer his guests a fancy room to eat their meals in? It was rare he had guests over anyway. If anyone was unhappy with where he seated them, then as far as he was concerned they could find someone else to visit.

He heard Lin's key in the door. The workmen he'd hired to help transform the dining room had left only half an hour before. He'd cut it fine.

Lin's keys clattered in the porcelain tray on the hallstand. He smiled, wondering if this would be the time she broke it. It had to happen one day. He'd never had the heart to tell her the exorbitant price tag that tray had come with. His interior designer had assured him it was worth it, of course. It was most certainly not a tray designed to have metal objects thrown into it. Not that he cared in the slightest.

She found him in the hallway and kissed him tenderly on the lips.

"Thank you," she said. "It was a great exhibition. I wish you could've seen it."

He laughed and she realized what she'd said.

"Oh, I'm so sorry. You know what I mean. I just wanted to share it with you. I know you going to an art exhibition is a fairly pointless exercise."

"Not really. Let's try it next time. You can describe all the paintings to me. It might be fun."

"That'd be great." She wrapped her arms around his waist. "You make me so happy."

"Do I?"

"Of course."

"Well, hopefully I'm about to make you even happier." He took her hand and led her toward the studio. One of the workmen had described it as an artist's dream. He just hoped he was right.

"Open the door," he said.

"But Matthew, you hate this room. You don't want to eat in here, do you?"

"Just open the door," he said, smiling.

He heard her turn the handle and then gasp in surprise.

"Matthew," she squealed. "Is this for me?"

"Well, it's not for me."

"I love it." She threw her arms around his neck and jumped up on him, straddling his waist with her legs and covering his face with kisses.

He walked into the studio, still carrying her, feeling as reluctant as always to break contact with her.

"Careful," she said, as he walked her into an easel, knocking the canvas to the floor.

"Oops. I guess it's going to take a while for me to get used to this room. Did I damage anything?" He set her down.

"No," she said. "No damage."

"Good."

"Where did all this stuff come from? It wasn't here this morning."

"Let's just say I had a little bit of help."

"But it's not my birthday." He could hear her opening drawers and rifling through them.

"Every day should be your birthday."

She came back to him and rested her head on his chest. He ran his fingers through her silky hair and breathed in her scent.

"Lin," he said. "I really do want to take good care of you. I can't give you some of the things Reinier gave you, but I can give you this."

"Shhh. Don't say that. In many ways you've given me so much more than he ever did. You mean different things to me. Don't you know that by now?"

"I know." And he did. The last few blissful months had reassured him of that. He and Lin were meant to be together.

"You do realize I'm going to have to learn how to paint now," she said.

"I thought you said you love to paint?"

"I love to draw. That's not the same as painting. It's like asking you to play the trumpet when you've spent your life on the piano."

"Oh, I'm sorry." His heart dropped.

"No, it's great. I love it. I've always wanted to learn. I just never had the chance. We could never afford the equipment. I can't wait to give it a try."

"Thank goodness for that," he sighed. "I thought I'd made a terrible mistake."

"You couldn't make a terrible mistake if you tried." She stood on her tiptoes and kissed his cheek.

"Do you see that canvas in the back corner of the room with the black cloth draped over it?" he asked. He'd already checked it had been placed it exactly where he'd asked.

"Yes," she said. "Did you paint me a picture?"

"I did, actually. Why don't you go and take a look?"

"Careful now," she said. "You're already a musical genius. You need to leave me something to be better at than you."

He heard her cross the room and then the flutter of the cloth as she pulled it to the ground. Then he heard nothing as she stood reading the message he'd painted onto the canvas. One of the workers had stood by his side and pointed out where the paint had failed to leave its mark. He rarely attempted to write and hadn't used paint since he was at school and still had his sight. But he'd been adamant that this message to Lin needed to be painted with his own hand. A marriage proposal just wouldn't be right if painted by anyone else.

Lin's silence continued beyond the point of comfort. He

walked over to join her at the canvas and knelt down on one knee.

"Will you marry me?" he asked.

She remained silent. This was one of the moments he wished for his sight. What was she thinking? Was she happy? Shocked? Frightened? Horrified?

"Lin?"

"Yes," she whispered, bending to kiss him on his lips. "Yes, Matthew. I'd love to marry you."

Her words were choked with emotion. She hadn't answered him immediately because she hadn't been able to.

His heart soared.

PART IV

REINIER

CHAPTER FOURTEEN

*R*einier had been in the dark for so long he'd forgotten what it felt like to bask in the glory of the light. How long would he spend in the darkness?

He never imagined having his soul extinguished would feel like this. He expected to be returned to Mother first, where he'd have the chance to change her mind. Then if he failed, he'd feel nothing. Not this. This was agony. Locked in a black and silent world with only his thoughts for company. Where was Lin? Had she found Matthew? Had the child been born?

He wished he could sleep. Turn his brain off for a few precious moments and stop the thoughts that swirled through his mind creating currents of regret and misery. How long had it been? It was impossible to tell if it had been weeks, months or even years.

He remembered all the moments of all his lifetimes that'd led to this point. He relived every memory of Lin. He saw her beautiful face cradled in his hands, looked deep into her eyes and felt her hair slipping through his fingers. Their wedding night had been his undoing. If he'd gone with her to Australia, things would surely be different now.

No, they wouldn't. He'd still have taken his life. That'd always been the plan. To fight Mother face to face, light to light. He'd expected good to triumph over evil, only this time it seemed evil had won.

Maybe it hadn't. Maybe Lin had found Matthew and the baby had been born. Maybe he wasn't meant to be part of the plan, beyond tracking her down and convincing her to seek out Matthew. Except that didn't feel right. He was sure there was more he was supposed to do. When he'd had visions of Lin's son saving the world, he'd seen victory through his own eyes. He was meant to be there. What had gone so terribly wrong?

He tried to reach out, but the darkness held him still. It was both his prison and his warden. It bound him in place. Left him helpless.

He thought of all the souls who'd taken their own lives before him. In their attempts to ease their pain, they were sending themselves to a world filled with pain of a different kind – the kind that came from endless contemplation and regret. Suicide didn't stop life from getting worse. All it did was make sure life never had the chance to get better.

He'd been so confident that day on the bridge. So sure he was making the right decision. In the split second it had taken for his feet to leave the security of the steel beam, his life had changed forever. He should've taken the time to think things through. *Really* think things through. He'd never even considered what would happen if his plan failed. He'd been cocky. No, that was too kind. He'd been incredibly stupid.

"I'm sorry!" His silent voice screamed to no-one. "I'm sorry!" And he was sorry. He was sorry he'd failed Lin. He was sorry he'd failed himself. He was sorry he'd failed the human race. He'd been wrong to take his life. Lin had been right. There must have been a different way. A better way. They could've done it together. He should've listened to her.

A small light flickered in the distance. He'd imagined lights before. This wasn't real.

This time the flickering came closer, growing larger, convincing him it might be real. He strained his eyes. Was this the end?

The light was blue. It wasn't Mother's golden light. Disappointment seeped through his soul.

The light continued to drift closer. He wondered if he should be afraid. He wasn't. Uneasy and curious, but definitely not afraid. At least something was happening at last. Maybe this wasn't the end. Maybe it was the beginning, and this light was his chance to make his way back to Mother.

He waited.

"Reinier." His name floated from the waves of bright blue light that circled before him. Slowly, the shape of a man emerged. His skin was as dark as night. His eyes the color of ash. Cropped, black hair lined his scalp, and his body was sculptured and strong. His every feature contradicted that of Mother, apart from his beauty. It radiated from his core. There was no doubt in Reinier's mind this man was good.

"Please, take me to Mother," Reinier said, stretching out his hand. "Please. Before it's too late."

"You don't need Mother." The man smiled at him yet didn't take his hand.

"Who are you?"

"I'm the Author. You're safe with me. I won't let harm come to you."

Reinier knew of the Author, of course. Most souls on Earth thought of him as the Creator. The Author was the one who brought life to Earth. His powers stretched across the skies. Why had he come to see him?

"You're the Author?" He could hardly believe it. This wasn't how he'd pictured him.

"Reinier, you know I'm not made from flesh and blood. You see what I want you to see," said the Author, breaking into his thoughts. "If it's helpful, I could look like this."

The Author faded. As his image disappeared, a new one formed. He was now an old man, his skin as white as a cloud on a summer's day, his long, gray beard stretching down to his waist. It was the exact image Reinier had always imagined.

"Or I could look like this." He faded once more, this time reappearing as a woman with long dark hair and green eyes that glistened in the blue light that cloaked her. She smiled at Reinier and transformed herself into the man who'd greeted him only moments before.

Fear seeped its way into the corners of Reinier's soul. This man was the Author – the supreme being who'd created the universe. He owed him not only every moment of his past, but his future lay in his hands. A future that was anything but promising. Please let him be merciful.

"I'm sorry to have questioned you, Author."

"Do not fear me." His eyes radiated kindness and love. They were eyes that put Reinier at ease.

"Where am I?"

"You're with me. We're in the Loom."

"This doesn't look like the Loom. How long have I been here?"

"You've been here as long as you needed to be. You took a human life. Your life. That was a life I created. Until you were truly sorry for that, you needed to stay with me."

Reinier wished he'd repented for his sin long ago. Perhaps then, he needn't have spent what had felt like eternity, floating in agony. Except he knew that would've been useless. Saying sorry is easy. Meaning it is a whole lot harder.

"What would've happened if I were never sorry?" he asked. "Would I have floated here for eternity?"

The Author smiled at him. "Every soul is sorry eventually. Some just take longer than others to figure it out. Your case is a complicated one."

This made him feel like a child. He'd thought he understood all the secrets of the universe. It seemed he was far from it.

"Please. I need to see Mother. You don't understand."

"I do understand. You don't need to see Mother, Reinier. While you've been with me, I've been studying your thoughts. I was unaware of what's been going on with Mother. She's on the wrong path. She won't help you."

"You were unaware? How's that possible? You're the Author. Surely you must know what's going on?" He knew he shouldn't speak in such a way to the man who held his life in his hands, but the endless torture he'd just experienced put his words beyond his control.

"Reinier, take my hand. I want to show you something."

He hesitated before reaching out his hand. The Author took it gently and wrapped it in his firm grasp. The darkness around them shimmered. Lights switched on like an impossibly large city coming to life at dusk. He saw stars, suns, planets and moons moving in circles around him.

He recognized planet Earth and, as it came closer, he saw movement and light. It was alive with souls. They lit the planet with an energy so powerful it shot like flares into the sky. He felt a surge of love. This was his planet. His home. Mother couldn't take that from him. The collective force of all the human souls on Earth had to be more powerful than Mother. She could be beaten. She *would* be beaten.

As Earth moved away, the depths of the Milky Way came closer and he saw planets from other solar systems. He saw more movement and light. Souls lit these planets in the same powerful way they'd lit planet Earth. Their energy shot into the sky and Reinier realized that although his home was unique in so many ways, the life that existed on it was in no way unique. Although each planet looked and felt different to Earth, Reinier was certain the energy pulsing from its core was human. These weren't alien souls. These were human souls, living and breathing in the same way as those on his planet.

The galaxy continued to speed past and soon he felt as if he were the one moving, and the stars and planets were standing still. He flew through the sky, letting the breeze caress his soul. He passed solar system after solar system, stretching far beyond the Milky Way to neighboring galaxies, all containing planets bursting with life. More souls woven from hopes and dreams, not at all unlike the lives he'd lived.

The universe was larger than any mind could possibly grasp, and it was heaving with life. Earth wasn't the center of the universe. It was a small cog in a gigantic wheel of life.

They came to a stop and Reinier watched the universe before him, only this time he looked at it with different eyes.

"Do you understand?" the Author asked, and the lights faded, leaving them in darkness once more.

"Yes." Reinier's voice was a whisper as he became enveloped with a sense of awe.

"Each of these planets is like one of my children. I love them all. As important as Earth is to me, I cannot be watching it every moment. Just as a mother cannot watch every breath her child takes, or every blink of his eye."

"I'd no idea there was so much out there."

"You couldn't have known. I've never shown it to you before."

"I should've known. How could all this exist to serve only one planet?" He swept his hands through the darkness, the vastness of the universe etched in his mind. "Of course there are others out there. The universe is too big to contain life on only one small planet."

"There are thousands of planets with life, just like Earth. I appoint each planet a Soulweaver to help me care for its souls. It's the Soulweaver's job to collect the planet's souls and lead them through their journey. It's only when a soul is extinguished or completes its journey that I take over."

"I'm not sure I understand." Reinier still had so much to learn. He'd always thought the Soulweaver was the one to extinguish a soul. He'd imagined the Author as the one who sat back and admired his work from a distance.

"When I created the universe, I scattered many planets throughout its depths. I gave each planet a spark of life – tiny organic molecules that washed into the oceans and began reacting with each other, multiplying and mutating into fascinating forms. Over billions of human years, these molecules evolved into plants, then reptiles, then mammals, until we have the humans you know today. Each planet has evolved in a similar way. With some differences of course."

Reinier listened, wondering how the human soul came into this picture. At what stage did strands of molecules become important enough to warrant a soul?

"Souls were there from the very start," said the Author, reading his thoughts. "Each tiny molecule contained a soul in its most basic form. Souls have evolved in much the same way as the bodies they reside in."

This answer raised more questions than the one it'd satisfied.

"Have humans completed our evolution?" he asked, wondering if this was the final human form.

"Nothing in life ever completes its evolution. That's what makes the universe so fascinating." Love burned in the Author's eyes. He was proud of what he'd created.

"Then it's possible humans could one day fly through the

sky or breathe under water?" It seemed ridiculous, although if what the Author was saying was true, then anything was possible.

"That's in the hands of the human souls themselves."

This answer surprised Reinier. He'd expected the fate of humankind to be predetermined. "Are you saying you don't have the ultimate power over how we evolve?"

"There'd be little purpose to life if the person living it had no power to influence it. I can steer the way, I can step in when needed, but how life evolves on a planet is up to the souls themselves."

"And the Soulweaver," Reinier added.

"To some extent."

"If the future of the universe isn't predetermined, how can we trust in it? How can I have visions of the future, if the future hasn't yet been set in stone?" There was an edge of frustration in Reinier's voice. He felt like his whole world had been spun upside down.

"Your visions are possible and likely outcomes open to your own interpretation. When I authored the universe, I wrote the beginning and the end. The pages that lie within are up to you. Each soul has the power to have a happy life or one filled with pain."

"I think I'm starting to understand."

"If you're starting to understand, then why is it that so many questions are still bothering your thoughts?"

"Because starting to understand isn't enough for me. I want to know everything." Determination gleamed in his eyes. This was his chance to satisfy his hungry curiosity. He might never have a chance like this again.

"Go on then. We have all the time in the world." The Author smiled.

"You said earlier that you become involved when a soul either completes its journey or is extinguished. How does that work? They're two very different situations." He wondered which category he fitted into.

"That's true. They're the opposite ends of the spectrum yet meet the same fate. In your case, you reach across this spectrum."

"And what will my fate be?" His patience was stretching thin under his veil of curiosity. Would he ever see Lin again? Each thought of her sent a sharp pain of longing through his heart. He missed her.

"We'll get to that. There's much for you to understand first. Enlightened souls who've completed their journey have no need to live more lives on Earth. There's nothing more for them to learn."

"Does this happen often?"

"No, it's very rare. And becoming rarer still as humans have continued to evolve. The evolution of your bodies is overtaking the evolution of your souls. One glance at what you're doing to yourselves and your planet will tell you that. Mother, of course, hasn't helped."

"When do you extinguish a soul?" This was the question that concerned him most. He didn't want to be extinguished.

"As you know, a soul is extinguished for one reason only. The unforgiveable sin of taking a life, either your own or one that belongs to someone else."

"But people who take their own lives are in pain. Surely they can't be punished for that?"

"Being extinguished is not a punishment. I don't think you understand."

Reinier had barely heard this answer before he continued. "But when a life is taken it's not always clear who's responsible. What of the soldier who takes a life in war? Is he guilty, or is it the man who sent him to battle? Who judges souls for this?"

"The Soulweaver is the judge. If they decide to offer

forgiveness, then the soul is returned to Earth to live a new life."

"So, the unforgiveable is actually forgivable." Now he was getting very confused.

"Don't get caught up in words and their meanings. Unforgiveable is meant to imply it's a sin that's treated seriously. Far more seriously than any other sin in life."

"What happens when forgiveness isn't offered?"

"When the decision is negative or not certain, the soul is sent to me."

"That sounds like an appeal in the human justice system."

"Every soul deserves a fair trial. There can be no mistakes."

"Surely souls who take a life have plenty left to learn in their journeys. Why would they be extinguished and turned to dust?"

"A soul can never be turned to dust. Souls are too precious for that. They're extinguished from life on Earth. Preserving life is the only rule I give. The dominant souls on a planet should be finding ways to respect life and ensure its continued existence. It's not their decision when to take it away."

"It's yours."

"No, Reinier. It's not mine. I already told you I don't take away life."

"Then what do you do with these souls?" What he wanted to ask was "what will you do with me?"

"I decide on which planet the soul should begin its new journey. There are many waiting for new souls to expand their growth."

"Is that why Earth's population has been expanding? We're taking souls from other planets?"

"Exactly. Earth is experiencing a period of growth. Other

planets are in decline. It's necessary for souls to travel between planets at times."

"Exiled to another planet? Forgive me, but this sounds a little harsh. I thought you said it wasn't a punishment."

"It's not harsh. It's necessary. Just as each planet is evolving, so is the universe as a whole. Don't think life on other planets is alien. They're human, just like you. I know you felt that when I showed them to you. Humans on other planets have lives just as satisfying as those on Earth. Quite often even more so."

"Where will you send me?" Reinier tried to accept his fate, despite the fact it sent shivers through his soul. He didn't want to leave Earth, no matter how satisfying a life he was promised. He needed to get back to the one planet that contained his reason for living. He needed to get back to Lin.

"You're assuming I'll be sending you away."

"I took a life. You just said if I'm found guilty of this, my life on Earth will be extinguished. And I am guilty."

"I said when you take a life I must judge whether your life on Earth will be extinguished. The unforgiveable can be forgiven, remember?"

Hope flooded Reinier's mind. He waited for the Author to continue.

"Your case is an unusual one. You took your life as a way to fight Mother and protect Lin. You were wrong to believe this plan would work. However, it did draw my attention to Mother. You showed me things I'd overlooked. I've never had a Soulweaver stray from their path in the way Mother did. I'm afraid I made a terrible mistake when I appointed her. She's failed me. Since learning of her deeds, I've removed her from her position. For the moment, I've taken on her responsibilities."

"For the moment?"

"Until I appoint a new Soulweaver, I'll care for Earth's

souls. There's a lot of work to be done to restore it to a sustainable and harmonious planet, but I believe it can be done. It can still be saved. There's a chosen one who'll make sure this happens."

"Lin and Matthew's baby. He's the chosen one, isn't he?"

"He is."

"Please don't send me to another planet. You must return me to planet Earth. I'd like to help Lin's son with his task. It's going to be a big one."

"Do not fear. You'll be returned to planet Earth. You have more to learn. But I'm only granting you one additional lifetime, Reinier. You must use it wisely."

"I will, Author. I promise. Are you certain it must be my last?" Panic rose in his words. If this lifetime were his last on Earth, then next time he'd be sent to another planet. The thought of leaving Earth – of leaving Lin – was terrifying.

"You're an enlightened soul, Reinier. You're not like the others. Your lessons are almost complete. Earth has taught you nearly all there is to know."

"That's not true. I have plenty left to learn."

As he spoke these words, he knew they were a lie. In his lifetimes he'd learned many different lessons. He'd learned what it was like to be oppressed, to be brave, to be blessed, to be filled with hope. He'd been ridiculed, loved, beaten and victorious. He'd learned to look within himself for the answers instead of leaning on others. Most importantly, he'd learned to find goodness in even the darkest souls.

The Author nodded, the kindness in his eyes filling Reinier's soul. "It's important you learn the final lesson life has planned for you. That lesson will be the most important one you'll learn yet. Your next life won't be an easy one, but it's crucial."

"Where are you sending me? Will I be close to Lin? I need to find her. I need to help her child. It'll be a lot to have on his shoulders, being the chosen one. We don't have much time."

"Oh, you'll find Lin very easily. I'm surprised you haven't guessed yet."

"Haven't guessed what?"

"You'll be Lin's child. Reinier, *you* are the chosen one."

PART V

SHEN

CHAPTER FIFTEEN

*S*hen was a curious child. It didn't satisfy him when someone explained how something worked, he wanted to know why. Why did the light switch turn on the lamp? Why did a balloon burst when a pin pricked its surface? Why did his ball float in the bath, yet he didn't? They were both filled with air.

As Shen grew older, his questions grew more difficult to answer. Why did he dream of strangers when he closed his eyes? Why did his mother cry when she thought she was alone? Why did his father see so much, yet his eyes were blind?

He lived a life so privileged that even at the age of eight he knew he was unlike his peers. His father was a successful composer who traveled the world, making people weep with joy and sadness. That seemed a strange profession, yet Shen respected his father's ability to move a room of people in such a way. He was a man of few words, so Shen had quickly learned to listen to what he had to say through his music. In some ways he felt his father's fans knew him as well as he did, for if you understood his music, you understood him.

Shen had inherited his father's passion for music, and they'd sit side-by-side playing the piano as if lost in a deep conversation. These were some of the happiest moments of his childhood, for these were the times he felt his father's love the most strongly.

When Shen was a baby, his family moved from London to New York. Their home was a penthouse with spectacular views, and more rooms than they had furniture to fill them with. Instead they filled them with dreams.

He spent hours by his mother's side, their noses pressed against the windows, imagining the city as a forest. This was a game his mother had played as a child and Shen reveled in it as much as she did. He loved the impressive view of the city he got during this game, but it was the view of his mother's mind he liked the most. Hulking concrete skyscrapers became thousand-year-old trees, helicopters became swooping eagles and Central Park became a clearing his mother had said she'd visited with his father long before he was born. Back in a time when his eyes still worked.

"I thought he was blind when you met him," Shen said, confused.

"He was," his mother replied. "But when I was Hannah, he could see me perfectly well."

Shen nodded. His mother often spoke of her life in Australia as Hannah. Just as she spoke of growing up as a girl called Lin in Hong Kong. For this reason, it had never seemed strange. There was more to life than the here and now.

"Could Dad see you when you were in Hong Kong?" he asked.

"No, darling. Dad's never been to Hong Kong."

"Have I?"

"No. You were born in London and now we live here."

"Then why do I feel like I was with you in Hong Kong?"

She smiled. "You've always been with me, Shen."

"Is that why I have memories that don't belong to me?"

"They do belong to you," she said. "Shen's new to this world, but you've been here many times before, just as I was here as Hannah. You're an old soul."

"Am I as old as you?"

"You're even older."

He liked the idea of this and smiled. It made sense to him and he accepted this information as easily as if she'd explained that leaves drop from the trees in fall.

When he wasn't staring out of the windows of their apartment, he'd wander around it looking at his mother's paintings. As a girl, she'd loved to sketch with pencil on paper. As an adult, her passion lay in paint on canvas. The walls of their apartment were lined with huge landscapes of Australia's dense forests, Hong Kong's overcrowded streets and London's most famous landmarks. As Shen looked at them he felt almost as if he were there, standing beside his mother as she painted. These scenes felt like home and he was never sure if it was because he'd studied them so closely, or if there was some other reason.

He directed many questions at his mother and she always answered him with honesty and love, but there were still so many he hadn't yet asked. So many things he didn't understand.

"Mom, do you remember when I was little and I was calling for you from my crib and you didn't come? So, I started calling out "Hanlin". And you came running in and you cried so much I got scared and I started crying, too."

"Yes, darling. I remember."

"Were they happy tears or sad tears?"

"Both. You see, the moment you were born I knew who you were. I don't mean my son, Shen. I mean that I knew your soul. When you called me Hanlin, you confirmed for me that I'd been right. You were telling me that you knew me, too."

"Of course, I knew you. You're my mother." His dark eyes blinked at her with the innocence only a child can possess.

"I mean that you knew me from your memories. The ones you have that you don't think are your own."

"And that made you happy and sad at the same time?"

"I was happy to have you back in my life and sad that I'd had to lose you in the first place." She looked at him with the same happy sad face he'd seen that day.

"Have I always been your son?"

"In this life, yes. But in other lives, no. You've always been important to me, though."

"More important than Dad?"

"A different important to Dad."

They lapsed into silence, becoming lost in the concrete forest that stretched out before them.

"Why did Dad buy this apartment?" Shen asked.

"What do you mean? This is a fantastic place to live. We're very lucky."

"I mean, why did he want a view of a city that he can never see?"

"Because maybe he'll see it one day."

He thought about this for a moment. "Maybe he bought it for us, because he knows we love it and he loves us."

"I think you might be right." She put her arm around him and drew him near.

"Mom?"

"Yes, Shen."

"Do you miss your parents? Is that why you cry?"

"I don't cry."

"Yes, you do. I hear you when you think I'm not listening. You cry a lot. You're crying now."

"So I am." She wiped a tear that had begun to fall down

her cheek. "Yes, darling, I miss my parents. That's one thing that makes me sad."

"Why don't we visit them?" It seemed so simple.

"We can't. They don't want to see us."

"But why, Mom? Why don't they like us?"

"They do like us."

"Then why can't I meet them? I want to meet them. I have your father's name. I want to meet him. I want to see your forest in Hong Kong."

"Life's full of wants, but we can't always have what we want." Her voice was firm.

"Why?"

"It's very complicated." His mother had never refused to answer a question before. This told him it was important. He couldn't let it go.

"Why, Mom? Please tell me."

She sighed.

He waited.

"When I was young I was married to another man and went on a holiday far away. The next time my parents heard from me I was living in London with your father. They didn't approve of me marrying him."

"You were married before?" She'd never told him this. He thought he'd known everything about her.

"Yes, darling. But only for one day."

"What was your husband's name?"

She paused. "Reinier." He heard pain in her voice.

"Reinier? But that can't be, Mom."

"Why, darling?"

"Because I'm Reinier. I know I'm Reinier."

"How do you know that?"

"I just know it. But I wasn't married to you. You're my Mom."

"I know. I told you it's complicated. But yes, we were

married when you were Reinier."

"Are you in love with me?"

"No, Shen. I love you with all my heart and soul, but no, I'm definitely not in love with you." She laughed.

"Was that a silly question?"

"None of your questions are silly, Shen. You just make me laugh sometimes. What do you remember about Hong Kong?"

"I remember walking in a market with you and sitting at a table with you, but I don't remember the day I was married to you. There are bits missing."

"Well, that's a relief." His mother smiled.

"Why's it a relief, Mom?"

"Some things are not helpful to remember, that's all. The universe is clever like that."

As the years continued to pass, Shen remembered more and more of his life as Reinier and his lives before that. He continued to sit with his mother at one of the many windows in the apartment, as he made sense of the complicated existence he'd been born into.

It wasn't until he was sixteen years old that he began to worry about the implications of everything he'd learned. He was the chosen one. He'd known that even before his mother had told him. But there must have been a mistake somehow. How could *he* be the chosen one? He was just an ordinary teenager growing up in New York.

That was where he knew he was fooling himself. There was nothing at all ordinary about him or the life he lived. For a start, he lived in one of the most expensive penthouses in the city yet attended a public school. This set him apart from his peers immediately. He was a source of intense fascination and interest to the other students and making friends was challenging. He hated the stares and whispers that followed him though the school corridors and into each of his classes.

He begged his parents to enroll him in a private school, but they insisted it was important he grow up in touch with ordinary people. His father often said the most ordinary people were the ones who did the most extraordinary things. Shen had argued that people who attended private schools were still ordinary people, but his father disagreed. He wanted him to work hard and learn to get along with people from all walks of life, not just those who lived a privileged existence.

"If it's so important to be ordinary," Shen had said once, "Then why don't we give all our money to charity and be ordinary people?"

"One day we will," his father had replied.

Shen couldn't tell if he was being serious.

He tried to make the most of his ordinary school life. He had a handful of friends and enjoyed spending time in their homes with their families. Having them visit him was a little more difficult and something he avoided. He hated the look of awe on their faces the first time they saw where he lived. It wasn't that he didn't want them to like his home, it was the way it changed how they saw him. Almost as though they were intimidated by him. And whenever his father walked in the room, they'd either fall over with fright or burst into gushes of praise about his work. Either response was irritating.

The only person who seemed truly relaxed in his father's presence was his Uncle Jarred. But he was his father's brother and had plenty of money of his own, so of course he wouldn't be intimidated. As his father's agent, Uncle Jarred had moved with them to New York. Shen wished he'd provided him with some cousins to grow up with, but there was no such luck. Apparently, he'd gone through an expensive divorce in London and had sworn off relationships ever since.

It wasn't just the size of Shen's family's bank account that set him apart at school. It was the way he saw the world. He had an intense interest in politics and was never shy in voicing his opinions. Other students found this odd. While they were at home on the weekends worrying about new blemishes on their chins, Shen was attending rallies crying out for world peace or an end to the destruction of our rainforests. While his friends sent each other text messages about what to wear to a party, he was sending letters to politicians demanding change.

"One person can't save the world all by themselves," a girl at school had said once when he handed her a petition to sign.

"Perhaps," he replied. "But one person can move thousands to follow and those thousands can move millions. Surely you'd have to agree that millions of people working together can change the world."

The girl had rolled her eyes and signed his petition. He liked the sound of what he just said, but even he had to wonder if it was true.

Shen knew his attitude was too much for some people, although he'd rather offend some than sit back and do nothing. He had to speak up. It was the only way he knew how.

The only thing he never spoke up about was his memories. He learned very quickly at a young age that speaking about your past lives was frowned upon. People looked at him like he was strange. One of his elementary school teachers kept him in at lunchtime for lying when he insisted he once lived a life as a Maasai warrior in Kenya.

It was easier to keep these memories to himself. And his mother, of course. He was grateful to have her to talk to. He remembered how hard life had been as Reinier, with nobody to talk to about his memories. He'd spent most of that childhood running away, never really knowing what he was running to. He had known something was missing from his life but couldn't work out what it was until he saw Hannah walk past him in the street. He'd stopped still. *She* was what was missing. A flood of memories had seeped into every crevice of his mind. Then the visions had started – visions of Mother taking Hannah's life to prevent the chosen one being born.

A shiver ran through him. He was the chosen one, and therefore the one Mother had been so desperate to put a stop to. If it weren't for him, Hannah would still be alive. Only then his mother, Lin, wouldn't have been born, and that wasn't a thought he could easily accept.

But Mother had made a mistake. In taking Hannah's life, she'd actually brought about his birth. She'd sealed his fate. If Hannah and his father had conceived a child in the clearing that day, it couldn't possibly have been the chosen one because he had still been alive as Reinier. When Mother killed Hannah, she'd set in motion a series of events that had led to the very thing she'd been trying to prevent.

Him.

It seemed destiny was something nobody could change, not even the Soulweaver herself. If it's meant to be, it will be.

That brought him back to his worries about being the chosen one. If destiny really was set in stone, then there hadn't been a mistake. He was the chosen one and expected somehow to save the world from destroying itself.

"Not much pressure for a sixteen-year-old," he muttered, sinking onto his bed and closing his eyes. He wondered how long the visions would take to start this time. Usually, within a few minutes his mind would be taken over, either by a series of memories, or flashes forward into the future. Lately it'd become exhausting as the pressure to perform his duty as the chosen one approached.

He asked his mother for advice on this, and she gently but firmly insisted all he needed to do was follow his instincts. She didn't seem to believe he actually had to do anything special at all. She said maybe all he was meant to do was say one thing to one person and that would be the event that would change the world.

This couldn't possibly be true. How could his whole life, and the lives of all the other people who lived on this planet, all boil down to one simple action or moment? It had to be more than that. He was meant to do something, and it was meant to be something big. If only it was as simple as signing a petition.

There was a gentle knock at his bedroom door.

"Come in," he called out.

His father entered. It was unusual for him to visit him in his room at such a late hour. In fact, it was unusual for him to visit him at all. Normally, he was the one who sought out his father.

He sat up in bed not bothering with the bedside light. It was of no use to his father and he liked the idea of talking with him in the dark. That way neither of them could see and it put them on a more even plane.

"What's wrong, Dad?"

"I'm worried about you." His father sat on the edge of the bed.

"Why? I'm okay."

"You're not really okay, are you, Shen? You're feeling the pressure."

"Yeah." He leaned back on his pillow. He'd learned very early in life there was little use in telling his father lies. One advantage of being blind was the ability to hear even the smallest inflection in spoken words. Without being distracted by visual clues, his father could spot even the most innocent untruth.

"This is what I was worried about all those years ago."

Shen was surprised. "You mean when you and Mom decided to have me?"

"Well to be honest, when I agreed to have a child with your mother I didn't actually give *you* a whole lot of thought. I just wanted to keep your mother happy. I was frightened I'd lose her if I didn't give her what she wanted. She believed in you so much. She still does."

"You didn't want me?" He couldn't help but feel a little offended. Every child likes to believe their parents wanted them desperately – even children born to be the chosen one.

"Of course, I wanted you. The idea of having a child with your mother was a beautiful one. I just never really thought too much about exactly who you'd be and the pressure you'd be under if what your mother said was actually true."

Shen felt his father's hand on his knee.

"You don't believe I'm the chosen one?"

"I do believe it now. I've believed it since the day I heard you call your mother Hanlin. That was when I started to worry."

"You heard me say that?"

"Just because I don't say much doesn't mean I don't hear nearly everything that goes on in this apartment."

"I don't remember you being there that day, that's all. I remember Mom holding me in the crib, but you weren't there."

"I didn't want to intrude so I left your mother alone with you."

"That's crazy, Dad. You're her husband. You're my father."

"Your mother and I were intended to be together. We have an extraordinary bond and I love her with all my heart, but the bond we have is different to the bond she has with you. Your soul has been interwoven with hers over many lifetimes. You're connected in a unique way."

Shen thought about this for a moment. "Does that make you jealous?"

"Occasionally, but not often. You're my son, Shen. I love you. What greater joy could I have than to see the two people I love most, joined by their souls as well as their blood?"

"That's very big of you, Dad." It was, too. Shen knew his father loved his mother in a way that seemed to be absent in the way his friends' fathers loved their wives. It was as if his whole world depended on every breath she took.

"I'm not trying to be big, Shen. I'm just being realistic. I had no idea how much I was going to love you until you were born. You're a miracle. You make me glad that I hung in there when times were tough."

His father had told him he loved him many times, but never like this. Maybe now was the right moment to ask him the question that had burned at him for years.

"So, you love me, even though I tried to kill you once when I was Reinier?" he asked.

They'd never discussed his actions toward his father when he was Reinier. This unusual conversation his father had opened up had finally given him the courage to ask.

"That's a good point. I might have to ground you for that." This wasn't the answer Shen had expected. He laughed and the somber mood of only moments ago shattered, taking the tension with it.

"I'm serious, Dad. I gave you no reason to like me when I was Reinier. Why would you love me so much as Shen?" He had to press him on this, now the subject had been opened. He needed to know.

"When you were Reinier, you dedicated your life to protecting the woman I love. You also encouraged her to find me. If it weren't for you, I wouldn't have her in my life.

What's not to love about that?" This also wasn't an answer Shen had expected, but it was more than satisfactory. It was a relief beyond anything he'd ever experienced. His father wasn't angry with him as he'd always feared. He seemed thankful.

"Dad." Shen paused. "Why haven't we talked like this before?"

"We have."

"No, this is the first time we've ever talked about stuff like this."

"It's not easy stuff to talk about, I suppose. You know the art of conversation is not really my specialty."

"You're actually quite good at it when you try."

He heard his father snort. "Your mother said the exact same thing to me once. If the pair of you agrees, it looks like I'll have to try it more often. I'm sorry I've been distant at times. Life hasn't been easy. I feel like I've spent most of my time thinking about what's happened to me rather than actually living it. I'll try to make things different from now on."

He hated to hear his father talk like this. He was the most successful person he'd ever come across and he admired him deeply. He shuffled out from under the covers and sat next to his father on the edge of the bed.

"You've achieved some pretty magnificent things for someone who claims not to have spent much time living life."

"You do know that the most magnificent thing I ever achieved was you, don't you?"

"Because I'm the chosen one?"

He shook his head. "Because you're Shen."

His father put his arm around him and squeezed him so tightly his arm hurt, yet he didn't pull away.

"Let's get back to my original question," his father said, loosening his grip. "About you feeling the pressure."

Shen sighed. "What do you think I need to do as the

chosen one? Really. Is it as simple as Mom says? I can't just sit here and wait for a random moment to change the course of the world."

"I wish I knew. It's certainly possible, but it can't hurt to try your hardest to make a positive difference, even if that's not what's ultimately the one thing you're destined to do. I'm really proud of the way you throw yourself into your causes. You've already made more of a difference to the world than any other teenager I've come across." Shen heard the pride in his father's voice.

"Thanks, Dad. Although it's hardly enough of a difference to save the world from destroying itself."

"Just keep doing what you're doing. I'm sure you're on the right path. Every day you're learning something new. One day it'll all make sense."

"Did you mean it when you said we were going to give all our money to charity?" This was another thing that'd been bugging him. His father had such a dry wit, sometimes he didn't know when to take him seriously.

"Of course, I meant it. How can we have so much when so many have so little? I'm just waiting for the right time."

"You'd even give up this apartment?"

"It's not like I can see it anyway. But don't worry. I won't leave you homeless until you're at least eighteen." There was that laugh again. His mother had always said it was more beautiful than any music she'd heard him compose.

"Don't make jokes about being blind, Dad. It really isn't funny."

"All the money in the world hasn't brought my sight back, Shen. I know it'd be hard to give all of this up, but it's not like I grew up having much. And your mother certainly didn't grow up with these privileges. We'll keep a small amount to live comfortably, but really, nobody needs the luxuries we're surrounded by. It makes me feel kind of guilty, actually."

"Then why do we still have it?"

"I told you. I'm waiting for the right moment. Money opens doors and I suspect there might be a few doors you're going to need to open in order to do what you need to do. The time isn't right to give it all away now. Anyway, enough talking. I've used up my quota of words for the day. Perhaps the year."

He stood up, indicating that the conversation was most definitely over. Shen had hoped they'd talk all night but decided to be grateful for the time they'd just had.

"Goodnight, Dad."

He crawled back into his bed. He was lucky to have his father. He doubted there was anyone else in the world like him. For someone who saw so little, he saw so much.

He closed his eyes and wished for sleep to claim him. It seemed an impossibility with all the thoughts swirling through his mind. The conversation with his father had been wonderful, though not entirely helpful.

He still had no idea what it was he was supposed to do. Whatever it was, he was prepared for it. He didn't want to spend his life waiting.

"I'm ready," he whispered to the night.

CHAPTER SIXTEEN

*S*hen woke several hours later in a sweat. He'd been falling. Falling down to the water, his body riddled with fear despite his certainty that falling was the answer. As his body hit the water, he woke. He always woke when he hit the water. He closed his eyes and willed himself back to sleep. He wanted to see what happened after the water. Not his lifeless body sinking to its depths, but the rising of his soul into the heavens.

Where had he gone when he left the earth as Reinier? Did he see Mother or was he sent elsewhere?

He squeezed his eyelids tighter and brought his mind back to the falling. He remembered climbing over the railing of the bridge. He heard cars honking their horns. Felt the smooth iron platform under his bare feet and smelt the fear as it seeped from his pores.

It wasn't the thought of death that frightened him – he'd been there before – it was the act itself that caused him fear. Despite all he'd experienced and knew, he was still a man. And man was designed to fear death, not walk toward it. Man is meant to run, scratch and fight until the last breath leaves his lungs. Still, he knew he had to die. It was the only way.

He remembered looking upwards as he stepped off the edge. His hands reached up to the sky. Onlookers thought he was grappling for the bridge. He wasn't. He was reaching for the clouds. His body was falling, but his soul was soaring. Death was near and he'd be able to keep Lin safe in a way that was impossible while he was alive.

Then he hit the water and the world turned black. It was over. Reinier was no more. The fact he couldn't remember what came next convinced him it must be important.

When he'd taken his own life, he'd committed an unforgiveable sin. He shouldn't have been reborn. Something must have happened that caused this universal law to be broken. Why else had Mother sent him back to Earth? By that stage she should've known he was the chosen one.

It didn't make sense. Had he been able to convince her of her wrongdoings? Maybe he'd been able to guide her back to her rightful path and she'd let him live again. If so, perhaps his task as the chosen one was already complete. He'd served his purpose before he was even born. Mother would now take care of the rest from the Loom. She'd make sure the right people were born at the right times to change the grim fate of the world.

"Am I right, Mother?" he called into the darkness. "Am I right?"

A shadow crossed the room. He thought his tired eyes were deceiving him until the shadow grew darker, taking shape as a solid form. He sat still and waited. The shadow wasn't here to hurt him.

The form of a man appeared before him. He was tall, muscular, his skin and hair as dark as the night that surrounded him.

"Mother's no longer with us," the man said.

"Who are you?" Shen asked, his voice trembling with anticipation rather than fear.

"Who I am doesn't matter, Shen."

"Why are you here?"

"I'm always here."

"Tell me what to do."

"You don't need me to tell you that, Shen."

"Then why are you here?" he asked again.

"I told you, I'm always here." The man smiled at him, reminding him of how his father smiled when he talked to him. Was that pride that lay beneath his smile? Who was this man, to be proud of him?

"You're the Author, aren't you?" Shen asked, the realization dawning on him. "I've heard of you, but we've never met."

"You're wrong about that."

"Then who are you?" He couldn't let it go. If this man wasn't the Author, then who was he?

"Shen, you said you were ready. Part of being ready is learning when to fight the universe and when to accept what it's offering you with grace. Have you learned that?"

"I'm ready. I've been ready for a long time now. I can't continue living like this, knowing I'm expected to do something important and not knowing what it is. Please, tell me what it is I'm meant to do, and I'll do it immediately."

"I'm going to give you a challenge and ask you to trust in the universe. This isn't the time to fight. Can you do that?"

Shen nodded as fear laced its way through his body.

The man reached out, placing his hand on the top of his head.

"This won't be an easy challenge. Are you sure you're ready?"

"I'm ready," he said, remaining still.

He felt an energy pass from the man's warm touch into

the center of his brain. It tingled at first, then as it settled, became a dull ache.

"Trust in the universe," the man said. "Because it's trusting in you."

"What have you done to me?" Shen put his hands to his head and rubbed his temples. There was an ache in his head. It was like the shadow of the worst headache he'd ever experienced. His stomach retched in response to the pain.

"Trust," the man said, searching his eyes. "Trust." He faded, his form melting into the shadows as quickly as he'd appeared.

Over the following days the ache in Shen's head grew. He knew he couldn't hide it from his mother any longer. She found him sitting at the kitchen table, his head cradled in his hands.

"Shen, what's the matter? Are you hurt?" She put her hands on his shoulders, drawing him to her as she'd done since he was a child.

"I'm okay," he said, pulling away. "It's just a headache."

She felt his forehead and closed her eyes.

"I don't like this," she said. "It doesn't feel right."

"I don't like it either," he said, giving up the pretense.

"What's happened? I know you've been hiding something from me."

She knew. She *always* knew. He wished he could tell her that she wouldn't understand, but she would. For the first time in his life, he longed for a "normal" mother. One who'd laugh at the suggestion that a strange man appeared in his bedroom and left him with a pain in his head. His mother wouldn't laugh at this and he hated wiping joy from her eyes.

"I had a visitor this week."

"Here in the apartment? Who was it?"

"Yes, here in the apartment, but not the kind of visitor you're thinking of."

"An intruder? Shen, why didn't you tell me?" Her dark eyes filled with fear as she glanced around, trying to figure out how this could have happened. The security in their apartment was state of the art.

"He wasn't an intruder, Mom. He was more of a middle-of-the-night apparition kind of visitor."

"How do you know he wasn't real?"

"Because he appeared first as a shadow and then he took shape. Before I knew it, he was standing before me looking as real as you do now."

"Who was he?" Fear remained in her eyes. This new information had done little to soothe her concerns.

"I don't know. He wouldn't tell me who he was. He said Mother's gone. He said he's with me now."

"Mother's gone? That's fantastic news." Her eyes lit with both relief and delight. "She was working against us. Against you. Maybe this man was the new Soulweaver."

"Maybe. I asked him if he was the Author. It was the only thing that made sense at the time, but he said I was wrong. Perhaps I should've asked him if he was the Soulweaver."

"What did he say? Why was he here?"

"Other than telling me Mother had gone, he didn't really say much at all. Just that he thought I was ready."

"You're not ready." She said it firmly, as if she could make it a fact with her voice alone.

"I'm ready, Mom. You've been preparing me for this moment since the day I was born."

"You need more time."

"I think you need more time." He looked into her eyes. "It'll be okay. I promise."

"What else did he say to you? I need to know everything."

"The only other thing he said was the importance of recognizing when to fight the universe and when to accept what it has to offer you. He said now wasn't the time to fight. He kept telling me to trust."

"Was he a good man? Could you feel his energy?"

"Everything about him radiated goodness. Except…"

"Except what? What are you hiding from me?"

Shen hesitated. He was hoping to avoid telling her about the final moment of the man's visit. He took a deep breath. She needed to know. "Except when he put his hand on my head and I felt an energy pass into me."

A shadow crossed his mother's eyes. "What kind of energy?"

"It wasn't anything I've felt before. It moved from his hands to the center of my brain and… well, it's still there."

"When did this happen?"

"Four days ago."

"And you're telling me this now? I wish you hadn't kept this from me."

"What good is it to tell you? It makes no more sense to you than it does to me. Look at how upset you are."

"We need to take you to the hospital." She crossed the room and picked up her keys.

"Mom, come on. It's a headache."

"We don't know what it is. What did this man look like? Did he look like a Soulweaver?"

"You mean did he look like Mother?"

"Yes."

"Well, no. He looked… the opposite. Where she had light, he had shadows. But as I said, he was a good soul. Kind."

"I don't like this."

"You don't like what?" It was his father speaking. He walked across to them. His mother turned to him and rested her head instinctively on his chest. He closed his arms around her.

"Shen's sick," she said, her voice a whisper. "It's not good. I know it."

"What do you mean he's sick?" His father turned to him. "Shen, what's she talking about?"

"I have a headache."

"It's not just a headache," his mother said. "He needs to see a doctor."

"I'll take him," his father said, his face turning gray as he registered the fear in their voices. "I'll call a car now."

"No, I'll take him." she said.

"Can both of you take me?" Shen said, suddenly smelling death around him. It reminded him of his last moments as Reinier on the bridge. "I'm scared."

A cloud of anesthesia settled around Shen's shoulders. He watched his visit to the hospital as if it were happening to someone else. The doctors. The tests. The questions. The needles. The machines. This wasn't happening to him. He was the chosen one. He wasn't supposed to get sick. He was supposed to save the world. He was ready, but he also wanted more time.

When the diagnosis came through, he heard it with ears that were no longer present. He'd wrapped himself in thick layers that no doctor could penetrate. He didn't react. Nothing would get through. Except his mother's scream. She wailed as only a mother who's losing her child can wail. It was the sound of agony in its purest form. It pierced every layer of Shen's mind, stripping them away until he was left a bare shell.

She threw herself on him and her pain sliced through him

like a razor. Soon he was crying too, with tears made from acid, burning though his skin to the core of his soul. The pain was too great. He'd been told this challenge wouldn't be easy, but this was too much.

"I will not lose you again," his mother screamed. "I will not."

He held her to his chest and looked over her shoulder. His father was staring at them. A look of shock had turned his face to ice. Something wasn't right. His face was frozen, but his eyes... his eyes were warm. They were burning with energy as it bounced from his heart directly to Shen's.

"Dad," Shen said, gently prizing his mother away from him and standing to face him.

"My son," his father said. "Look at you."

"You can see me?" He didn't really need to ask. He knew he could see him. His familiar eyes looked as if they belonged to someone else. They were lit from behind and drinking him in.

"Lin," his father said, pulling his gaze from Shen to look upon his wife's face for the first time.

"Matthew." His mother turned and put her hands on his cheeks. "Do you see our son?"

"You're both so beautiful," he said. "More beautiful than I'd dared to imagine." He wrapped his arms around them and there they stood, holding each other as if they could stop time and stay like this forever.

For at that moment they were a mother, a father and their son. Nothing more. No chosen ones. No lifetimes before. No lifetimes to come. This was now.

Now was all that mattered.

A tumor had grown inside the center of Shen's brain. Even if the doctors could access it, removing it would be impossible. It had wrapped itself around critical blood vessels, making it too dangerous an operation to perform. This was the opinion of not one but four of New York's best surgeons. His fate had been sealed. The only way to extend his life would be with radiation therapy. It would buy him time, but not a cure. This wasn't an option Shen was convinced he should take. He'd been asked to trust in the universe.

The tumor was more aggressive than his doctors had ever seen before. Within days of his diagnosis he began to experience dizzy spells, disorientation and numbness in his face and hands. This tumor was on a mission.

"Why don't you want the radiation?" his mother asked for the twelfth time in as many minutes.

"Because it won't work."

"No, it won't work if that's your attitude. You have to fight this, Shen."

"That's exactly it. I was told to accept this, not to fight it."

"You're prepared to stake your life on what someone tells you? Someone who wouldn't even tell you who he was. I'm your mother and I'm telling you to fight."

"Please don't do this, Mom."

"Listen to me. I've been reading up on cancer survival and do you know what all the people who beat this disease have in common? They fought it. They fought it and they won."

"And what of all the people who fought and lost?"

"I'm sure it's normal to feel like this, but you have to—"

"There's nothing normal about this at all and you know it! This isn't a normal tumor and I didn't get it in the normal way, whatever that is. I don't want to spend the time I have left feeling any more ill than I already do. I want to use my time to come to peace with this. I want to accept this as I was asked to do. I don't want to fight."

"I can't lose you again." His mother clutched at his hand.

He closed his eyes. He hated causing her such pain, but he knew what he was saying was true. The man who visited him had given this to him. There was no radiation therapy in the world strong enough to do battle with a force like that.

"You're thinking about him again, aren't you?" his mother asked. She had a knack for knowing what he was thinking.

"Of course. I'm trying to understand who he could be. If he's not a Soulweaver or the Author, then who was he?"

"Tell me again what he said. Every word, if you can remember it."

"I asked him if he was the Author and he said I was wrong. That's it."

"What were the exact words?"

"I said, 'Are you the Author? I've heard of you, but we've never met.'"

"And he said?"

"He said 'You're wrong about that.'"

"But what were you wrong about? Him being the Author or the fact that you've never met?"

"Do you think...?" He paused. Despite replaying the conversation in his mind countless times, he'd never thought of that possibility. "Oh, Mom, I think you could be right. He was telling me we had met before. He *is* the Author. He must be. It's the only thing that makes sense."

"You're wrong again, Shen. That's the only thing that makes no sense at all to me."

"What do you mean?"

"I mean if he was the Author then he's supposed to love and protect us, not give us brain tumors. I'm not sure I can believe in an Author who's so cruelly taking my son from me."

"People lose their children all the time, Mom. You know that. It's never stopped you believing before."

"This is my child. This is different."

"It's not different. What have you told yourself all these years when you've seen people suffering? Why did you think the Author was doing that to them?"

"It was a necessary part of their journey. They were suffering to strengthen their soul for their next life."

"Exactly. Think about it. If that man was the Author, and we had met before, then we must've met when I died as Reinier. He was the one who sent me back. There must be a reason he needs to take me away again. Maybe my work as the chosen one isn't supposed to take place with me as Shen at all. Maybe there's a job for me up there."

A thought flashed across his mother's face with such strength she couldn't hide it. Her dark eyes opened wide, her lips parted, and her fingers fluttered to her throat.

"What is it, Mom?"

"You're the next Soulweaver. It has to be you." Her eyes filled with tears.

"Me? Why would you think that?"

"You said yourself that Mother's gone. So, who's guarding the Earth?"

"The Author, I guess."

"Well, he can't do that forever. Why do you think he's always appointed a Soulweaver? I'm telling you, Shen. It's you."

"Then why wouldn't he have just appointed me as Reinier? He didn't need to send me back again."

"You must have needed to learn something or do something as the chosen one. Something important."

"But Soulweavers are the purest souls to walk the earth. It can't be me."

"Shen, you *are* the purest soul to walk the earth. You wouldn't hurt another creature. Who else catches spiders in their apartment and carries them sixty stories down in an elevator to release them to safety?"

"And that makes me Soulweaver material? I don't think so."

"It's more than that and you know it. You're always working to make the world a better place. You always have. You've made me proud every day of your life."

"Which life?"

"Every day of every life."

He closed his eyes. His head was throbbing with both the tumor and the new information he was trying to absorb.

"You're tired. This conversation is draining you. I'll leave you to rest." She kissed him on the forehead. "Dad will be in soon."

He opened his eyes. He didn't want her to leave just yet. "How's Dad today? Is he still staring at you like you're made from diamonds?"

Her lips pursed into a weak smile. "Yes. I don't think he's taken his eyes off me for a second. I'm not even sure he's been blinking. The funniest thing was when he looked in a mirror for the first time. I'm sure he expected to see a sixteen-year-old boy staring back at him. He got quite a shock. Lucky for him he's aged so well."

The doctors were amazed that his father's sight had returned. It seemed the shock of Shen's diagnosis had somehow been responsible. He was the talk of every medical journal in the country.

"Has he seen Uncle Jarred yet?"

"Yes. He couldn't get over how much he looks like their father."

"I wish I could've been there. You must be happy for him."

"I'm not sure I can call it happy just yet. My heart is far too heavy at the moment for any joy to squeeze its way in."

"I'm going to be all right, Mom. You know that. We've said goodbye before. We'll see each other again."

"I'm not sure saying goodbye to you was ever this difficult."

"Even the last time?"

"You didn't say goodbye last time. And anyway, that was nothing compared to this."

"But you loved Reinier."

"He wasn't my child. You're my child. I carried you in my womb for nine months when I was a mere child myself. I thought I knew what love was before you were born, but when I looked into your tiny face for the first time, I saw love in its purest form. I still see it now when I look at you. I'm not sure how I'm going to continue on without you."

"But you love Dad. You'll still have him."

She smiled a sad smile. "Yes."

"We need to be strong. Trust in the universe. This is happening for a reason. Everything happens for a reason."

"I know, but that doesn't mean I won't miss you."

"I'll miss you, too."

Shen returned home later that week, after convincing his parents that radiation therapy would be useless. He wanted to die at home.

He walked into the apartment with his father's help. His dizzy spells had become worse and walking without assistance was no longer possible. His father had his arm placed firmly around his shoulders as he led him to the bed he'd set up in front of Shen's favorite window in the living room.

"It's about time you repaid me for all the times I had to

lead you around," Shen said, noticing how their roles had reversed.

"I'll try not to bump you into any walls," his father said. They laughed, remembering when ten-year-old Shen got distracted by a street performer and led him straight into a brick wall, almost breaking his nose.

Shen lay down on the bed, allowing his father to fuss over him, propping him up with pillows and arranging a blanket over his legs.

"Are you comfortable?" he asked.

"Very. Thanks, Dad."

His father hovered, clearly wanting to say something and not knowing how.

"What are you thinking, Dad?"

"I was thinking about my own mother, actually."

Shen smiled. He loved his grandmother, despite having only met her twice in person. Their relationship was conducted mainly over internet calls. His grandfather had died in a car accident when he was still young. Sadly, he never got the chance to meet him. Shen felt sorry for his grandmother. It couldn't be easy to be a widow and have both your sons live so far away. They sent her money and she lived a comfortable life, but how happy was it? He decided to give her a call later in the day.

"What were you thinking about her?" he asked his father.

"I was remembering her sadness when I first lost my sight. It was as if she'd lost her own sight. I know she would've changed places with me if she could. I never really understood her grief until now. I'd trade places with you in a heartbeat."

"I love you, Dad."

"I love you too." He sat on the bed next to him and forced a smile to his face. "You know, I still can't believe how handsome you are."

"You thought I'd be ugly? Thanks." He smiled.

"No, I knew you wouldn't have taken after Uncle Jarred."

They laughed. Uncle Jarred was certainly not ugly, but they'd always enjoyed teasing him.

"Look at you, Shen. You're amazing. I'm so proud."

"Was being handsome all I had to do to make you proud?"

"You've always made me proud. You're the best thing that ever happened to me. I want you to know that."

"Thanks, Dad. And for what it's worth, I'm glad I didn't kill you in the clearing that day." He grinned at him.

"Gee, thanks. Hey, um, Mom told me about your conversation with her earlier this week."

"Which one?" He rubbed his temples. It was getting harder to hold onto information now.

"About you being the Soulweaver."

"Oh, that."

"Do you believe it?"

Shen saw at that moment whether it was true or not, he had to ensure his parents believed it. It was easing their pain to think his death had some greater purpose. They'd cope so much better if they believed he was being called to fulfill his role as the chosen one.

"I do believe it," he said.

His father smiled, relief smoothing out the wrinkles that had creased his forehead. Now his sight had returned, his ability to see through white lies had completely evaporated. The visual clues he was being swamped with were distracting him from distinguishing the truth.

"Who's that?" asked Shen, hearing the voice of a woman in the next room.

"That's Kate. She's from the nursing agency I told you about. If you press this button next to your bed she'll be right by your side."

"Who's she talking to?"

"Uncle Jarred. He's taken it upon himself to help her settle in."

"I bet he has. Let's meet her, then," said Shen, pressing the button.

A woman in her late twenties entered the room, closely followed by Uncle Jarred. She smiled at Shen, her perfect teeth gleaming. Her blonde ponytail swished from side to side as she approached the bed. Shen couldn't help but notice the athletic frame she hid under her conservative agency uniform of black pants and a stiff blue shirt. No wonder Uncle Jarred was following her around like a puppy dog.

"Hi," she said. "You must be the new man in my life."

Uncle Jarred raised his eyebrows and Shen felt heat rush to his cheeks. "Y-y-yes."

"I'm Kate. Nice to meet you, Shen."

"Thanks for coming at such short notice," his father said, noticing his discomfort and trying to deflect the attention away from him.

"No problem. I'm just going to take your temperature now if you don't mind."

"You can take mine later if you like," said Uncle Jarred.

She ignored him and rolled over a trolley, filled with now-familiar hospital equipment and busied herself with taking Shen's temperature and blood pressure. He complied with her requests, sneaking looks at her when she wasn't looking at him.

"I'm going to leave you to rest for a bit now," she said, finishing up. "I'll come back in shortly. Just buzz me in the meantime if you need me."

"Sure. Thanks."

She left the room. Shen concentrated on her swinging ponytail, not daring to drop his gaze.

"That's some nurse you've got," said Uncle Jarred, who most definitely hadn't averted his gaze.

His father laughed. "She's a bit old for Shen, don't you think?"

"Like an age gap stopped you with Lin."

"That's different. She chased me."

"Sure she did," said Uncle Jarred, leaving the room to follow Kate.

"Leave her alone!" called out his father.

"Mom did chase you, though," said Shen. "She went all over the world to find you."

He loved the story of how they'd met.

"True, except you have to realize we were technically the same age when we first met."

"When she was Hannah? That doesn't count."

"It does. Does it count that technically you used to be married to your mother?"

"Don't say it like that. That sounds revolting. It's not like that and you know it."

"Do you remember any of that? You know, being married to her." He'd never asked this question. Shen wondered how long he'd wanted to ask.

"None of the mushy stuff, if that's what you mean. I just have vague memories of walking down the street talking. That kind of thing."

"Lucky for you. You might be scarred for life otherwise."

Shen winced as his headache took hold with a new force.

"Are you okay?" his father asked, pressing the buzzer.

Kate appeared within seconds. Uncle Jarred stood behind her, his face filled with concern.

"Everything all right?" Kate asked.

"He's in pain," his father said.

"Shen, what's the pain like out of ten?"

"Twenty," he gasped.

She marched over to her trolley, retrieved a vial of morphine and injected it smoothly into his forearm. He felt the drug flow through his veins, spreading through his body in a wave of relief.

"Thanks," he said, closing his eyes, hoping he wouldn't be made to suffer for too long. If his death was meant to be, then let it come quickly.

———

Exactly one week after his diagnosis, Shen felt himself begin to slip away. Moments of haze overtook moments of clarity. Darkness overtook light. His legs no longer walked, his eyes no longer saw, his tongue no longer spoke. He was trapped in a world of fog that swirled around him.

Occasionally, something would break through the fog and he'd glimpse his mother's dark eyes or hear some notes from his father's piano. He'd hold onto these moments, pasting them into the scrapbook of his mind before they were snatched away, leaving him lying in the fog once more.

He knew the end was near when the curtain of fog began to lift. First, he heard the voice of his mother singing him a lullaby from her childhood. It was a song she'd sung him many times in his early years. The gentle melody floated him back to a time when the world felt safe. He became aware of her softly stroking his forehead, tracing the lines of his brow.

"Under the moonlight, my son, you will sleep," she sang in Cantonese. "Tomorrow your mother has to go to the field."

His eyes fluttered open and her singing halted as the breath caught in her throat.

"Matthew," she called. "Quickly. He's awake."

His father appeared by her side and they leaned in, their eyes filled with grief and love in equal measures.

Shen parted his lips. "Don't... stop." His voice was so soft it failed to reach even his own ears.

"Don't... stop," he tried again. The effort of each word felt like climbing the highest mountain.

His parents glanced at each other with confusion. "Don't stop what, my darling?" Tears streamed down his mother's cheeks and landed in large drops on her shirt. He hated leaving her. If only things could be different. If only he could stay.

"Don't... stop... singing."

She began her song again, her voice trembling with the effort of holding herself together. "Under the moonlight, my son, you will sleep."

"We love you so much," his father said. "Be brave."

He took one final look at their beloved faces and closed his eyes.

CHAPTER SEVENTEEN

*T*he tunnel was dark. Peaceful. It had a beauty that couldn't be seen but felt. It took hold of Shen, hypnotizing him, entrancing him, seducing him. Had death taken him, or had it let him go?

He looked for the light he knew he'd find. It wasn't there. He walked along the tunnel, breathing in the calm. He'd accepted his fate, but he hadn't wanted to leave. The peace he'd found in his final days came from complete trust in the universe. There was a bigger plan for him.

With each step he took, his life as Shen faded further away, until he wondered if it had ever existed. Of course, it had. His body must still be warm in his bed, his parents' cheeks wet with sadness. Only that body was no longer him. It had never been him.

This was him. His spirit, his energy, his core. He hadn't died. The vessel he'd used to walk the earth had released him, that was all. It was time to find out why.

A blue light flickered in the distance. He blinked with surprise. Where was the familiar yellow light? Then he remembered it wasn't Mother who'd be greeting him. It would be the Author. A being whose light burnt brighter, stronger and hotter than any other being to grace the skies.

He walked closer.

"Shen," the light called. He stepped forward and the last of the pain of his final moments of life as Shen lifted. The light was making him feel warm and safe as it continued to draw him in. It began to spin, spitting bold colors of light from its core. They jumped at him like sparks from a fire. He put out his hand to catch one of the sparks. It landed on his palm and lit his fingers, turning them blue. He stared at them with amazement as the energy from his fingers traveled up his arm and warmed him to his core.

"Shen," the voice called again. It was a male voice, deep, powerful, exactly as a human would imagine the voice of their god.

He stepped into the light and was cocooned in its loving embrace.

A darker blue light spiraled toward him and took form. The silhouette of a man slowly appeared.

"Author," Shen said, recognizing him. "Is it you?"

"Yes, Shen. It's me."

So, he was the Author. His mother had been right. He'd expected to feel anger at this moment for the torment that had been inflicted on him and his parents, but instead he felt joy, forgiveness and understanding. The Author had a plan for him. He trusted in that. He knew it to be so.

"I'm sorry for your pain, my son. Thank you for believing in me."

"Is that why you sent me back? You were testing my belief."

"I needed to see if after all the lives you've lived, you were able to develop complete trust in the universe. I threw you the worst and you gave me the best. As Reinier, challenges came your way and your response was to fight. Then you took your life. As Shen, you proved you can trust in the greater plan. You made me proud. You showed me that I chose well when I picked you to be the next Soulweaver."

Shen gasped. "It's true? My mother was right." He could hardly believe it. *He* would be the Soulweaver. Was he worthy of such an honor? Whether or not he was the best soul for the job, he knew one thing for certain. He'd do his best. He'd give everything he could to guard the human souls in his care and never stray from his path. He'd make the Author proud.

"You've already made me proud, Shen," said the Author, reading his thoughts. "And Lin's a perceptive being. Your souls are uniquely bonded. It isn't possible to keep you apart. You've proven that more than once. When Lin's time comes to leave Earth, I'll reunite you. She'll sit by your side as a Soulweaver. Earth will have both a Mother and a Father."

As perceptive as his mother had been, this was something she hadn't guessed. "What about my father?" he asked. What will become of him?"

"He's a young soul compared to you both. He has more lives to live. In time you'll figure out where he can best serve the world. He'll never be far from you. Souls like his will be crucial to help return Earth to what it was always meant to be. Do not fear for him."

"Why did you have to take me so young?" Despite his pain having lifted, the wound of being separated from his parents remained raw. A few more years on Earth would be a mere drop of water in the ocean of time.

"I needed you here."

Shen closed his eyes and breathed in the Author's brilliant blue light. His lungs filled with confidence and hope. He'd do his job as the Soulweaver to the best of his abilities. He wouldn't fall for the same traps that had ensnared Mother so viciously.

"Please, tell me where Mother went so wrong. I cannot make the same mistakes."

"She lost her trust. That's why it was so important for me to test you in the way I did. It cannot happen again. She began birthing the wrong souls to the wrong parents at all the wrong times. It was just a few careless errors to begin with and then slowly humankind began to spread like a cancer, devastating the environment and treating each other as expendable pawns in their games of power. The more humans lost respect for Earth, the more Mother lost respect for humankind. She decided to watch you destroy yourselves so she could start again."

"How do I turn that around?"

"By birthing the right souls to the right parents at all the right times. It won't be easy, but it can be done. I have faith in you."

"What's happened to Mother?"

"She got her wish. She wanted to start again, and so she has, only not in the way she intended. I washed her soul clean and sent her far away. She'll start her journey again somewhere else."

"Where?"

"On another planet far away from your own."

"Another planet?" A memory deep in the recesses of Shen's mind tried to fight its way to the surface.

"Do you remember what I showed you when you last came to me as Reinier?" the Author asked.

"I'm trying, but I can't."

"Close your eyes."

He did as he was told. The dark soon became light and he felt energy pouring into his soul. Each memory that'd been cleansed from him was returning. Every lifetime was being handed to him one by one. Finally, he came to Reinier and saw his meeting with the Author and the tour of the universe he'd been given.

He saw galaxies bursting with life and understood once more the place his small, blue planet held in it all. He was connected to Earth in a way he couldn't explain. His soul was wrapped around it so tightly, he didn't feel it would be possible to separate from it. His planet was one small piece of a puzzle that'd be incomplete without it, yet beautiful beyond imagination once it was in place.

The universe was a complex and delicate structure with a billion splinters of light layered into it.

Shen was proud to be Earth's Father. He'd work hard to weave love and hope into its fabric, until every dream trapped inside was released into the heavens above.

Earth would be beautiful once more.

EPILOGUE

*M*atthew and Lin sat in the living room of their luxurious Manhattan apartment, feeling nothing but pain. It throbbed deep in their hearts, threatening to swallow them whole. With each heartbeat, the pain radiated throughout their bodies, until it was felt in the tips of their toes and shadows of their minds. There was no way to escape it. No way to turn back time. No path that would take them back to Shen.

Just one more moment with him in their arms would ease the pain. Just one blink of an eye with his face before them. How could he have been taken so young? So quickly. They hadn't had enough time.

How much time would be enough when it came to saying goodbye to your son? One thousand moons would barely make a start.

"I didn't tell him that I love him," said Lin, her eyes wide with panic.

"You did," said Matthew, running his hands down her soft hair. "You told him all the time."

"But I didn't say it at the end. I didn't say it, Matthew."

"I said it. Remember? I told him that we love him. You were singing him the most beautiful love song I've ever heard. He knows you love him."

She looked across at the hospital bed still sitting in front of the window. It was empty now. Cold. It was hard to believe it had been warmed by Shen's tired body only the day before.

"I want it out of here. The bed, Matthew. Get it out of here. Please." Her voice was panicked. Irrational.

He knew not to argue. He stood, unlocked the wheels of the bed and rolled it into the hallway. Out of sight, but still held firmly by their minds.

"No," she cried. "Bring it back. I'm sorry."

Quietly, he rolled the bed back into the room. He sat on it and patted the space beside him. "Come here, sweetheart."

She sat beside him and ran her hand across the pillow. They both saw Shen lying there, gripped by pain, free from fear.

"Our son was amazing," he said.

"Our son *is* amazing," she corrected.

"You're right. He is amazing."

If her lips could remember how to smile, she would have. Instead a flicker of warmth moved across her eyes. That was all she could offer right now.

"Where do you think he is?" he asked, looking around the room. "You came to me as Hannah. Do you think he's here now?"

"No." Her answer was as certain as it was simple.

"Really? I'm surprised to hear you say that. You don't think he'd come back to say goodbye?"

"He already said it. When I was Hannah I was ripped away from you before I had the chance to say goodbye. I wasn't expecting it. I wasn't ready."

"And you think Shen was?"

257

"I know he was."

Matthew sat up straight like he'd received an electric shock. "I nearly forgot. I'm sorry." He ran out of the room.

"What's going on?" Lin called after him. "Matthew."

He returned moments later holding a letter. "Jarred gave this to me last night. He said Shen had asked him to give it to you after he…"

"Died, Matthew. The word's died. We can't hide from it."

"You're right. Sorry." He handed her the letter and sat beside her.

She held it in her lap, staring at it. "Why didn't you give this to me last night?" There was the definite sound of a reproach in her voice.

"I forgot. I'm sorry. I could barely remember my own name yesterday." His voice cracked with the strain of the past twenty-four hours. He'd been trying so hard to be strong for his wife. He'd thought he had the strength to hold them both together. He realized now he barely had the strength to keep himself from falling apart. His son was dead. His only son. Nothing would ever be the same again. He put his head in his hands and wept.

"Matthew." She reached for him, still clutching the letter in her hand as she wrapped her arms around his neck. "Of course, you forgot. I'm sorry. He was your son too."

He buried his face in her hair and closed his eyes, drawing comfort from the familiar feeling of darkness. *This* was the woman he'd married. All sweet-smelling softness and warmth. As beautiful as she was, he barely recognized her with his eyes open, but when he closed his eyes, he found her. The woman he knew and loved.

"Read the letter," he said, opening his eyes and pulling her arms from him. "Go on."

She drew in a deep breath. Why had her son written to her? What was it he'd wanted to say that he couldn't say to her face? She wasn't sure if she should be frightened. The last time he'd written her a letter like this, he'd been Reinier and that note was filled with sadness.

She handed it to Matthew. "Would you read it to me, please?"

He hesitated. He'd not yet told her that his reading had suffered in his years of darkness. Those years had cost him in many ways. He could still read, of course, but found he now needed to take his time and concentrate on each word.

He opened the envelope and slid out the letter, relieved to see it was only one short sentence. He could do this. His wife needed him to. He began to read.

"Thank you for being exactly the mother I needed."

"Go on," Lin said.

"That's it," he said, handing her the note. "That's all he wrote."

She clutched the note to her chest. "It's perfect," she said.

"Is there a hidden meaning in that?" he asked, confused.

"No."

"Then why go to the trouble to write that note if that's all he wanted to say?"

"He had nothing else to say. I know that he loves me. I know that he wants me to be brave. I know that he's going to be okay."

"And you didn't know that you were the mother he needed?"

"Not really. I always tried hard to be the mother I thought he deserved. It means so much more than that to know I was also the mother he needed."

"I'm still not sure I understand." He closed his eyes, trying to make sense of the meaning behind the note. It was so much easier to think when his eyes were closed.

"I never told Shen how much I worried that I wasn't doing enough for him. That I wasn't telling him the things he needed to hear or teaching him the things he needed to know."

"You never told me that."

"I guess I never told anyone. Shen knew it anyway. He knew the words I needed to hear."

He nodded. That made sense. Shen had always seemed to know what his mother had needed.

"He wrote the words down to make sure you heard."

"Exactly." She smiled her first smile since Shen's diagnosis. Her son was a beautiful soul. She was honored to have been his mother. He'd made her a better person. He'd taught her how to be brave, how to fight and how to trust in the spectacular universe she lived in.

She wasn't just the mother he'd needed. He was exactly the son she'd needed, too.

The Soulweaver stood quietly in the corner of the room watching two beautiful humans reading the words he'd written only days before, in a time when he'd had slender fingers made from flesh for the words to flow through. In a time when his name was Shen.

He saw the tears on their cheeks and the sadness in their eyes. He also saw a cloud of light surrounding them like a fog. In this fog hung the memories from their lives gone by.

He looked at Matthew and poured love into his gentle heart. He was a soul to be admired. How little his adoring fans really knew of him. They saw him as a tortured genius who spoke with his hands, instead of his tongue, when in fact it was with his heart that he spoke. For this was a man whose life had been built on a foundation of love. First his love for Hannah, and then Lin. Two women with the one soul. A soul that'd captured him and held him so close he'd forgotten how to breathe on his own. Only she wasn't Matthew's soulmate. She was his intended, and in his lifetimes to come he'd have other intendeds. There'd be other souls who'd touch his heart in the same way.

The Soulweaver shifted his gaze to Lin and for a moment he saw Hannah. Innocence shining from big, blue eyes, and blonde hair flowing down her back like a goddess. Her innocence was a gift from the lives she'd lived before. She'd learned tough lessons as a beggar on the streets of Jakarta, as a nun in the mountains of Spain and a healer deep in the jungles of Africa.

Her life as Hannah was meant to bring her peace. A quiet life in Australia, daughter of a preacher and friend of the forest. But what her life lacked in struggles, it also lacked in years. It was always intended to be a short life, for Hannah needed to make way for her life as Lin.

He looked at Lin. *Really* looked at her, in a way that's impossible for a son, a brother or a lover. For where there was a face, he saw a soul. Where there was a body, he saw a wave of energy. He didn't see his mother, as he no longer felt like Shen. In the hours since he'd left Earth, his life as Shen had merged into his other lives, as his new role as Soulweaver had taken hold.

This pure soul that sat before him with tears staining her face was destined to sit beside him forever, weaving Earth's souls, making it the paradise the Author had intended it to be.

For the moment it was a task he must tackle alone. The thought didn't trouble him. Lin deserved to live her final years in peace, with a husband who loved her in a way he hadn't been able to when he was Reinier.

He'd just wanted to look in on her one last time. Not to say goodbye, for he'd be seeing her again soon enough, but to give him the strength he needed to fly alone. In all his years on Earth, she'd been there, traveling on the same path. Now there was a fork in their road and, despite the fact it would meet again, he'd feel her absence.

"See you soon, Soulweaver," he whispered in her ear.

Her pupils widened. "He's here," she gasped, her hands reaching out before her.

She was wrong.

He'd already gone.

THE END
Ready for the next lifetime?
Check out Book 2, The Truthseeker, now
http://mybook.to/hctruthseeker

THE TRUTHSEEKER

BOOK 2 THE SOULWEAVER SERIES

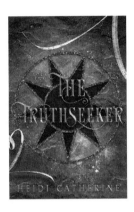

Two sisters. Two worlds. One truth.

In a future where humans have been driven underwater to hide from the deadly rays of the sun, a soul has been reborn. Maari is the new girl in town and her arrival has upset a powerful force in the sky. The Soulweaver will do anything to keep her away from Nax, the boy she's inexplicably drawn to. Including trying to take Maari's life.

Nax and Maari must travel to the depths of the ocean to visit an old woman known as the Truthseeker. She warns them to run as far away from each other as they can. But staying apart isn't possible when you've found the person who brings your soul to life...

We discover that when soulmates meet, there's nothing that can keep them apart.

Except love.

Grab your copy now!

http://mybook.to/hctruthseeker

ALSO BY HEIDI CATHERINE

The Kingdoms of Evernow
Five kingdoms. Five senses.
One secret that will change them all.
The Kingdoms of Evernow (Prequel)
The Whisperers of Evernow
The Alchemists of Evernow
The Empress of Evernow
The Guardians of Evernow
The Angels of Evernow

The Soulweaver series
Two girls. Two lives. One soul.
The Soulweaver
The Truthseeker
The Shadowmaker

The Sovereign Code
Humans saved bees from extinction...
and created the deadliest threat we've seen yet
Harvest Day
Hive Mind
Queen Hunt
Venom Rising
Sting Wars

The Thaw Chronicles

Four tests. Seven days. Nine teens.

Only the chosen shall breed.

Burning (Prequel)

Rising

Breaking

Falling

Reckoning

Extant

Exist

Exile

Expose

Tournaments of Thaw

Conquer the Thaw

The Oasis Trials

The Oasis Deception

The Last Oasis

Domestic Suspense

Written as HC Michaels

The Woman Who Didn't

The Girl Who Never

FREE NOVELETTE

Sign up to Heidi Catherine's newsletter and receive a FREE novelette: https://www.heidicatherine.com/freebooks

Heidi loves to connect with readers, so please say hello on social media, leave a review on Amazon or Goodreads, or visit her at www.heidicatherine.com

facebook.com/HeidiCatherineAuthor

twitter.com/HeidiCatherine

instagram.com/HeidiCatherine

amazon.com/author/heidicatherine

tiktok.com/@heidicatherineauthor

ABOUT THE AUTHOR

Heidi writes fantasy and dystopian novels, which gives her a chance to escape into worlds vastly different to her own life in the burbs. While she quite enjoys killing her characters (especially the awful ones), she promises she's far better behaved in real life. Other than writing and reading, Heidi's current obsessions include watching far too much reality TV with the excuse that it's research for her books. She also writes domestic suspense novels under the name HC Michaels.

Made in the USA
Middletown, DE
03 September 2023

37858376R00163